# Bittersweet Memories

# Bittersweet Memories

a novel

by

## Lynn Osterkamp

PMI Books

Boulder, Colorado

ISBN: 978-1-933826-51-6

Cover by R.L. Sather
www.selfpubbookcovers.com/RLSather

Published by
PMI Books
an imprint of
Preventive Measures, Inc.
254 Spruce St.
Boulder, CO 80302

Printed in the United States of America

pmibooks.com

"Our memory is a more perfect world than the universe: it gives back life to those who no longer exist."

Guy de Maupassant

# Chapter 1

Nowadays I flip to the obituaries in the *Helena Independent Record* before I read the front page. When you're seventy-three and you've lived in the same town most of your life, the frequent funerals of high-school classmates become strange social situations where you drink coffee at post-service receptions and catch up on the lives of the living, while wondering which of you will be the focus of the next gathering.

Mostly I'm able to "go with the flow," as my younger sister Meadow suggests, recognizing death as a natural part of life, but not on that Tuesday morning in June. I had been dreading that day for the last year—the day I would be saying goodbye to Martha. Looking back now, I also recognize it as the beginning of my obsession with my family's past.

Martha and I were best friends always. I can't remember when I didn't know her. We were like sisters all through school, sharing every important event and just hanging out. As kids we spent hours at the pool in the summer, seeing who could swim the farthest under water, practicing fancy dives like the swan and the jackknife, and playing cards in the shade during the one hour we had to stay out of the water after lunch because in the 1950s our mothers believed swimming right after eating might cause drowning from stomach cramps.

In high school we practically lived at each other's houses, sharing our clothes, record albums, and secrets. Our friends called us "Martha-Anne." And even though we went off to different colleges, we both ended up back in Helena, Montana, where we married high-school boyfriends, worked in our families' businesses (law for me, banking for her) raised our kids, and retired and got old. Best friends forever as the teenagers say today. Only nothing lasts forever.

Now Martha was gone and I had to accept the loss. Cancer had been slowly killing her for more than a year. All through the harsh icy Montana winter she fought with every fiber of her being, enduring the horrible chemo and radiation and, when those failed, enrolling in clinical trials. She lost her hair, her energy, and her appetite, but never her spirit.

I had hoped we would share one more Montana summer in which Martha might feel well enough for a leisurely picnic in a sea of colorful wildflowers, or an evening watching the sunset with a glass of wine on my patio. But those were pipe dreams. Three days ago she lost the battle.

I already missed her. A lot. I had an overwhelming urge to call her to share my grief. She always said the perfect thing to cheer me up. She was my go-to person and she left a huge hole in my life.

In my head, I heard Martha say, "Quit feeling sorry for yourself, Anne. Buck up and move on with the day." Her one rule for visitors in her last weeks and months was "no crying." I had stayed strong for her then and I could be brave again today.

I pulled on my pantyhose, wiggled into my favorite black dress, and went to check on Jerry in the living room. He was sitting on the couch staring into space with his usual vacant look. "You look distinguished, sweetie," I said. "I'm glad you picked this jacket." I smoothed the front of his gray jacket and buttoned two of its five buttons. He had put it on inside out this morning, but after I gently pointed that out, he had changed it by himself. I encourage him to do as much as he can for himself, but buttons are beyond his ability. Arthritic fingers are part of his problem, but mixed-up brain connections are the primary culprit.

My cell phone rang. My twin brother, Dan. "I'm on my way to pick up you and Jerry for the funeral," he said. "I'll be there in ten minutes."

"But you hate funerals and you hate church," I said. "Why would you go? I thought Debby was picking us up."

"She can't. Your hardworking daughter is hung up here at the law firm finishing a reply brief, which is due today, so I told her I'd take her place. I'll call when I'm out front."

I knew Dan was busy too. He always is. Even though he is seventy-three, as the main partner at Weller & Associates Dan is still the rainmaker who brings in the business, so he's either on the phone or out with clients most of the time.

Ever since my great-grandfather Edmund Weller struck gold in the nearby mountains in 1883, Wellers have been prominent Montana ranchers, lawyers, and politicians. Daddy started Weller and Associates in 1940; I joined the firm in 1966 and Dan in 1970. After Daddy died and I left to be a judge, Dan brought in two young attorneys, and two years later Debby joined the firm right out of law school. They all work hard but Dan takes overall responsibility. So his taking time off to go with us was sweet.

"Dan's coming to pick us up," I said to Jerry. "Let's get your shoes on so we'll be ready." He stuck out his feet limply, and scowled as I struggled to press his apathetic toes into his shoes.

"Why does Dan need to pick us up?" he asked. "I can drive us." Jerry's refusal to accept that driving with dementia is dangerous is the reason I try to find someone else to drive us whenever we are going somewhere together. I am perfectly capable of driving and I do when I go places on my own, but Jerry is old school and getting in the car with me driving wounds his pride and triggers his stubborn side, leading to an emotional roadblock that can quickly become a permanent detour. He is more comfortable accepting someone else driving with the two of us sitting together in the back seat.

I gave him a quick hug. "I know you can drive, but Dan offered, so why not take it easy and enjoy the trip. Let's go. I don't want to be late."

The funeral, a beautiful ceremony at the historic Cathedral of St. Helena, left me numb and tired, so I was grateful Dan was there to drive us to the cemetery for the burial. As we gathered around

Martha's gravesite, the gorgeous June day mocked my misery. Warm and sunny, not a cloud in sight. In movies mourners often stand beneath a heavy gray sky holding black umbrellas to protect themselves from the pouring rain that matches their mood. But no cameras were rolling, and the universe did not provide the verification of tragedy I so desperately needed for Martha. Instead I got distracting summer sounds of kids playing catch with their dog. Probably Martha sending me notice that I should cheer up.

After the burial ceremony, Dan offered to take us out to lunch. But Jerry was slumping and asking me repeatedly, "What are we doing?" so I didn't think he'd do well at a restaurant.

"Come on back to the house for lunch," I said. "I'll make your favorite meatball sandwich. I have lots of my homemade meatballs in the freezer and they heat up in about a minute in the microwave."

A wide smile spread over Dan's face. "Can't turn down your meatball sandwich. You feel like cooking after all this?"

I took a deep breath, straightening my spine. "I'm sad," I said "but I've been grieving my loss of Martha for the last year, and she kept telling me I'd have to get a grip and move on once she was gone. So the best way to honor her memory is to do that."

By the time we got home, Jerry needed help to get up the ten steep steps to our front door. I was glad to have Dan there. Even though Jerry has lost muscle and shrunk in the last year, supporting his weight is still a heavy lift for me. But for Dan it was nothing.

To look at us you'd never think we're twins. Dan looks the part of a Montana politician, which I think helped elect him to three terms at the state legislature. He's tall, well-muscled, ruddy-faced, broad-nosed, with a firm jaw, leathery weathered skin, deep laugh lines on the sides of his face, and crinkly brown eyes that invite you in. His hair—what's left of it—is gingery reddish-gray, which matches his mustache. I, on the other hand am short with blue eyes and curly blonde hair, which shows no gray thanks to my hairdresser's magic. My body has thickened a bit over the years, which, according to Martha, gives me a soft comforting appearance that along with my round face makes me look more like a housewife or a preschool teacher than the retired judge I actually am.

"Hang on, buddy." Dan smiled at Jerry, propping him up while I unlocked the front door. "I hear we're going to get Anne's famous meatball sandwiches for lunch if we're nice to her and don't cause any trouble."

Jerry perked up a little. "I like meatballs," he said. "Let's go."

Soon we were sitting at the kitchen table chowing down. After a small struggle, Jerry had agreed to take off his jacket before eating—but only after Dan took his off first. Watching the tomato sauce dribble down Jerry's chin to his shirt, I was glad we'd prevailed. At least I could bleach the shirt.

"Do you remember those barbecues we used to have out at the ranch when we were kids?" I asked Dan. "That delicious sauce Grandma Clara made was SO messy and drippy. Somehow she never got any on her clothes, but I always did. The more careful I tried to be, the more I'd spill. She'd say 'Anne, you need a bib,' and I'd be petrified she'd actually get me one and embarrass me even more than she already had."

Dan washed down the last of his sandwich with a big swig of coffee before he replied. "I try not to think about Grandma Clara," he said, "for so many reasons."

I never get anywhere arguing with Dan about family stuff. His recollections are facts in his mind. But he wasn't being fair to Grandma Clara and I couldn't just let it go. "She could be tough, but we had some good times, and she really helped us out when we needed her," I said.

"Much as I'd like to stay here and debate that premise with you," Dan said with a laugh, "I have to get back to the office. Thanks for the lunch."

After Dan left, and Jerry settled in for a nap, I got myself a glass of wine and sat in the living room in my favorite wing chair. The room's sunny memories surrounded and soothed me—Jerry and I restoring the hardwood floors and original woodwork; our children growing from babies and toddlers to kids and teenagers; and friends and family gathering for lively celebrations. Their voices echoed in my ears as I sat in front of the bay windows overlooking the garden and sipped my wine.

Alcoholism runs in my family, so I don't usually drink wine in the early afternoon, but I gave myself a dispensation in Martha's honor. My mind drifted past my miserable memories of her suffering and deterioration during the last year, back to better times together. After a bit—and a couple of glasses of wine—she popped up in my mind's eye, laughing as we celebrated one of her birthdays with a decadent chocolate cheesecake, then hiked the Mount Helena Ridge Trail the next day to work off the extra calories. More old memories surfaced, bittersweet, like the wine in my glass, yet fortifying, like the love we had shared. Taking time to remember gave me strength to move forward.

I reflected on how reminiscence comforted me, and I wondered why that wasn't true for Dan. At lunch he had, as usual, quashed my cheerful childhood memory of Grandma Clara. He and I had such different memories of growing up. His were largely negative, while mine were predominantly positive. Yet we're twins who grew up together. How could I get him to see he was choosing to see the mud instead of the stars?

That was when I remembered the rusted old tin container of super-eight movies our parents took of us as kids. I'd been planning to go through them to identify the parts that were worth getting digitized to make into videos for our children and grandchildren, but it was one of those projects that kept falling to the bottom of my list.

The next day, I dug out the films and began playing them on the ancient projector. It was like time travel, the past alive again. Scenes of us as kids romping in the fall leaves with our dog, celebrating birthdays, hanging up our Christmas stockings. So long ago, yet so achingly familiar.

Jerry sat next to me on the couch watching with me. The old-time flickering images kept his attention, but who knows what or who he thought they were. The films did not have sound, so I narrated for him as I went along, both to keep a connection with him and to sort out my own feelings. "Look, there's Dan and me on our second birthday, " I said, squeezing his hand. "It would have been 1943, so it was wartime. Daddy was off in the Navy and we were living on the ranch with Mama and Grandma Clara and Granddad. Mama put together a party for us—cake, candles, presents, everything. She must have had a hard time getting all that with the wartime rationing and all, but nothing ever stopped Mama. Look—two cakes. Mama always said that just because Dan and I were twins who had to share the same birthday, didn't mean we had to share the same birthday cake."

"It's your birthday," Jerry said, with a smile. "You have cake."

The film stopped abruptly, ends flapping as the reel continued to turn. I jumped up, labeled this reel with its year and occasion, put it in the "to be digitized pile," and pulled out another. This one started out dark, then streaks of light appeared, and then suddenly it was Christmas. Dan and I were gawky teenagers, Sandra was a tiny baby and Ned and Meadow were little kids.

"A Christmas tree," Jerry said, pointing at the screen.

Christmas Eve. The movie panned across all five of us children sitting next to the tree, Sandra in my lap, Dan next to me, Ned and Meadow in front of us. Then the camera moved slowly up and down the tree, showing the angel on top, the European glass ornaments so fragile we kids weren't allowed to touch them, and the popcorn chains that were our contribution. My parents filmed the tree like this every year, even though the trees and their decorations were so similar that the only way you could tell one from another was by the ages of the kids next to it. "It must be 1954," I said, "because Sandra is only a few months old. So Ned was eight, Meadow was six (of course her name was Nicole then), and Dan and I were thirteen. Daddy was home from the war and we'd long ago moved from the ranch into the big house in Helena."

Now it's Christmas morning. Mama and Daddy always made us wait until they got the blinding floodlights set up for the movies before they allowed us into the living room. Then they directed us as to what to do and how to move, while reminding us to act natural. The film's imitation of normalcy was as surreal as a Magritte image.

Ned and Meadow walked haltingly toward the fireplace to retrieve their stockings full of toys and candy, rather than rushing toward their gifts like children would if they weren't being filmed. Dan and I stood awkwardly on the sidelines watching.

The movie took me straight back. I could almost smell the cinnamon buns, bacon cheese pie, and pancake corn fritters I knew we'd have later for Christmas breakfast.

As I worked my way through more films, I was startled at how vividly they recreated childhood days. My memories were like old washed out photos in comparison. The more I watched, the more I longed for those long-ago times. Mama and Daddy still alive, us kids so young and carefree, our lives still stretched out in front of us. All of us happy just being together as a family.

But that togetherness was gone. We didn't have that close family anymore. Too much stood between us. I wished I could push rewind and go back and redo those years when it all fell apart.

# Chapter 2

When my cell phone rang the next day, I had no premonition of the impact the call would have on my life. I was straightening up the living room while Jerry napped, and pondering the state of disrepair of the historic home Jerry and I had poured endless time and money into restoring in years past. I could almost hear this room begging for repair.

As I returned books to their shelves and gathered magazines and newspapers for the recycling bin, my eyes flicked over the scratched hardwood floor, chipped wall paint, and cracks in the crown molding. The blemishes pained me, but I couldn't think of a way to have restoration work done now that Jerry got agitated when anyone cleaned or disturbed his surroundings. There was no way he could tolerate the noise, fumes and disarray workers would bring.

The phone call from Joyce at Weller & Associates was a welcome distraction. "Hey, hon, you got a way-out-there call just now, so I figured I'd go ahead and give you a ring," Her raspy voice pulled me away from my gloomy thoughts.

I have all the calls from my landline phone forwarded to the law office. As a retired judge, I am flooded with requests, but I retired to be with Jerry, not to spend time giving speeches and serving on boards. Joyce screens my calls and mail, deals with most of them on her own, and passes on the stuff that requires my personal attention.

"What's up, Joyce? Someone wants me to … ?"

"Listen, hon. You have a brother name of Ned?" Joyce is kind of folksy, but she's very efficient and reliable.

"Seriously, Joyce? Ned called?" I asked in a shaky voice. Adrenaline surged through my body. Close friends and family all had my cell number, but of course Ned wouldn't have it. I hadn't talked to Ned for more than forty years.

"No, some guy named Keith. Said he's from San Diego and he needs to talk to you ASAP about your brother, Ned. I tried to get more out of him, but he clammed up. I offered to let him speak to Dan, but the guy said the message was for you, only you. Kind of flaky-sounding. I wouldn't give him your cell number, so he said you should call him. ASAP."

Getting a message about Ned was like finding a beautifully-wrapped anonymous gift on my doorstep. I wanted to know what was inside, but at the same time I was afraid it would blow up in my face. My mind zigzagged across possible actions. At first I was inclined to wait and see if Keith called again. But on second thought I told myself that if there was any chance I could reconnect with Ned, I didn't want to miss that opportunity. My feelings about Ned had long been deeply layered—sadness, guilt, and annoyance, topped with hope and wishful thinking.

On the other hand, I knew nothing about this Keith or his connection to Ned. If Joyce thought he sounded flaky, did I want to respond to his call? I weighed the options and settled on making the call using my landline so the guy wouldn't get my cell number.

Keith answered on the first ring. He thanked me for returning his call. Then he got to the point, his voice muted and breathy. "I'm sorry to have to tell you this, Judge Barnes. Ned passed away last week. I know you haven't been close, but he left you something—something very important to him—something he wanted only you to have."

Ned reaching out from the grave to reconnect after all these years? Could this be for real? I could believe Ned had died, but I was dubious he had left me something. More likely this was some new version of the Nigerian scam. I was in judge mode, collecting information before accepting the reality of Keith's news. "What's your connection to Ned?" I asked. "And how did he die?"

"Ned and I were together for twenty-seven years," he said, his voice choked with tears. "He was the love of my life. He died of liver cancer."

Whew. Maybe he was genuine. But this wasn't my first rodeo. Decades of experience with crooks and con artists had made me a skeptic. "I'm sorry, Keith" I said, "but if you were close to Ned, you know I haven't seen him or even spoken to him in over forty years. So I don't know anything about you and your life with him. How can I know you are who you say you are? How can I know you knew him? How can I know he is dead? You must understand I need some proof that what you're saying is true."

"I'm not asking you for anything, Judge Barnes," he said. "I'm trying to give you something—something your brother wanted you to have. It would be easier for me to forget the whole thing, but this was important to Ned. His dying wish was that I make sure you got what he left you. I can't break my promise to him."

I was doubtful, but as long as he wasn't asking me for information like my bank account number, I decided to play along, see where it would go. What could it hurt to have him send me whatever it was? "Okay," I said. "You can send what Ned left me to our family law firm, Weller & Associates. Do you need the address?"

There was a long silence on Keith's end. I figured I had called his bluff and that would be the end of it. But no. "Here's the thing," he sputtered. "I can't send what he left you. I don't have it and I don't even know what it is. All I have is instructions. Ned was very clear and specific. He said you need to come out here and you need to come alone. When you get here, I will give you a key to a storage locker where he has left you something along with an explanation. I know this sounds strange, but I assure you it's all true."

"Keith," I said. "You have to know I need more information before I agree to make a trip like that. Is there an obituary or a death certificate you can fax? Any other proof you can give me?"

"No obituary," he said. "Ned didn't want that. And he didn't want a funeral or memorial service. But he was cremated. They might have some sort of certificate or something they can send." He paused. "Oh, and we had hospice at the end. I can give you their number and you can talk to them."

"Okay," I said. I took down the names and phone numbers and said, "I'll do some checking and call you back tomorrow or the next day."

The first thing I did was Google Ned. I found the usual demographic info—stuff I knew from having goggled him before. He got his PhD in behavioral neuroscience at the University of Washington, Seattle in 1971. He was a professor in the highly rated Neurosciences Graduate Program at the University of California, San Diego. I found links to some of his academic publications, a short article about a bike race that he placed in, and one about a sailing club he belonged to, but no death notice or obituary. No mention of Keith or other ties to the gay community.

Next, I called an attorney friend in L.A. to get a recommendation for a private investigator in San Diego. I gave the San Diego PI all the information I had about Ned. He promised to get back to me in twenty-four hours.

Then I let down my guard, sat back and thought about Ned, and all of us, and what happened, and how it broke our family, most of all Ned. Waves of emotion crashed over me, knocking me down, dragging me under, pulling me back to Christmas Eve 1964 when our mother died so shockingly.

One day she was alive and vital, laughing, decorating, wrapping presents, making cookies, and loving the holidays in the way she always did. She was the center of us all, the flame that kept us warm. Then suddenly that flame was snuffed out. She was dead, gone forever. The hole she left in our lives was unbearable, unthinkable, impossible to even begin to believe. How could she be gone? Couldn't we go back a day and change it all? Couldn't it be a nightmare we could wake up from, relieved that our worst fears had not come true? No. It was real.

The tragedy happened on a snowy Christmas Eve. Ned was eighteen, and home for Christmas vacation from his freshman year of college. Daddy and Mama had waited for Ned's arrival to take our youngest sister Sandra on her first family hunting trip. Hunting was an important activity in our family. Weller men have always been hunters and Daddy loved to hunt. He told me once that when they were first married, Mama hated the idea of killing, but Daddy persevered until he convinced her that killing for food is acceptable. He taught her to shoot. Took three long frustrating years, but finally she shot her first deer.

That year—1964—Daddy gave Sandra her first shotgun, a 20 gauge, on her tenth birthday in October. She was so excited, had been waiting years to be old enough to go hunting like the rest of us. Daddy had taken her along on hunting trips to teach her about the outdoors, gun safety, and the joy of hunting. But like the rest of us she had to wait until she was ten for her first real gun. Once she got it, Daddy spent the next couple of months teaching her to shoot, and now she was ready.

Daddy and Mama and Sandra and Ned headed out to the family ranch to hunt pheasant. Only the four of them went. I was home on vacation from law school and planned to go with them, but at the last minute something kept me at home. Dan was in the Air Force stationed in Thailand. Meadow was sixteen and had been partying late at a Christmas gathering the night before. She had said she'd get up and go with them even if she stayed out late, but that morning she couldn't drag herself out of bed. So only Sandra and Ned watched Mama die from the gunshot wounds after Daddy ran off to get help.

Daddy called me and Meadow from the hospital. We raced over. Sandra and Ned were in shock. They couldn't remember anything about the accident. Meadow and I kept asking Daddy what happened, but all he would say was "She was shot by accident … it was an accident."

We all went in to say goodbye to Mama. I'll never forget the sight. They had cleaned up her body and she looked peaceful. We were sobbing. I can still hear Sandra wailing, "No, Mama. No. You can't be dead." I wanted to yell with her, but kept the words locked inside.

The priest came to give her the last rites and he blessed us all and told us she was in a better place. His words hit me like a bomb. How could she be in a better place than with us, her family who loved her?

I think that was when I started to give up on religion.

Finally we all went home. The next few days were a blur of family, friends and funeral arrangements. Friends and neighbors brought casseroles, baked hams, coconut cakes. Grandma Clara came in from the ranch and stayed and cooked and took care of all the food people left for us. Dan came home from the Air Force and he and I and Daddy met with the priest and the mortuary people to make funeral arrangements, and with the coroner and the sheriff about the accident.

The sheriff talked to Daddy and Ned and Sandra separately. Neither Sandra nor Ned could remember what happened, no matter how many questions they were asked. By then Daddy was drinking a lot, but he insisted he did remember. He said Ned had fired at a bird and accidentally hit Mama because he didn't see her through the brush and the thick snow falling. Daddy kept repeating that it was an accident, not Ned's fault.

Ned was devastated. He couldn't believe he had killed Mama, couldn't remember shooting her, couldn't cope with the guilt. But Daddy said neither he nor Sandra had fired, only Ned, so his shot had to be what that killed her.

Ned stayed in his room, refused to come out, refused to talk to anyone, even the priest. Meadow and I tried to help, brought him food, told him through his closed door that no one blamed him. But, even though Mama's death was ruled an accident and no charges were filed, people did blame Ned.

Daddy never blamed him to his face, but I could tell he didn't want to be around Ned. Dan blamed both Daddy and Ned. He didn't mince words. "I refuse to call Mama's death an accident," he said. "More like gross negligence. Before you pull that trigger, you should be one hundred percent certain what you're shooting at, and what the backdrop is if you happen to miss. You're responsible for every shot you deliver. It's the abc's of hunting and shooting. There is no excuse for shooting another human being in the woods." Dan went back to Thailand right after the funeral and he and Ned never spoke again.

Ned went back to college and didn't come home after that even for holidays. I went back to law school at Stanford and I visited him several times in Seattle, where he was in college. But he was depressed and didn't want to talk about anything. I had no idea what to do or how to help him.

Daddy and Sandra and Meadow (who was still Nicole then) needed me, so when I finished law school two years later, I moved back to Helena. Ned cut himself off from all of us after that.

But for years I refused to give up. I called him and wrote him letters trying to set up a meeting. He must have screened his calls, because he never answered. I left messages but he never responded. Long before Google, I hired an investigator to find out where he worked, and I was on the brink of traveling to San Diego and looking him up at the university, but I never went. I told myself that showing up there when he obviously didn't want to see me would be an invasion of his privacy, but I also feared provoking his in-person rejection of me, which could forever quash my hopes of a reunion.

As I let myself relive that time, the vein of sadness ran deep in me. The events of fifty years ago were as vivid as ever, and the effects on our family as tragic as ever. Over the years, the massive cracks Mama's death made in our family structure spread like roots splintering the foundation of a building. I didn't know whether we could have fixed them at the time, stopped the spread in some way, but we didn't. And Ned suffered the most. I regretted we had never been able to talk about it, and now—if he was truly gone—we never would.

The San Diego PI called the next day with confirmation of Keith's story. Ned had indeed died of liver cancer the week before. At the time of his death, he had been living with his longtime partner, Keith Kalford, a violinist with the San Diego Symphony Orchestra. I wasn't surprised Keith's story was true. I was sad that any possibility of repairing my relationship with Ned was lost forever. All I could do for Ned now was comply with his last request.

I called Keith again on Friday. "I'll come next week to pick up what Ned left to me," I said. "I have some things to do here first. Will Tuesday work for you?" He agreed, so we were set. Now I had to tell the rest of the family.

# Chapter 3

## Anne

I debated calling everyone to pass on the news about Ned without delay. But this announcement wasn't urgent. Like me, Dan and Meadow hadn't seen or spoken with our brother for many years. I didn't know whether Sandra (aka Sister Mary Margaret) had been in touch with Ned, but I doubted she would take my call. My three grown children, Debby, Bill and Clint, had never met Ned.

I didn't expect any of them to grieve, but I did want them to know he was gone. Keith had said Ned didn't want a funeral or memorial service. Still, I wanted us all to at least take a minute together as a family to acknowledge his death. I was afraid that if I called them, told them about Ned, and tried to bring them together to remember him, most of them would have reasons not to come. The best way would be to tell them in person as a family group.

As it happened, I had earlier invited them all to birthday brunch for Jerry on Sunday. There would be ten of us: Jerry and me; our three kids, Debby, Bill and Clint; Bill's wife Amelia and their daughters Vicky and Miranda; and Dan and Meadow. Gathering them together isn't easy because of their complicated schedules, but they would never refuse a celebration of Jerry's birthday. Even though Alzheimer's had him in its grip, making him confused and disoriented, he was still his sweet loving self. He still recognized them (most of the time) and was happy to see them. They loved him and would put their schedules aside to celebrate his birthday.

I had planned a fun family gathering, a time to enjoy each other's company, but I decided that after the birthday celebration, I would also tell them about Ned. Combining a death notice with a birthday party might seem strange, but Ned's death was more of a news announcement than a tragic tale, and Jerry wouldn't tune in to that news, so it wouldn't affect his experience of the party. I could start by showing them one of the old movies that featured Ned before I told them he was gone. Seeing Ned as a child would give them a context to recall him with affection, rather than distaste.

## Debby

Fifteen voicemails to answer and about a hundred emails and the clock only said 10:00 a.m. Debby stared out the window of her Weller & Associates, LLC office at the glorious sunshiny day. If she didn't have to finish this contract by the end of the day, she'd chuck work and head over to the park to watch the ducks. New baby ducks were out. She'd seen them at lunch yesterday. Sweet adorable babies instinctively swimming in a line behind their mothers.

Josh had been her sweet baby once. She closed her eyes and let the feeling wash over her. His warm tiny body held close, his soft hands exploring her face, his trusting eyes meeting hers. What she wouldn't give for just one hour with him like that today.

Her phone interrupted the fantasy. Caller ID said Teen Rehab Institute. Her stomach lurched. What now?

"Ms. Barnes?"

"Speaking."

"I need to let you know that Josh had an incident this morning involving another patient. He has a black eye, but otherwise he's fine."

Debby fought back angry tears. Josh fighting again. Wasn't he making any progress at all? "What am I paying you for? Can't you …" She caught herself before she finished the accusation. After all she'd gone through to get Josh into this treatment center, she couldn't wreck it now. She had to be patient.

She took a deep breath. "Can you tell me what happened?" she asked in a slow steady voice.

"They got into a disagreement at breakfast. Nothing serious, but they punched each other. They've both lost privileges as a consequence, so I doubt they'll do it again."

She closed her eyes and managed to ask, "Is there something I should do?"

"No, no. Don't worry. Josh is adapting. It just takes time."

When Debby hung up, her stomach was in knots. As a single mom she always worried about whether she was doing enough or doing too much for Josh. She looked out the window again, but the peaceful feeling of a few minutes ago didn't return.

Her phone rang again. Mom calling. Debby tried to sound cheerful, but Anne picked up her mood right away. "Is something wrong?"

Debby sighed. "Just Josh. He's having a few bumps in the road settling in at the rehab center. They're handling it, but I wish he'd shape up and get with the program."

"Rehab's never a smooth path," Anne said, "but are you sure TRI is the best place for him?"

Oh no, Debby thought, here it comes. There are better places in California or Colorado or Washington and Mom will pay if I'll send him there. But I want him here where I can visit easily. Mom never understands that. After all her years as a judge, she's so focused on results she brushes aside other important details.

"It's fine. Mom. He just needs some time. Anyhow, what's up with you?"

"I just wanted to say don't bring presents to Dad's birthday party on Sunday. There's nothing he wants or needs. So it will just be brunch and a birthday cake and lots of love from the family."

Debby was in no mood for a family gathering. Same old stuff. Too many expectations, too little fun. Her brothers were difficult, judgy, and often snarky toward her. She loved her dad, but doubted he realized it was his birthday. Also, he wasn't at his best in a large group. Debby preferred to spend time with him one-on-one. She'd rather use her Sunday morning to take a long bike ride with her new friend, Luke. But she knew better than to argue with Anne. If she did, she'd end up going anyway and there would be tension between them. So she promised to be there.

"Sure, Mom, I'm looking forward to it," she said with as much enthusiasm as she could muster. "I have to go work on a contract now. Talk to you later."

## Bill

Bill Barnes was thinking about the upcoming birthday party as he drove to show a property to a client. A family gathering wasn't his first choice for Sunday morning. Bill liked his days to be smooth and tranquil, and they most often were. He enjoyed selling real estate and he did well because he had a knack for listening to people, for hearing what they wanted, what was vital to them. He matched that up with his listings of available properties. People liked him and he liked them, which translated into strong sales and a substantial income.

Bill was relaxed from his daily workout at the gym. He had been a NCAA champion skier in college, and his memories of his strength and vigor at that peak level of fitness kept him committed to working out. He knew he looked good for forty-five, dressed in his usual Levis, Frye boots, and lambskin leather blazer. His wife Amelia, who was ten years younger than him, tried to interest him in more stylish clothes. She said that with his tall toned body and his thick brownish-blonde hair, he would be a knockout in the right outfit. But Bill wasn't interested in wowing people with his appearance. He didn't like to draw attention to himself. He'd rather just blend in.

He believed he'd made excellent choices in life so far. But his sister Debby and his brother Clint didn't see it that way. They both looked down on him for selling real estate, even though Barnes Real Estate had been their dad's firm and the money it brought in was plenty good enough for them when they were growing up. Now Debby was always telling him he'd settled for too little, that he should go into politics like Uncle Dan so he could make a difference in the world instead of just selling real estate and collecting commissions. And Clint accused him of sucking up to the establishment, catering to the greedy, materialistic elite.

Bill didn't enjoy spending time with either of them and neither did Amelia, but his dad's birthday was special and their daughters

Miranda and Vicky would be excited. At ages six and four, they loved birthday parties and Jerry was one of their favorite people. So of course they would be there.

## Anne

The Sunday birthday brunch was shaping up. Our youngest son, Clint, would be coming by later to stay with Jerry while I went to the grocery, so I needed to make a list. I'd make a couple of quiches—one vegetarian for Meadow and one with sausage for Jerry and Dan. I'd get some bagels and smoked salmon, Amelia's favorite, and put together a big fruit and cheese platter. I'd make blueberry muffins and cinnamon coffee cake and of course a birthday cake—chocolate, Jerry's favorite.

I was glad Jerry was in the bedroom napping after lunch when Clint showed up with an ugly black cloud hanging over him. Sometimes I worried about leaving Jerry with him. Clint served three tours in Iraq with distinction. He was an infantry platoon leader and company commander. He cares about the world, but since he's been back from Iraq he sees emptiness everywhere. Clint's dark moods sometimes upset Jerry who can't understand the source of them. But Clint needed the money I paid him to stay with Jerry and he also needed to know he was doing something valuable.

Today Clint looked down and irritable. He stood in the middle of the room, his lean angular body and sharp-featured face drawn tight as if poised to pounce on an unsuspecting prey. His brooding brown eyes looked right through me.

"I don't think I can come on Sunday, Mom. I have an important meeting at Electus." He plopped down on the couch and began digging through his backpack.

Electus had been soaking up more and more of Clint's time in recent weeks. My web research had confirmed my suspicions that Electus was a New Age cult. Its members believed its founders were extraterrestrial beings sent ahead by a more advanced planet to prepare the most evolved humans to evacuate in flying saucers. Good grief! Hard to imagine anyone believing that! But I saw Clint sinking in the quicksand of hope for a utopian future.

I sat gingerly in a chair across from him and tried to throw him a lifeline. "I know you like Electus, but don't let them replace your family. Your father's birthday is special."

He jerked his head up until his fierce face—accentuated by spiky black hair, black mustache and goatee, and five-o'clock shadow—was right in mine. "If it weren't for Electus, I would either be completely insane or dead by now. You can't begin to imagine what was going on inside my head before I found them. So back off, okay?"

I debated for the thousandth time how to reach Clint without alienating him even more than I had up to now. How could he not see Electus is a cult? I smoothed my face and sighed. "I'm not sure I understand why Electus is suddenly so important to you."

I winced as Clint's intense dark eyes burned into me. "Look, Mom, this society is sick. You should know that better than most, after being a judge all those years. Haven't you seen the sickness up close and personal?"

"Of course," I said. "But the people we see in court don't represent mainstream society. We get the outliers—the ones who have screwed up."

Clint clenched his jaw and stiffened his shoulders as he leaned in to me. "You're right that they're not the mainstream. They're just the ones who got caught and were too poor or powerless to work the system. The real filth are the elite power-brokers who run everything to their own advantage and screw the little guy every chance they get. Wall Street is a vampire corporate entity, sucking money from the many for the few."

I answered in a calm voice I hoped would engage his rational brain. "You know I agree with you about inequality and the concentration of wealth and power. You know I support progressive politicians and their policies."

Clint scowled and fidgeted as he pushed on with his blaming agenda. "And yet you own stocks and property, a lot of which you inherited." His voice rose in a challenging tone. "You're part of the one percent, so don't try to wash your hands of the problems."

I kept my voice low-key. "I'm not washing my hands of the problems, I'm supporting solutions."

"Never mind. This planet is going to be recycled and renewed. The only way to survive is to leave. I have to be ready when they come. I have to give up my attachments to this planet. That means family, friends, jobs, money and stuff."

That was when I lost control, my restraint slipped and I stuck the knife in with a cheap shot. "Since you don't have a job, I guess that makes giving up that attachment easier."

As soon as I spoke, I regretted the jab, but it was too late. Storm clouds gathered over Clint's narrow face as he got up, turned away from me, and walked toward the kitchen. "Forget it," he said. "You can't see because you're blinded by tradition. We've talked enough. Go do your shopping."

When I got back, Jerry and Clint were on the couch, legs stretched out on the ottoman in front, watching old reruns of Bonanza. Both were smiling and looked relaxed, so I went on in to the kitchen to put away my groceries without disturbing them.

Later, after Clint left, I snuggled up with Jerry on the couch. When he was holding me wrapped in his arms, I almost fooled myself into believing I had the old Jerry back.

My eyes drifted to our framed wedding photograph on the side table—me in a long-sleeved white lace dress with silver accent stitching of roses, and Jerry in a tux—standing next to a multi-tiered white wedding cake decorated with pink spray roses and baby's breath. We had eyes only for each other as I stuffed sugary cake into Jerry's open mouth with one hand, while my other hand caressed his face. We looked so young, so sweet, so in love. After fifty years, I loved him more than ever. But losing him to the shadows overtaking his mind was slow torture. I longed for him to be his old self laughing and talking with me.

"We're going to have a party for your birthday on Sunday," I said. "We'll sing Happy Birthday, and eat cake and have fun like we used to do."

# Chapter 4

## Jerry

On Sunday Morning, Jerry sat on the couch watching the flickering faces on the television screen, trying to follow the thread of what the two men were saying on *Meet the Press*. Their words confused him and their argumentative tone worried him. He looked around for Anne, but he didn't see her. A familiar ache came over him. His chest tightened. His heart raced. He was alone. He needed her. He wanted her next to him. "Hon, what are you doing?" he called.

"Just getting the food ready for brunch. I'll be right back."

He squirmed in his seat, unable to get comfortable. His eyes darted around the room. She wasn't there. He couldn't see her at all. "Hon, where are you?" he yelled.

"Sweetie, I'm right here."

There she was, running into the living room.

Jerry lit up at the sight of her. "There you are," he said, his whole face smiling.

Anne returned his smile as she stretched out her hand to help him up. "Come on into the dining room with me," she said. "You can help me set the table before everyone gets here."

Jerry followed along, happy so long as he was with Anne. The food smelled yummy and his stomach rumbled. "Let's eat," he said. "I'm hungry."

"Soon," Anne said. "When they all get here."

## Anne

My sister Meadow arrived early with bunches of colorful flowers for the table. "I know you said no gifts, but I wanted to bring him something," she said.

Meadow and I are very different but we "get each other," as they say. I knew she loved Jerry, but I also knew she found it hard to get into a celebratory mood for his birthday. When I talked to her on the phone about the party, she had asked me what I thought another year meant for him now. And if I were in his situation, would I be celebrating another year coming up? Meadow has been meditating for years and reading Eastern mystics and she's thought a lot about the meaning of life. She told me recently she had tried thinking of Jerry as a sort of enlightened being with a beginner's mind, but she never could see holiness or wisdom in his eyes. Sadly, I couldn't disagree with her assessment. When I looked into his eyes I saw a blankness, not the deep-pools kind, but the kind like there's nothing there.

"Jerry, sweetie, I brought you spring flowers," Meadow said, holding them up to his face so he could sniff their delicate fragrance. "Let's fix them in some vases." She put one hand on Jerry's arm and led him to the kitchen. I followed, admiring the way her long silver spiral earrings picked up the silver threads in her curly black hair.

"I went out with Roger last night," she said to me over her shoulder.

"You could have brought him," I said.

"Nah, he's not family, and I don't want him to be. I've been thinking about signing up for internet dating," she said. "Here I am, sixty-six, still looking for my soulmate, and I've run out of possibilities in Helena. I know all the available men, I've slept with most of them, and the earth hasn't moved." Meadow helped Jerry into a chair at our weathered wood farmhouse kitchen table while I got out three crystal vases.

"So you'd be looking to meet men from other places?" I asked. My heart sank at the thought of Meadow moving away. Now that Martha was gone, Meadow was the only person I could talk to openly about absolutely anything. Dan is my rock, strong, solid, reliable, and always there for me, even more since Jerry's descent into dementia. But we're both opinionated and stubborn and we disagree on lots of stuff.

Meadow arranged the flowers in the vases, artistically the way she does everything. Jerry watched her, while I got the muffins and coffee cake out of the oven. "I'd hate to leave Helena," she said. "I'd miss teaching pottery at the Archie Bray Center, and I'd miss you—but we could Skype or talk on the phone. I'm not sure what I'd do if it came down to making a choice to move, but after all these years of failed relationships, I still want to find true love. You and Jerry have been so lucky to have each other all these years." She gave him a hug and a kiss on the cheek. He smiled and patted her arm.

When the doorbell rang, we moved into the living room. Bill and Amelia were at the front door with our grandchildren Vicky and Miranda dressed in lacy party dresses. Vicky's dress was pink, her current favorite color, and Miranda's was a more sophisticated purple. With shouts of "Happy birthday, Granddad," they ran to Jerry and gave him the cards they had made. "How old are you Granddad," Vicky asked with her usual four-year-old's directness. "Vicky!" Miranda scolded, "Mommy said not to ask him that."

Vicky's face crumpled at the rebuke from her six-year-old sister, so I leaned down and gave her a hug. "Never mind," I said. "He's seventy-five. Can you count that high?"

"I can," Miranda said, tugging on my arm. "One, two, three, four …"

Miranda's counting went on in the background through the arrival of Dan, and Debby, and Clint, who'd decided to show up after all. By the time she got to seventy-five, we were taking our seats at the table in the dining room with its high ceilings, flocked wallpaper, and french doors that open out to a patio lined with perennial flowers. It's my favorite room in our house. To me a dining room represents family warmth, closeness and love. It's a place where generations bond through holiday celebrations, family rituals and traditions.

So there we were, the happy family celebrating a birthday—the exact scene I'd pictured. But the happy-family-thing lasted at most ten or fifteen minutes while we passed food around and filled our plates with fruit, cheese, quiche, bagels, and muffins, and I poured coffee, tea, juice and milk. Then the squabbling started, with Dan first out of the gate.

"Hey, Bill," Dan said. "I heard John Rasanen and Phil Lemon are trying to recruit you to run for City Commission. What's the word?"

"Not interested," Bill said.

"Come on, Bill," Debby said in a teasing tone. "With your charm and good looks and the family name, you'd be electable with no sweat. Why not give it a try?"

"Too much trouble and takes too much time," Bill said, methodically spreading cream cheese on a bagel and topping it with smoked salmon. "Why don't you run if you think it's such a great idea?"

"Um, never-married single mom with son in drug rehab. Don't think I'd make a viable candidate." Debby said.

"Elections are rigged anyway," Clint said, waving a forkful of pineapple in the air. "Why would either one of you want to support that phony racket? Politicians are just out to line their pockets."

"Hang on, Clint," Dan said, putting down his fork. His face reddened. "That's a little harsh. I'll admit there are some shady politicians out there, but not all of us are corrupt."

"Sorry, Uncle Dan, but I can't agree," Clint said sharply. "Every time we have an election, challengers promise to come in and end the corruption so we can have a fresh start, but once the new ones get in they're as corrupt as the ones they replaced."

Both Vicky and Miranda looked worried. And Jerry was frowning. "Clint," I said, in an attempt to smooth things over. "This isn't the time or the place for this discussion. You and Dan can argue about this some other time."

"Mom," Clint was shouting now. "Why is it always my fault? Uncle Dan and Bill and Debby started this conversation."

Vicky began to cry. "Mommy, why is everybody so mad?"

Amelia picked her daughter up and put her on her lap. "They don't have good manners," she said. "They don't know how to behave at a party like you and Miranda do."

I jumped into fixit mode, hoping to distract everyone with a family birthday story. "Hey, Dan," I said, "Do you remember Meadow's tropical birthday party?" I turned to Miranda. "Meadow was eight—just two years older than you—and she wanted a Hawaiian party, so our mama made fake palm trees and a friend of my dad's played the ukulele and some woman gave hula lessons. Our mama made fancy drinks out of pineapple and cherry juice with little paper parasols stuck in pineapple chunks. It was so much fun. We wore grass skirts—or at least the girls did— and we danced and ate birthday cake decorated with yellow and orange tropical flowers."

"Ha! That's not how I remember it," Dan said, tilting back in his chair like the teenager he was recalling. "What I remember is that Mama made us all dress in dorky Hawaiian clothes. I was fifteen and I had to wear a stupid shirt with palm trees on it and when we were outside in the front yard, some of my friends rode by on their bikes. I never heard the end of it. They called me 'hula boy' for years. So thanks for the fond memory, Meadow."

Meadow cocked her head to the side and smiled. "Poor Dan," she said. "But I don't remember that party being so great myself, "What I remember was that Daddy was putting booze in his fancy drinks and he had a lot of them and he and Mama were arguing about it. Then when he was bringing out the cake with the lighted candles on it, he stumbled and got the candles too close to the tablecloth and set it on fire and Mama had to throw water on it. She managed to save the cake but she was smoking mad herself."

Clint was listening eagerly. "Sounds like one more terrific family time all right," he said with a smirk.

I gave up. "Come on Miranda and Vicky. Let's go in the kitchen and light the candles on Granddad's cake."

"We'll do it carefully," Vicky said, "so we don't set anything on fire."

After the cake, I got them all into the living room to watch the family movie. "I just remembered these and got them out the other day," I said. "I'm going through them and then I'll get the best parts digitized. But I want to show you one short snippet today."

They looked more wary than eager as they moved chairs around and took seats facing the screen. I turned on the projector and there were a much younger Ned and Meadow frolicking in the snow. They made snow angels, threw snowballs, built a snowman, and pulled each other on one of the old wooden sleds we had back in the 1950s. Vicky and Miranda giggled.

Meadow clapped and grinned. "Wow! It's great to see that. I must have been about eight and Ned about ten. Look—Mama made us wear those silly hats Grandma Clara knit for us. Ned and I used to have so much fun playing together." Her face took on a pensive look.

I turned off the projector. "I wanted to show you all the film because most of you never met Ned and those of us who knew him haven't seen him for a long time. I got a call from California last Wednesday telling me he died a week ago from liver cancer. I wanted to tell you all together so we could take a minute to think about him.

Long silence. Jerry had dozed off. Everyone else, except Vicky and Miranda, looked like they'd rather be almost anywhere else but here. When I planned this announcement, I thought it was a good idea, but now I wasn't so sure. Perhaps I should have called them individually after all.

Vicky pulled on my arm. "Gramma, can we watch some more movies?"

Amelia pulled Vicky onto her lap. "You know what? I think you and me and Miranda could help your Gramma by putting away some of the leftovers in the kitchen while these grownups talk. We might even find some extra cake out there to snack on." She put Vicky down, stood up and moved toward the kitchen, with the little girls scampering after her .

I appreciated her quick thinking. At this point I was uncertain what turns the conversation might take.

After another minute silence, Meadow spoke. "Poor Ned," she said. "I know I should feel something, but it's been so long since I've seen him that he's like someone from another life."

"I know," I said. "The last time I saw him was about forty-five years ago. His choice, not mine, but maybe I should have tried harder."

"It was so painful, though," Meadow said, grimacing. "I remember seeing him a few times when I was living in Oakland and he was in graduate school in Seattle. We both tried to connect—or at least I did and I think he did too—but all that stuff we couldn't talk about sat there like a mountain we couldn't get over or around. He was my brother and a terrible thing happened to him. I wanted him to know I cared about him and I didn't blame him, but he was so tense and standoffish he'd flinch if I even put my hand on his arm."

"Exactly," I said. "I had no idea how to repair my relationship with him. So I just gave up."

Dan had his arms crossed in front of him, staring off into the distance. Finally he turned toward me and said in a flat voice, "I don't have anything to say about Ned that I haven't said years ago. You know how I feel about him, Anne. I can't pretend to care about him now, when I haven't cared for the past fifty years."

In my opinion, Dan did care, but he didn't want to deal with his feelings about Mama's death and Ned's part in it. So he just stuffed all that under and pretended it wasn't there.

I poked a little with my response. "Isn't that kind of harsh, Dan? He was our brother after all and Daddy and everyone said what happened wasn't his fault. Can't you at least give him a break now that he's gone?"

"I'm not some sanctimonious guy who changes his mind and pretends to like someone just because he died. That would be hypocritical. You may not like my point of view, but at least I'm consistent."

This wasn't going anywhere. I'd pushed one of Dan's "cannot undo" buttons.

"What about the funeral?" Bill asked. "Should some of us go? I'll go with you if you want, Mom."

"Thanks. You're sweet to offer. Apparently Ned didn't want a funeral or a memorial service, so there won't be anything. But Keith—the guy who called—says Ned left me something very important that he wanted me to pick up in San Diego personally and by myself. I plan to go next Tuesday, just for overnight."

"I can stay with Dad during the days you're gone," Clint said, "if someone else can be here that night."

"I can do Tuesday night," Debby said. "I'm alone at home now that Josh is in rehab.

A comfortable warmth came over me. My kids have their issues, but I can count on them to rise to the occasion when I need them. "Thank you all," I said. "I appreciate the help and support."

"Are you sure it's worth the trip?" Dan asked skeptically. "Why can't this Keith just send what Ned left you?"

"Keith doesn't have whatever it is. All he has is instructions and a key to a storage locker."

"That sounds risky to me." Dan sounded exasperated. "Have you even considered that this may be some sort of trap Ned set for you? His last revenge? You don't know much about this Keith guy and you don't know what you're getting yourself in to." When I didn't respond, he sighed and continued, "Okay. I know how stubborn you can be, Anne. If you insist on going, I'll go with you."

"Thanks for the offer, Dan, but Ned asked me to come alone and that's what I'm going to do. You don't need to worry. I'm no patsy walking blindly into a trap. I've done my research and I'll be careful."

Dan held up his hands, palms out in a gesture of surrender. "Okay. If that's what you want. Have a nice trip," he said, in that automatic tone he uses when he has mentally moved on. "Call me when you get back."

After we cleaned up the dishes, they left and Jerry settled in for a nap. I was left alone with my thoughts. The cake, the candles, the whole family singing the Happy Birthday song had taken me back to other pleasant memories of family birthday parties, but an emptiness had replaced my happy expectations for the day.

I'm crazy about family gatherings and traditions. They jump out at me everywhere I go. Families gathered together at restaurants, on picnics, on vacation—sharing festive times, celebrating weddings, birthdays, holidays. Generations laughing, joking, and enjoying that intimacy that comes with long familiarity.

I crave the warmth and closeness that envelops them. The old World War II song, "I'll be Home for Christmas," always brings tears to my eyes. It's a far-from-home soldier's yearning to be with family for the holidays, and saying he will be there "if only in my dreams." Home in that song isn't a place, it's a family, people who care about you, who always love and welcome you.

But today's gathering hadn't been what I had envisioned. I wanted the affectionate family in The Waltons *Thanksgiving Story*, not the prickly one in *The Ice Storm*. I wanted the family of my childhood, the one I remembered, the one I saw in our old movies.

# Chapter 5

## Anne

If you live in Helena, Montana, you're stuck with expensive plane tickets and undesirable schedules to most destinations, so I wasn't surprised to find no ideal choices for flights to San Diego. The best I could do was a flight leaving Helena at 6:30 in the morning, which would get me to San Diego at 9:30 a.m., after a stop in Salt Lake City. To leave later in the day, I'd have two or three stops resulting in a ten- or eleven-hour trip. So I steeled myself and left early Tuesday morning while Jerry was still asleep. Of course he'd be upset when he woke up and I wasn't there. He wouldn't remember where I had gone, but Clint was there and would remind and reassure him.

My plane got in to San Diego right on time and the address Keith had given me was only about twelve miles from the airport. So I pulled up to the house in my rental car at exactly ten forty-five, the time Keith and I had agreed to meet. It was a gracious Spanish-style ranch with a burnt sienna stucco finish, surrounded by tropical landscaping. Seeing Ned's house after all these years was like judgment day—where I was both the judge and the accused. Why was my first time here on a day when it was too late to make amends?

I marched myself up to the front door, like a kid sent to the principal's office. My heart was pounding, my hands were clammy. Very unusual for me. I've been in plenty of tense situations, and I'm known for keeping my cool under pressure. But this was different. This was family. I took a deep breath, straightened my spine, and rang the bell.

The man who answered was slight and balding, with a smattering of gray hair on the sides of his head. His steely blue eyes took me in at a glance as his wide smile welcomed me. "Hi, I'm Keith. It's so nice to meet you at last, Judge Barnes." He ushered me in to a small living room decorated in warm southwestern colors—brown, beige, turquoise and red. I looked around the room and saw what I imagined was Ned's life. Art. Books. Mozart piano sonatas playing. Was this who Ned was? What had I missed by not being part of his life?

Keith walked me through to a wide inner courtyard landscaped with flowering bushes and palm trees surrounding a kidney-shaped pool, a waterfall and a small hot tub. "This is our favorite part of the house and where we spend most of our time when we're home," he said. I noticed he was still referring to Ned in the present tense, which I saw as testimony of their loving bond.

Keith led me to a padded chair under a large palapa facing the pool. Then he excused himself, went back into the house, and returned with a tray holding two mugs of coffee and a plate of warm bite-sized pastries. "I'm so sorry we have to meet this way," he said, his earlier wide smile replaced with a thoughtful expression. "I wanted Ned to invite you before, but the thought of getting back in touch with his family overwhelmed him after so long. You understand."

I nodded. What else could I do? It was too late to be part of Ned's life. But in truth I didn't understand. I never had. Why had he cut us off forever? What could I have done to change that?

Now that he was gone and I was sitting here in his stunning courtyard, I found myself descending into a deep pit of regret. Why hadn't I tried harder? Pushed more? Was I too busy? Too polite? Too scared?

But it was too late for all that. I could take time for regrets later. Today was about Ned's instructions, his bequest, and learning anything Keith could add to my understanding of my brother's life. I was a bit wary of Keith, though. I didn't know what to make of this man who had been Ned's partner all these years. I couldn't decide whether I was a jerk for doubting Keith's connection to Ned, or a fool for taking his word that I needed to travel all this way to get what Ned left me.

I sipped the rich coffee, inhaling its nutty aroma. "Do you know why Ned left me whatever it is?" I asked, keeping my tone neutral and my voice soft. I didn't want Keith to feel attacked or on the defensive in any way.

Keith looked down at his hands, avoiding my eyes. "No. Ned was very secretive about his personal life. I don't even know why he was estranged from his family—your family. We both mostly left our pasts behind."

"Do you have any idea what he left me?"

He hesitated, then spoke slowly as if choosing his words cautiously. "No. I don't know that either. We owned this house together and he left his share to me, along with some stocks and such. But he didn't have as much as you might think. He'd been spending a lot on a project he'd been working on for years. He had his own lab for it, not at the university. But I don't know anything about that either. I'm a musician. He was a neuroscientist. We talked about my work because Ned loved music, but he preferred not to talk about his work and I respected his wishes about that."

"Of course," I said, nodding in agreement. I knew how unapproachable Ned could be. Apparently Ned compartmentalized his life even with Keith.

We talked a bit more, Keith sharing his experience of Ned's cancer and the anguish of his last months. I listened, but did not reciprocate by disclosing any of Ned's past. If Ned hadn't revealed his past to Keith, it certainly wasn't my place to do so.

After about an hour, Keith said he had an appointment, so he needed to give me Ned's instructions, which turned out to be directions to a storage unit, a code to open the front gate, and a key to unlock the padlock on unit number 180. I found myself wondering why Keith hadn't succumbed to curiosity and gone there himself to discover what was inside. Either he was a man of honor whose loyalty to Ned trumped everything, or this whole thing was an elaborate setup designed to suck me in. I decided to trust Keith, thank him for his help, and move along with the task.

I plugged the address for the storage place into my GPS and drove off, my curiosity suppressing my doubts.. When I spotted the sign for the storage site, I turned in, drove up to the metal gates, and punched in the code Keith had given me. The gate swung open like it knew me, admitting my car to a land of dark-green single-story cement storage units. As I drove slowly up and down the rows looking for unit 180, I saw only one other customer—a guy closing and locking his unit. Once he drove off, the place was eerily silent. After about ten minutes, I spotted unit 180, the second to the end of a long row.

I stopped in front and got out, the key to the padlock clutched in my fist. The mid-day sun beat down on me as I stood contemplating this spot Ned had brought me to. Unit 180 did not stand out from the others in any way, but rather blended into the row, its padlocked corrugated metal door hiding whatever treasure or trash lay within.

I hesitated, doubts rising to the surface again. "Why me?" I asked myself. "Why did Ned leave whatever is inside to me? And why did I have to come all this way alone to get it?"

What if Dan was right and this was a trap? Would a bomb go off when I opened the door? Or would something sharp or heavy land on my head? Or would I trip a wire connected to a gun that would shoot me in the face? Was I crazy to put myself at risk? Who would take care of Jerry if I didn't make it home from here?

"Stop," I told myself. "You don't need those negative thoughts. You've come all this way. You want to get this last message from Ned. You'll be fine. Now unlock the door and go in."

I planted my feet, stuck the key in the lock and turned it. It opened. I removed the padlock from its fastenings, took a deep breath and lifted the metal door by its handle at the bottom. The door went up and nothing else happened. No noise, except the sounds of the door going up. Nothing blew up or fell on me. All I saw was a small table with a chair next to it. On that table was a black metal box whose contents would change my life forever.

I walked over to the table and examined the dust-covered box. On top of it was a thick white envelope addressed to me, with the added instruction, "Please read this before you open the box." Inside the envelope was a handwritten letter:

Dear Anne,

I've been a neuroscientist for more than forty years, teaching and doing research here at UC San Diego. I expect you know that. What you may not know is that the focus of my research has always been the science of memory, specifically the recovery of lost memories. This won't surprise you when you remember my horror and disbelief when I was told at age eighteen that I had fatally shot Mama in a hunting accident—an accident that I was unable to remember at all.

For years I tried to reconcile my own memories with what our father told me happened on that terrible day. I needed to remember so I could accept what I had been told as reality. Psychotherapy, cognitive therapy, hypnotism—nothing worked. Later, in my scientific study of memory, I learned that these methods are as likely to implant false memories as they are to recover actual ones. So I took another approach.

I can almost hear you saying, "Get to the point, Ned," so here it is. I did finally discover a reliable way to recover memories. It's the culmination of my life's work—a device I call the Memory Enhancer. I have only recently perfected it and have used it many times but kept it to myself because I haven't had the time or the energy to thoroughly consider its implications. With the progression of my cancer, I know my time is short now, and I will not be able to control the Memory Enhancer's future.

If you are reading this, I have died and left you the Memory Enhancer (I'm going to call it the ME from now on, which is a very appropriate acronym as you'll learn later). I realize I should have talked to you about it rather than leaving it this way. I meant to do that, but so many years have gone by with no contact between us. I know that was my choice and that you wanted to keep us all together. But I could never forgive the way Dad handled Mama's death, and you were so close to him. Plus, you're close to Dan and he blames me for everything. So, bottom line, I thought about calling you, but I never could bring myself to dial your number.

I paused in my reading to consider what that phone call might have been like if he had actually made it. Or what might have happened if I had persevered in trying to contact him? It sounded like at some point he was open to talking with me. But he didn't and I didn't and now here I was reading his dying wishes. With tears in my eyes, I picked up the paper and read on.

*So why am I leaving you the ME and what is it? I'll start with the why. Some inventions change the world in a profound way. I think the ME may be one of those. You're a judge, and from all I've heard and read, a fair and careful one. You have a lot of experience making decisions in difficult situations where the results are likely to affect many people. In that respect, I consider you more qualified than I am to decide what to do with the ME.*

I was touched that he had followed my career as if we'd been close over the years. At some level he must have seen himself as part of the family, even though he didn't want to spend time with us. That both warmed and wounded my heart.

*Now to the what. The ME uses transcranial direct current stimulation (tDCS) to apply low dosage electricity to the brain while the wearer is sleeping. I know this sounds creepy like Jack Nicholson having his brain fried by electroshock therapy in the movie* One Flew Over the Cuckoo's Nest. *But in fact it's nothing like that. Electroshock uses one ampere of electricity and tDCS uses 1.5 milliamperes, about a tenth of the amount of current flowing through the ear buds of an iPod. It's a painless process that produces only a slight tingling at the onset. The user wears a skullcap that produces a small surge of electricity that stimulates neurons into firing more readily and accessing information imbedded in memory.*

*Here's how it works for the person using it. There's a digital control on a laptop connected to the skullcap. You set it for the specific date and time you want to re-live, then you put on the cap, press start, and go to sleep. While you're sleeping you will vividly recall your experience from the time you set, exactly as if you're living the events all over again. It feels like the ME uncorks a bottle containing your memories with their original intensity, and those memories envelop you. When you wake up you will remember the time clearly and in detail.*

Whoa, this sounded like time travel. Could this work? Or was Ned trying to trick me in some way like Dan suspected?

*The ME ,with its complete instructions and specifications, including a laptop with the required software, is in the black box on the table. I am asking you to try it and decide what to do with it. I realize I am asking a lot of you. You may be worried about trying a device that sends electricity to your brain. Let me reassure you that I am an exceedingly cautious neuroscientist who would never use or ask anyone else to use a device that could be dangerous. I conducted years of animal trials before trying the ME myself, and then eighty volunteers tried it several times each. I found no bad effects from its use (and it's in no way connected to my cancer). If you look up tDCS, you'll find it's been used in many trials with healthy adults, again with no bad effects.*

*I can't give you documentation of the experiences of my human subjects who tested the ME because I destroyed that data. I didn't develop the ME at the university nor did I go through their Institutional Review Board to get approval for the use of human subjects. This work was all done on my own, the subjects were paid volunteers, who willingly agreed to participate and enjoyed their experiences. In fact many of them would like to continue using the ME, but I was careful to keep my identity and affiliations secret from them, so none of them would know how to find me, or be tempted to publicize their ME experiences.*

*Of course conducting unregulated research like this means I violated my agreements with the university. I did that because I didn't want the ME to be a project of a university or scientific institute where it would be embroiled for years if not decades in regulations and red tape. I'm sixty-eight and I've been fighting colon cancer for six years.*

*I wanted the ME to be completed in my lifetime and I wanted to use it myself before I got too sick to do it. So I made my choices.*

A loud banging sound from outside the storage unit shot a jolt of adrenalin through me. I jumped out of the chair, dropped Ned's letter, ran to the door and looked out. I saw a battered red pickup about seven units down the row from Ned's, but no person was in sight. Aware that I was alone in an isolated spot far from home, with no way to defend myself if I needed to, I considered my options. I could pull the door to the unit down, but there was no way to lock it from the inside. The lock was a padlock on the outside. And if I pulled the door down, the noise would not only call attention to me, I'd be inside in the dark with no way of knowing if someone was coming toward me. I had left my phone in the car, and even if I had it, who would I call? I couldn't call 911 about a banging noise. At that point, I wished I had accepted Dan's offer to come to San Diego with me.

But I was alone and needed to take care of myself. I decided I'd be safer in the car, which I could lock from the inside and where I could see any threats around me. So I grabbed the letter and the black box, ran to the car, jumped in and locked it. I decided to keep reading in the car in case, after I got done reading, I wanted to put the box back in the storage unit and leave it there. I settled myself in the front seat and read on.

*You may think the ME's potential benefits aren't enough for you to get involved with a project that violated ethical guidelines. If so, I encourage you to think again. The ME is an amazing device. I can tell you that you'll be stunned at the way the ME takes you back. It's kind of like a dream and kind of like a HD video. You're back there, you see and hear and feel what's going on. You are yourself there but at the same time inside your head you are yourself today. So you can re-live old times with today's perspective and remember your past accurately. We all have memories we'd like to re-experience, loved ones we'd like to see again, and questions about our pasts we'd like to have answered.*

*I'm not going to tell you more about the ME here because I want you to make up your own mind about it. I'm also asking you to keep it to yourself until you've made a decision about its value.*

*Having kept myself estranged from the family all these years, I may not have the right to a dying wish. But you know the history and the anguish of our past and how those long-ago events cracked our family apart. I am asking you as a judge to give the ME a fair chance. My dying wish is to give something back to the world that may improve the lives of others. The ME is yours now. Please try it, think about it and decide. You can choose to destroy it and its specifications (there is only one prototype and one set of specs) or you can decide to share it with the world in whatever way you choose.*

# Chapter 6

## Sandra (aka Sister Mary Margaret)

Sister Mary Margaret was not on the list to wash dishes after lunch, which meant she had one precious hour of free quiet time before beginning her afternoon work. She walked alone to a favorite spot on the Abbey grounds—a rock garden bursting with blue, pink and purple perennials. As always, she marveled at the imagination of the creator who gave the earth such a marvelous variety of plants and flowers.

She sat quietly on a bench facing the garden waterfall where water cascaded over rough gray stones into a koi pool. The splashing of the falling water soothed her as it always did, smoothing out the bumpy parts of her soul. She needed that rush of tranquility to bring back the serene Sister Mary Margaret she had worked so hard to become.

Meadow's phone call had unsettled her, leaving her disquieted in a way she hadn't been for many years. She could hardly believe Ned was dead. The news jolted her back to being Sandra again—that troubled girl she had been before she joined the contemplative Benedictine order forty years ago when she was only twenty. In Sister Mary Margaret's mind, Sandra was a separate person, a dreary and downcast young woman she didn't want to think about, much less be.

She fingered the sterling silver rosary she always kept in her pocket. Mama had given it to her for her first communion, and it was one of the few family remembrances she had kept when she entered her new life. Her contact with her family had been minimal since she joined the order. Although family members were allowed to visit the Abbey, she had not encouraged them. Back when tragedy struck their family, everything was chaos and misery. Daddy ignored Ned—couldn't or wouldn't speak to him. Dan only came home for the funeral and yelled at Ned and Daddy. Anne fluttered from one to the other of them trying to placate everyone. Nicole (who hadn't yet changed her name to Meadow) was out with her friends smoking pot. Ten-year-old Sandra laid low.

In the long cold winter months that followed, her sisters and brothers had left her floundering, forced to deal with her grief and an alcoholic father on her own. Dan went back to the Air Force, Anne went back to studying law at Stanford, and Ned went back to college in Seattle. Nicole was at home for two more years, but she was sixteen and immersed in her busy teenage life. Sometimes she'd take Sandra out to the mall or ice skating or cross-country skiing, but those times were few. Most of the time it was just Sandra, Dad, and Grandma Clara at home. They each withdrew into their own desolate grief space, unable to comfort each other.

Her mind flashed to a typical cold, dark, lonely winter evening eating supper in the kitchen with her grandmother, her father still at work and Nicole off with friends.

"How was school today, Sandra?" her grandmother would ask.

"Fine," Sandra would reply, stuffing a roll into her mouth.

"Did you learn anything interesting?"

A long silence while Sandra finished chewing. Then she'd mumble, "Not really."

"Eat your carrots," Grandma Clara would say, turning Sandra's plate so the uneaten vegetable was at the front.

"I don't like carrots," Sandra would say, reaching for another roll and slathering it with butter.

"You need to eat more vegetables and not so many rolls. You're getting a little chubby," her grandmother would admonish.

"I'm done," Sandra would say, standing up and carrying her plate to the sink, carrots uneaten.

Then she'd head to her room to do homework, listen to music, and take solace in the secret box of candy bars she kept hidden in her closet—but the chocolate provided only momentary comfort.

She'd never made friends easily and the extra pounds added by her secret candy stash and her love for buttered rolls didn't help. Extreme loneliness intensified her grief. For years, Sandra had cried herself to sleep every night missing her mother. She had not cried for her father when he died sixteen years after she came to the Abbey and she would not cry now for Ned. She prayed for them, but she could not weep for them. She wasn't angry at them, but she saw no connection to them. They had been dead to her for a long time.

## Anne

I put down Ned's letter and opened the box. Inside was a small red plastic headset with four round attachments that looked like earphones; also a laptop computer, a plastic bag of cords and cables, a notebook entitled "Instruction Manual," and an expanding folder with three sealed envelopes inside. A note on the folder said: *In this folder I've included several handwritten letters about my experiences using the ME. I planned each one for you to read as a guide as you go along when questions come up. Of course you could read them all right now, but I think you'll find them more valuable if you read them as you proceed over the next few weeks.*

It was 2:00 p.m. by then, and stiflingly hot in my car. I was tired—having gotten up at 4:00 a.m. to catch my early plane—and hungry—having eaten nothing since 5:00 a.m. except Keith's tiny pastries—so I searched on my iPhone for nearby restaurants.

I decided to put all the stuff back in the box and take it with me. I figured I could think about Ned's invention while I ate and if I wanted to put it back in the storage unit, I could always come back.

I was about to drive to one of the restaurants when my phone rang. Clint. Something must be wrong with Jerry.

"Mom, you need to talk to Dad. He keeps looking for you and calling for you. He won't eat or do anything except ask me, "Where's Anne? Where did Anne go?"

This wasn't good. It was 3:00 p.m. in Helena, If Clint hadn't been able to get Jerry to eat yet, things weren't going well. "Okay. Put him on."

"Here's Mom. You can talk to her."

I hear Jerry breathing into the phone.

"Hi sweetie. How are you? Did Clint give you some lunch?"

A long pause. Then Jerry said, "I'll have lunch with you."

"I had to take a short trip, sweetie, so I can't be there for lunch or dinner. Clint will fix you something yummy. How about pepperoni pizza? You love pizza."

"No." He sounded determined. "I don't want lunch with Clint. I want lunch with you."

"I can't be there until tomorrow. We can have lunch tomorrow. But right now you need to eat lunch with Clint."

Bang. Jerry dropped the phone. Clint picked it up. "Okay. You tried," he said. "If Dad doesn't eat until morning, so be it."

"Debby will be over later. Maybe he'll eat with her," I said.

"It's not like Debby has some magic I don't have, Mom. I can do whatever she can do."

Uh, oh. Clint was getting defensive. Anything I say that he can see as criticism sets him off. I needed to reassure him. "Of course she doesn't, Clint. I'm not saying she's better with Jerry than you are. But sometimes a change will defuse his stubbornness."

"Whatever, Mom. See you later." He hung up.

## Debby

Debby was wiped out from a grueling day in court and still buried in work piled up at the office when it was time to leave to go over to relieve Clint and stay with her dad. On top of her weariness, she missed Josh. He still hadn't been in rehab long enough for her to be allowed to visit or even talk to him on the phone. While she was glad he was there, being out of contact was like a punishment she didn't deserve.

As always before seeing her dad, she was a little tense. Debby had a close bond with Jerry growing up. He taught her to ride, skate and ski, encouraged her to join the high school hockey team and cheered loudly at all her games. She got her athletic ability and her love of the outdoors from him. She missed sharing athletic activities with him and she missed his sense of humor and she missed the long talks they used to have. He had given her so much. Now she wanted to return the favor, but he had slipped so far from reality that she didn't know how to reach him.

She had spent hours researching Alzheimer's disease and its treatments on the internet in hopes of helping him recover some of his memory or at least not lose any more. She found scholarly articles that reported on the effects of memory-boosting super foods like leafy greens, cruciferous vegetables, and fish rich in omega-3 fatty acids. She read that those foods could decrease the cognitive decline in people with Alzheimer's and sometimes improve cognition. But Jerry didn't want to eat those foods and Anne didn't push him. She just let him eat junk. When Debby confronted her on that, Anne's reply was always something like, "That research is inconclusive at best and your dad has so few pleasures left. I'm not going to deprive him of the enjoyment he gets from eating what he wants."

Debby had also found memory exercises and games that strengthen brain cells and neural pathways by keeping the mind active. She'd given some of these to her mom, but Anne said Jerry didn't like them. So Debby tried to stop by often and engage Jerry in a short memory game that required him to recall information. That was what she planned to do tonight.

Debby knocked, then turned the door handle. It was unlocked so she walked in. "Hi.? Are you upstairs or in the kitchen?"

"Kitchen," Clint yelled back.

In the kitchen Debby found Jerry slumped in a chair wearing sweatpants and an undershirt, no shoes. Clint had a plate of pizza in front of him, trying to entice him to eat some, but Jerry had his mouth clamped shut and was shaking his head 'no.'

"Come on Dad. You have to eat something. You don't want to get sick. Just try it. This is one of your favorites." Clint's voice rose in frustration.

Jerry kept his mouth zipped and turned his head away from Clint. Debby wanted to grab the pizza and throw it away, but she restrained herself.

Clint moved the pizza slice around to Jerry's mouth again.

"Clint, stop. Can't you see he doesn't want that? Why force him to eat it? It's not even good for him."

"He has to eat something and this is what Mom suggested."

"Well he for sure doesn't want pizza, so why not try something else?" Debby reminded herself to stay cool. "Never mind," she said. "It's not that big a deal if he doesn't eat right now. Let's give him a rest and I'll offer him something else later."

## Anne

Seething with frustration after my conversation with Clint, I drove the few miles to a recommended bakery cafe. At least I could eat lunch. I locked Ned's box in the trunk of the car, and went inside. The turkey cobb sandwich on rosemary bread and a large iced tea hit the spot. After eating, I was still exhausted, so I headed for my hotel. I had booked near the airport so as to be convenient for my early morning flight on the next day. When I got to my room, I flopped on the bed and fell asleep.

My phone woke me at 5:30 p.m. Debby calling. I'd been asleep about an hour and a half, and was much more alert.

"Mom, I don't think Clint's taking good care of Dad. When I got here after work, they were arguing—or I should say Clint was arguing. Dad was refusing to eat." Her exasperated tone reminded me of times when Clint was three and she was eleven and he kept sneaking into her room and drawing on her walls.

As I had done then, I tried to pour oil on by offering another perspective. "I know Clint was having trouble," I said. He called me earlier. Sometimes your dad just doesn't want to do what people want him to. It even happens to me."

She shook off my attempt to placate. "Well Clint was pushing pizza in his face and telling him he had to eat or he'd get sick. You know that's not the way to get Dad to do something."

Again, I grasped for calm and tried to toss some Debby's way. "Clint had been trying for hours to get him to eat. I expect he was very frustrated."

But she wasn't buying that. Like any first-rate attorney she had a point to make and evidence to back it up. "That's the thing. Clint has a short fuse. You know that. I don't know why you leave Dad with him. That kind of environment isn't what an Alzheimer's patient needs."

This was going nowhere. "Debby, I know you're concerned about your dad and I know you mean well, but you have to trust my judgment about how to take care of him. He's my responsibility."

"Well he's my responsibility right now and he's not doing well at all."

"Just do your best, Debby. I'll be home tomorrow and he'll be fine."

After Debby's call, I wanted to put the events back home out of my mind since there was nothing I could do from San Diego to help the situation. So I used the time to examine the contents of Ned's box. I opened the Instruction Manual notebook and found detailed instructions of how to use the ME—how to connect the various cables to the computer and to the headset, how to use the software that was on the computer and how to set yourself up for a ME session.

Everything was handwritten, and Ned began with the reason for that. He didn't want any computerized records of these materials that might be recovered even though they had been deleted. To make sure that only one copy existed, he wrote by hand.

Next I looked at the expanding folder. It contained the letters Ned said were inside. Each entry was in a sealed envelope with instructions on the front telling me when to read it:

*Letter #1 - Read after you've used the Memory Enhancer several times.*

*Letter #2 - Read when your trips raise questions about the ME's accuracy.*

*Letter #3 - Read when you're ready to put it all together and make a decision.*

I knew I was too tired and confused to make any long-term decision about the ME that night. I certainly didn't plan to try it then and there. But neither was I ready to discard it. I owed Ned at least a serious consideration of what he said was his life's work.

For years, guilt had clouded my memories of Ned. I was supposed to be part of the hunting party that day, but I didn't go. And it was for a stupid reason, not anything important. I just decided to stay home to do a little last-minute Christmas shopping because I wasn't satisfied with the gifts I'd bought in a rush before I came home from law school. I've always wondered whether if I had been on that hunting trip, the accident might not have happened. The butterfly effect and all that. One tiny change can affect everything that comes after it. Maybe Mama would have lived, Ned would have had a better life and our family would be as close and happy as the fictional Waltons from the TV series.

Okay, I didn't really believe that part about the Waltons, but I did have some guilt about Ned, partly because I wasn't there that day and partly because our family didn't help him back when tragedy happened. True, we didn't know how to help him then—but nevertheless we didn't help. Now he was gone and the least I could do was give thoughtful consideration to his dying wish. So I packed up the ME for the trip home.

# Chapter 7

## Anne

I am a careful person who believes in checking out the terrain before I jump into something new. So when I got home from San Diego late Wednesday morning I was itching to begin a web search for transcranial direct current stimulation (tDCS). But first I had to soothe Jerry, get him to eat, and settle him in for a nap. At the same time I had to deflect questions from Clint, who was there taking care of Jerry.

I had accepted Ned's conditions when I brought the ME home—essentially signing on to a contract with him to keep the ME secret while I checked it out. I was honor-bound to follow his instructions not to tell anyone about the ME until I had made a decision about its potential value and what to do with it.

Clint stood next to the kitchen table where Jerry was sitting waiting for the scrambled eggs, toast and applesauce I was fixing for him.

"So what did you inherit?" Clint asked. "And why the big mystery? Is it something illegal like drugs or a huge stash of guns?"

"Clint!" I exploded. "As if Ned would ever go near a gun again!"

He grimaced. "Oh, yeah. I forgot. So what is it then?"

I buttered Jerry's toast, put the eggs on his plate and put it in front of him, along with his dish of applesauce and a glass of milk. He smiled, picked up his spoon and began to eat.

I turned back to Clint and his question. "It's a scientific discovery," I said. "I don't understand it yet, so I can't explain it. I can tell you more after I've studied it."

"Doesn't sound all that earthshaking." He shrugged. "But what can you expect from a university researcher? They're all corrupt. He was probably paid off by some corporation like a pharmaceutical company to show results they wanted or hide something they didn't want."

As long as Clint wasn't pushing me for information about Ned's bequest, he could think whatever he wanted.

"I need to go now, Mom," Clint said as he gathered up his stuff. "Sorry I wasn't able to get Dad to cooperate better."

"It's okay. He misses me when I'm gone that long. I know you did your best. Thanks for being here."

After Clint left and Jerry was napping, I got out my computer and Googled tDCS. Just as Ned had said, it uses small electrodes to deliver constant low-current stimulation directly to the brain. I found that tDCS has been around since the 1800s, but wasn't used much until recent years when neuroscience developed tools that could study its safety and uses. It was developed to help people who have brain injuries, and is considered a safe method of brain stimulation that has shown some success in clinical trials with patients who have Parkinson's disease or have suffered strokes.

Some said it could also help healthy adults perform better on tasks that rely on memory, problem solving and other cognitive abilities. I discovered a research report from a major university where scientists found that a small surge of electricity improved name recall in adults by eleven percent. They concluded that tDCS stimulates neurons into firing more readily and accessing information available in the person's memory.

My most interesting finding was the commercial use of tDCS. Headsets that deliver tDCS, like the one in Ned's box, are produced and sold to gamers who want to get the edge in online gaming by making their synapses fire faster. Gamers report improved reaction time and improved ability to learn new skills using the headsets, which they can control from an iPhone, iPad, or similar device.

All the reports I read emphasized that tDCS has not shown any short-term risks. Of course jolting your brain with electricity, even a minor dose, is controversial, but the headsets have been approved by the FCC for sale in the United States.

This was reassuring. That tDCS had been found to improve memory was an indication that Ned's ME device might work the way he said it did. That tDCS had been studied and hadn't been deemed risky relieved some of my worries about trying it. Still, it was a little like playing with fire. Did I really want to follow Ned's instructions to put this thing on my head and turn it on?

I wished I had someone to talk to about it. Someone with some expertise. Maybe a neurosurgeon? But any physician or scientist worth his or her salt would warn me against trying the ME. They'd want way more study and evidence of its safety before giving approval. And giving the ME over to another scientist would be a betrayal of Ned. So I'd have to figure it out on my own.

## Debby - Wednesday afternoon

At 2:15, Debby stretched in her desk chair and decided to take a break to call her mom, who should be back from San Diego by now and settled in.

"Oh, Debby, hang on just a minute." Anne sounded distracted and Debby heard typing sounds. *Mom was already on the computer?*

After a few seconds, Anne picked up again. "Thanks for staying last night. I'm sorry Jerry wasn't more cooperative."

*Really?* Debby thought. *Do I need to remind her one more time what Dad needs?* Debby took a deep breath and plunged into the deep water. "He would have been better if Clint hadn't been feeding him junk food. Dad needs to be eating fresh greens and fish, not processed stuff like frozen pizza. Do you even know what's in that garbage?"

Anne sighed and came back with her usual oblivious response. "Clint gave Jerry what I told him to give him. It's what Jerry likes."

"If he likes it so much why wasn't he eating it?" Debby shot back. But she could tell Anne wasn't in a receptive mood, so she decided to let it go. "No, never mind. Don't answer that. I know what you're going to say, and I'd much rather hear about your inheritance. What did Ned leave you?"

Silence from Anne's end.

Debby waited about twenty seconds before prodding. "Mom,

are you still there?"

"Oh, sorry. Yes I'm here," Anne said nonchalantly.

This was not sounding like her mother. She was generally quick and direct. "Are you okay?"

"I'm fine, Debby. Just a little tired."

Anne still hadn't answered the question about the inheritance, so Debby rephrased it. "So what was in the mysterious storage locker?"

"It's a scientific thing. I doubt you'd be interested." Again the spiritless voice.

Curiouser and curiouser, Debby thought. It was as if Anne was deliberately hiding something from her. "Come on, Mom. Of course I'm interested. Is it an invention of some kind?"

"It is," Anne said in a strained voice. "But I don't know enough about it yet. Listen, I have to go now. I'll tell you more about it later."

Before Debby could reply, Anne hung up.

Debby was sitting at her desk processing her odd conversation with Anne when she noticed her uncle Dan walking by. She jumped up and followed him down the hall to his office. "Dan, do you have a minute?"

"Sure. Have a seat." Dan waved her toward an oversized brown leather armchair. Dan's office with its dark wood paneling, built-in bookcases, massive oak desk, leather-upholstered furniture, and Charles Russell paintings was just the way her grandfather, William Weller, had had it. The only concession to modern times was the computer on his desk.

Debby noted as she often did in Dan's office that she inwardly shrank into a smaller, younger and less capable version of herself there than she was in her own office. She had tried to figure out the source of this sensation and had come to believe that it was because she remembered visiting her grandfather there. He was a stern man who had been a gunnery officer in the Navy during World War II before he started the law firm. He worked hard and drank hard, and expected his children and grandchildren to meet high standards. Debby was nineteen when her grandfather died, but he always treated her as if she were much younger. Now, even though Dan was always friendly and approachable, his office had this way of summoning her younger self.

She took a deep breath and got to the point. "Have you talked to Mom since she got back from San Diego?"

Dan grinned. "No. I thought I'd give her a day to recover."

"Well I just had the strangest conversation with her. She wouldn't tell me anything about what Uncle Ned left her—just said it's a scientific thing. She sounded like she was hiding something."

"She could be. I wouldn't put it past Ned to have tricked her," Dan said with a smirk and a small chuckle. "She's probably embarrassed because the invention isn't much and she went all that way to get it. Or maybe there's nothing but she doesn't want to admit it."

Debby wasn't getting the help she had hoped for from her uncle. "Maybe you could call her? He was your brother, too. She might tell you more."

Dan shook his head. "No. I don't want to make her feel bad. I know my sister. She likes to be in control and she hates being backed into a corner. I'll wait until she decides to tell me what happened. Can you show me what you have on the Ferguson case so far?"

Debby's shoulders hunched a bit at this dismissal of her concerns, but she had learned to meticulously choose her arguments and marshal her evidence before pressing Dan, and she wasn't even close to doing that in this situation. And—even though she didn't think so—it was possible he was right about the inheritance. The whole thing might be a hoax that her mother didn't want to admit.

Back in her own brightly-lit office with its glass-topped desk, white upholstered furniture, plants and modern paintings, Debby reclaimed her self-confidence. Evidently Dan didn't want to pursue the question about what Ned had left her mother. But that was on him. It didn't mean it wasn't worth her concern.

Something peculiar was going on for her mom to be so remote. Why would this brother who hadn't spoken to anyone in the family for years leave mysterious instructions for her to come to San Diego by herself to get something from a storage unit? Why isn't she telling what it is? Is it something illegal or dangerous or embarrassing?

Debby decided she would wait a few days to see if she heard more.

If she didn't, she'd stop by her parents' house. It would be harder for her mother to evade her questions in person.

## Bill - Thursday morning

"Are you sure your mom wants Vicky over there today after she just got back from San Diego yesterday?" Amelia asked as she pulled Vicky's long blonde hair through a soft pink scrunchie to make a ponytail. If he'd had his camera handy, Bill would have snapped a picture of them, so adorable with their matching blond ponytails and pink shirts. Vicky was totally a mini-Amelia.

Vicky squirmed and grimaced. "Ouch, Mom. That hurts."

"Sorry, Vicky," Amelia said, "I'm almost done." She turned her face back to Bill. "Anne might be tired today. Did you call and check with her?"

"No. I didn't need to call. Mom would have let us know if she wasn't up for having Vicky over today," Bill said. "You know how organized Mom is. If it's Thursday, she has Vicky. If she needed to cancel, she'd call us." Bill thought Amelia worried too much about details. He wasn't one to anticipate problems. Why stir things up unnecessarily? He could deal with complications when he needed to, but he didn't like to create them.

"Have you told her we want to talk to her about the foundation? Because I'd like to do that today when we drop Vicky off."

Bill was anxious to get to the gym so he'd have time to work out on the elliptical and lift weights before his first client. "No, I haven't had a chance to bring that up to her with all that's been going on. It might be better to wait a few days or a week," he said.

"Come on, Bill." Amelia's cornflower blue eyes had that no-more-nonsense look. "I need to get on with this launch. I think we should talk to her today if she's willing."

Bill knew Amelia was right. They shouldn't wait any longer to ask his mom to serve on the board of their foundation. Getting the board set up was a step they needed to take before they could move on. "Okay, let's talk to her today if she has time."

When they got to his parents' house, Vicky gave Anne a hug and headed straight for the couch where Jerry was sitting and climbed into his lap to snuggle.

Bill turned to Anne. "There's something we'd like to talk to you about if you have a few minutes."

"Of course. I'll put *Curious George* on TV for Vicky and Jerry. We can go out to the kitchen and have coffee."

Once they were seated at the kitchen table with their coffee, Amelia began, "You know we're coming up to the one-year anniversary of our baby Evan's death." Bill could see she was fighting to hold back tears, so he caressed her back. She took a breath and continued. "Bill and I have given it a lot of thought and we've decided to start a website and a foundation in his name to promote pertussis vaccination. We're calling it Evan's Place. We plan to tell the story of babies like Evan who got sick with pertussis when they were too young to be vaccinated. Some of them recovered but had long-term complications. Others died like Evan did. Our mission is to make sure everyone knows that when they don't get their children vaccinated for whooping cough, they're endangering babies. We're hoping you'll agree to serve on our board."

Anne reached over and put her arm around Amelia. "It's an important cause and I applaud you wanting to honor Evan's memory this way, but you realize it will be controversial."

"We know," Amelia said. Bill sensed her slim body tightening as if she was preparing for a struggle. "We've seen plenty of anti-vaccine disinformation on the internet. Right here in Montana there are groups like Shot Free, and Montana Families for Health Freedom, fighting to, as they say, 'liberate' children from vaccinations by making it easier for parents to get their children exempted from regulations that require vaccination to start school."

Bill wasn't surprised his mom raised the subject of controversy. Anne was very aware of hot-button issues and most likely wanted to make sure they had thought through the implications of their cause. "We're not looking for a fight," he said. "We know how fiercely independent Montanans can be, especially when it comes to their individual freedoms. But when their freedom endangers someone else's baby, they've taken independence too far. We want to help them see that."

Amelia twisted in her seat. "Surely if they knew what they were doing, if they knew that not vaccinating their children killed our two-month-old baby, they would change their minds."

Anne took a long drink of her coffee before she answered. "Changing minds is never easy," she said, "but I'm certainly willing to help you get the word out about the importance of vaccinations. Let's go over the paperwork for your foundation together so I can be clear on the details, and you can sign me up for your board."

"Thanks, Mom," Bill said, with a rush of affection for Anne. Evan's Place was all Amelia talked about these days. She had done the research and was ready to go, but neither of them were lawyers. Having Anne as an advisor and a board member would give the foundation a huge boost in authority and credibility.

Amelia smiled. "Yes, thank you SO much, Anne," she said. "Now we can get this going." She got up, leaned over, and hugged Anne. "Is there a time that works for you to go over the details?"

"I have a few things to catch up on after my trip to San Diego," Anne said. "Can I call you in a couple of days to set a time?"

Bill smacked his forehead. He was a blockhead for not asking his mom what happened in San Diego. It must have been hard for her learning about her brother's death and going out there to find out what he'd left her. Anne always seemed so capable and in charge that it was easy to discount any distress she might be feeling. "Oh, sorry Mom, I forgot to ask how that went," he said. "What was all the mystery about?"

Anne stood up and took her coffee cup to the sink. "No worries, it was fine," she said over her shoulder as she walked toward the living room.

"Looks like *Curious George* is over," she said, stopping in front of the couch where Jerry and Vicky were still snuggled up. "Time to turn off the TV. Looks like Granddad has fallen asleep. Would you like to color now, Vicky? I got some new markers."

Vicky jumped up from the couch. "Can I see them? Where are they, Gramma?"

Bill had no trouble recognizing his mom's evasive behavior. She was a master at ducking a question when she didn't want to talk about something. For whatever reason, she apparently didn't want to tell them about her trip and what her brother Ned had left her—at least not right then. That was fine with Bill. He wanted to get to the gym and get on with his day, and he wasn't that interested in the uncle he had never met.

# Chapter 8

## Anne

Thursday evening after Amelia had picked up Vicky, and I was fixing supper for Jerry and me, Debby called again. Then Meadow called. I didn't pick up either call. My phone conversation with Debby the day before showed me how difficult it would be to keep the ME a secret as Ned had asked me to. I had told the family about the storage unit and now they wanted to know what was in it. Of course they did.

I hadn't lied to Clint or Debby or Bill and Amelia, but I hadn't given them straightforward answers either. Nor was I planning to tell Meadow or Dan about the ME when they asked, which was likely to be soon. In addition to my obligation to keep my unspoken promise to Ned, I was also afraid that if I told any of my family about the ME, some if not all of them would be so worried about its possible bad effects on me that they would try to stop me from using it.

I gave the issue serious thought all evening while I sat on the couch with Jerry watching *Animal Planet,* and later as I got him settled for the night. I'm a judge who has made many tough decisions, often with less substantiated and reliable information than I would have liked. My rulings always complied with the letter and the spirit of the law, but they also had heart. I have confidence in my system of considering the available evidence and reaching a conclusion.

At that point I hadn't yet come to a decision about whether to try the ME, but to be honest, I wanted to try it. If I could go back and see Jerry when he was still himself, that would be incredible.

And I told myself that the ME might be able to help Jerry. Of course I wouldn't try it on him until I had used it enough to understand how it works and how he might react to it. But what if the ME could help him remember? What if he could go back and see clearly? If he could even see last week or last month and remember, that would be gold for him.

Jerry was also my biggest concern when it came to using the ME myself. I was prepared to take a personal risk, but if something happened to me, who would take care of him? I'd just had a glaring example of what life was like for him when I was away for only one night. Shouldn't he be my first consideration? Yes, he should, because he was vulnerable and depended on me.

But I let that worry go, because I wasn't actually nervous about what would happen to me if I tried the ME a time or two. After all, Ned had said he had used it many times with no bad effects, and eighty volunteers had each used it several times with no problem. Given his academic credentials, I trusted Ned as a scientist. And as his sister, I believed he wouldn't have asked me to try the ME if it was risky.

By the time I went to bed, I had convinced myself that my best strategy was to try the ME the next day before anyone in the family got suspicious. As it turned out, keeping them all out of the loop that way ended up creating a lot of problems for me, but even now I don't see how I could have done it any other way.

On Friday, after I got Jerry settled in for his afternoon nap, I locked the outside doors, put my phone on airplane mode, went into my office across the hall from Jerry's and my room, and got Ned's box out of the back of the closet where I had hidden it.

I re-read the instructions, put on the headset, connected it to the laptop, opened the ME software, and set the date and time to September 17, 1966, 1:00 - 1:30 p.m. I needed a short time span because I couldn't be gone long in case Jerry woke up. Well, not "gone" exactly, but asleep with my door locked so he couldn't wander in and find me hooked up to the ME. Seeing me asleep wearing a strange-looking headset connected to a computer might freak him out. He doesn't even like me to wear earphones and will sometimes pull them out of my ears. I had no idea of what the implications might be for me if he pulled off the ME headset or otherwise woke me up while I was on this "trip."

As I lay down on my office couch ready to click the "start" button, my heart pounded like I was about to jump off a high cliff, but I knew from Ned's instructions that I needed to be calm and relaxed. Fortunately, my yoga training had taught me techniques to handle adrenaline rushes. I took some long slow deep breaths and let the tension flow out of my body. I closed my eyes and sank into the soft darkness. My body softened. My breathing slowed. Then I clicked the button.

*Suddenly I swoop through a dark tunnel, shed fifty years and emerge sitting in a grassy meadow on a sunlit mountain having a picnic with Jerry. I revel in the cool crisp air and suck in the piney mountain smell. The tart taste of apples explodes in my mouth, complemented by the sharpness of aged cheddar and the chewy texture of the crusty bread we are eating. I delight in my slim, light, energetic body and enjoy the relaxed muscles that follow a long hike.*

*Jerry looks young, trim and strong, and best of all his soft brown eyes twinkle with the intelligence and curiosity that drew me to him when we met. Joy floods over me. I try to tell him how wonderful it is to see him as he was so long ago. But I can't speak those words. I see myself and at the same time I am myself. It's like being in a movie of myself long ago. I know what the future will bring, but I can't change the scene. I can't change what my former self says or does. I can only re-experience the past as it happened.*

*Jerry reaches into his pocket and brings out a tiny silver box. A ring box. "Will you marry me, Anne, my love," he asks as he opens the box. The diamond sparkles in the brilliant sunshine. "I love you and I want us to be together always. Will you share your life with me?" He takes the ring from the box and holds it out toward my left hand.*

*I hold out my finger to accept the ring. "Oh, yes," I say. "Oh, dear Jerry I love you so much. We will have a perfect life together."*

*As he eases the ring onto my finger, I fall into his arms and we tumble onto the grass in a deep embrace. My current self savors his*

*strong arms encircling my former self, drinks in our deep kisses, and*
*revels in the passion between us. It's a glorious time that I vow to*
*relive again and again.*

I awoke from my ME session more relaxed than after the best massage I've ever had. I was enchanted. My memory of that glorious time with Jerry was now as fresh and sharp as if it had just happened. Unlike my usual nostalgic reminiscing where I focused on reconstructing past events in my mind's eye, the ME was a 3D movie with stereo sound—or maybe 4D since, in addition to seeing and hearing, I was able to smell, taste and touch my surroundings. It was time travel that put me back inside my twenty-five-year-old self and left me with a marvelous vivid memory.

I jumped up, put the ME away and hurried into our bedroom where Jerry was napping. I lay next to him on the bed, hugging him and kissing his neck. "I love you so much, sweetie, and I've missed you," I whispered in his ear. "Now that I can go back and relive our good times, it will be like having you back the way you used to be."

This ME had brought Jerry back to me in a way that was beyond my wildest dreams. I could hardly wait for him to fall asleep that night so I could go back again. While I was getting him settled, I gave some thought to pinpointing an exact date and time for my next trip. It was a little tricky. The marriage proposal one I had done earlier was easy. Who ever forgets the date and time they got engaged to the love of their life? I considered our wedding day, but rejected it because there were so many people everywhere that day and I wanted an intimate time with just Jerry and me.

Even with Jerry asleep, I couldn't be locked in my office long, which meant I needed to be very specific about the time of day I was going back to so I could set the ME for a short time span. While I waited for Jerry to fall asleep, I made a list of possible dates: May 23, 1959—my senior prom; December 31, 1968—our first New Year's Eve in this house; March 17, 1969—the day Bill, our first baby, was born;

I decided to start with my senior prom just because it was the farthest back. Jerry is two years older than me, so he had graduated and gone off to the University of Montana in Missoula, but we were still high-school sweethearts, dating whenever he could get home for the weekend. By prom time, his semester was over and he was home for the summer, so we were celebrating in the intoxicating live-for-the-moment way of teenagers in love.

*I swoop through the dark tunnel and find myself in a dimly lit ballroom decorated to be an evening in Paris, featuring an imitation Eiffel tower, artificial trees with twinkling lights, and softly glowing street lamps. Jerry holds me close as we dance to the romantic strains of Elvis Presley's "Love Me Tender," played by a live band. It's all perfect.*

*I'm wearing a drop-dead gorgeous strapless baby pink tulle full-skirted long dress, trimmed with romantic lace and ribbon. I think it's the prettiest dress I've ever owned. My blond hair is caught up in back in a mass of curls secured by a silver filagree barrette that matches my dangly silver earrings. I have a wrist corsage of baby pink roses, and my shoes are high-heeled silver sandals. I'm as much a princess in a fairyland fantasy as my granddaughter Vickie is in her princess dress-up clothes.*

*Jerry is wearing a white-dinner-jacket tuxedo, with a black bow tie. He had balked at my suggestion that he wear a pink cummerbund that matched my dress, but he is wearing the boutonniere of a single pink rose that I got him. He looks so adorably handsome I want to kiss him all over, except I don't want to mess up his outfit or mine. Jerry croons the words to the song into my ear. My young body tingles as I snuggle closer to him.*

*I see Martha dancing with her boyfriend Mark. It's so great to see her alive again and looking amazing in a strapless ivory chiffon dress embroidered with tiny black leaves and flowers. With her raven black hair, the effect is stunning. I want to stop and give her a hug and tell her how much I miss her, but of course my 1959 self isn't going to do that. I'd also like to warn her that Mark is going to dump her right after prom, but I can't do that either.*

*Seeing and being my former self dancing in Jerry's arms, I think about how lucky we've been to have so many joyful years together.*

*I resolve that whatever it takes to keep him happy now at the end of
his life will be my pleasure to give.*

*The song ends and we drift around talking to friends until the
band launches into the rock-and-roll song "Peggy Sue." Jerry and I
join the crowd of fast dancers swinging to the beat.*

Without warning, I plunged through time to my office in the
present moment. It happened so fast that the lithe, agile sensation of
my eighteen-year-old dancing body was still with me. I leapt off the
couch—or I should say, tried to leap—to continue the dance, but my
seventy-three-year-old body was too slow and stiff to make the jump
I saw in my mind's eye. I landed in a heap on the floor.

I lay there thinking. This was mind-boggling. One minute I was
eighteen and Jerry was twenty and we were dancing in each other's
arms, our whole lives in front of us. Then, like I had hit fast-forward,
we were back in our seventies, much of our lives past, Jerry disoriented
and confused, me frustrated as I tried to connect with him. How had
our lives gone by so fast? How had we ended up here?

No matter. The ME let me push rewind to re-live tender romantic
times from Jerry's and my past. That filled a deep hole in my current
life.

Like a kid with a new toy, I couldn't stop without one more ME
trip that night. But first I unhooked the ME and went in to check
on Jerry. He was sound asleep. I gave him sweet kisses and pulled
the blanket up over his shoulders, then returned to my office and
hooked myself up.

I chose March 17, 1969—the day Bill was born. I remembered
that heavy snow was falling in the late afternoon as Jerry carefully
drove me to Helena's new St. Peter's hospital building east on Broad-
way. By the time Bill was born at 10:12 p.m., travel was hazardous, so
Jerry had stayed the night at the hospital. I set the ME for midnight,
a time I remembered being in my hospital room with Jerry when a
nurse brought Bill in for me to hold and feed for the first time. Surely
a happy time to revisit.

*I'm sitting up in my hospital bed, Jerry in a chair next to me. I'm tired and achy, and groggy from the medications. I'm holding Bill in my arms a little awkwardly, kind of afraid I will break him. It's so real to me that I'm a mom now. Tears are running down my face.*

*I smell the hospital antiseptic odors, the meatloaf and gravy on the tray they brought me after they moved me into this room, and the roses Jerry had somehow gotten for me in the midst of the snowstorm.*

*"He's so beautiful and perfect," I say, looking up from the baby to gaze into Jerry's eyes. My throat is so thick with emotion that I choke on my words, but at last I manage to say, I love you both so much." Then my tears intensify.*

*Jerry gazes back at me, his face melting. "Our son is here. Our son, Bill. I'm so happy, Anne.*

*Suddenly Bill scrunches up his face and lets out a piercing cry. I'm so startled I almost drop him. "He must be hungry," I say to Jerry, "but I'm not sure how to start this breastfeeding thing."*

*A nurse comes in and shows me how to cradle Bill close to my breast while at the same time supporting his head. Very tricky. "Now tickle his lower lip with your nipple," she says. I try it and Bill opens his mouth, takes in my nipple and begins to suck. It hurts a little, but not much." There you go, Mom," the nurse says. "You're doing fine." She walks out, leaving me to manage on my own.*

*Bill stops sucking, lets go of the nipple, and begins to cry again. I keep trying to get the nipple back in his mouth, but he turns away. I'm so frustrated and tired that I begin to cry along with him. "He won't drink," I say to Jerry.*

*He pats my arm. "I'll get the nurse," he says, walking out.*

*Oops. It all comes back to me—the difficulty I had getting Bill to latch on and drink enough to satisfy him, and the nurses supplementing my feedings with formula in the nursery, which made Bill less interested in nursing. I'm sad for my frustrated new-mother self. I want to tell her/me that it all works out, and that once he gets the hang of it, Bill nurses happily for months.*

Back in the present again, I took time to reflect. This memory didn't have the glow of the first two, but it had just as much impact. It brought back so much I had forgotten. I was amazed at how over the years I had painted my memories of being a new mom with a rose-colored brush, forgetting the emotionality, the worry about being a good mother, the frustration when things didn't go as I thought they would.

# Chapter 9

## Anne

I conked out that night until Jerry woke me up at 4:00 a.m. He got up to pee and then wandered to the kitchen. After a few minutes, I got up and followed him out there, hoping to entice him to come back to bed. But he was wide awake and wanted breakfast. I've learned that once he gets set on something it's hard to dissuade him, so I fixed him some toast and hot cocoa. I managed to get him back to bed about 5:30 and we got a couple more hours sleep, but I got up groggy and grouchy.

I knew I should try to keep Jerry awake so he would sleep better that night, but he was sleepy and didn't want to do much. By 10:00 a.m. he was sound asleep on the couch. His naps usually last at least an hour, so I figured I could squeeze in one more ME trip. I did hesitate briefly before going into my office and locking the door behind me, though.

What if Jerry got up, climbed the stairs and fell? Our house is a two-story house and Jerry wasn't safe on stairs any more. His balance was so iffy, I had worried he would fall down the long staircase that goes to our second floor. I had considered moving to a one-story house, but Jerry knows and loves this house, and moving could exacerbate his memory issues.

Plus this is the house we bought together just after Debby was born and Bill was two. It's a fabulous old historic house, built in 1889. Being in the real estate business, Jerry saw the listing right away and insisted I see it that day. Houses like this can go quickly. We fell in love with its high ceilings, kitchen cabinets with glass doors, tile fireplace surrounded by built-in shelves and cabinets, hardwood floors, and more.

We restored the house, raised our children here, and built years of loving memories. I couldn't imagine living anywhere else. So when Jerry's Alzheimer's progressed and his balance deteriorated, we simply stopped using the second floor. We didn't need it. The main floor has two bedrooms—one is our bedroom and I use the other for my office—and a full bathroom, and the living room, dining room and kitchen are all large.

To make sure he didn't go up there, I had a waist-high expanding gate installed across the stairs. It looks a little strange, since the staircase is opposite the front door so the gate is the first thing you see when you come in. But it worked. Once it was there, Jerry ignored the stairs.

So I didn't think Jerry would go on the stairs. Even if he did wake up—which I doubted he would—he'd most likely just lie there on the couch waiting for me and watching the TV, which I left on.

I went back to the ME, eager to return to my childhood, to see Mama again and relive a scene like the ones in our old family movies.

*It's June 20, 1950, my ninth birthday—and also Dan's, of course. We're in the sunny kitchen of the large Helena house Mama and Daddy bought in 1948, just before Nicole was born. Jolts of energy course through my tiny nine-year-old body. The smell of baking cakes, mixed with the scent of the Chanel No. 5 perfume Mama wore every day of her life, surrounds me. Mama is making two birthday cakes—chocolate for Dan and lemon for me. Mama always says that just because we're twins who share the same birthday, doesn't mean we have to share the same birthday cake.*

*Mama looks amazing. The first thing everyone always notices about Mama is her sparkly smile and vivacious energy. Her dark wavy hair is pulled back into a pony tail, tied with a red ribbon. Her fitted green-and-white striped pedal pushers and green wrap blouse that ties around her tiny waist flatter her slim figure. She's thirty-one, but looks years younger.*

*My best friend Martha and I are at a white formica table licking* the bowl from my cake, getting what's left of the batter after Mama filled the tins for baking. The rich, buttery lemon shocks my taste buds, so much better than I remembered it. Too bad kids can't lick batter like that today. Too much worry about getting salmonella from the raw eggs. Amelia would have a fit if I let Vicky or Miranda eat raw cake batter or cookie dough.

Dan is behind us at the green tiled counter licking his chocolate bowl, first with a spoon, then bending over and sticking his face inside to lick it with his tongue.

Mama laughs. "You're going to get chocolate up your nose, Danny."

Then I hear myself launch into the childish rhyme Mama taught us, that we recite every year when she bakes our cakes:

"When Mama bakes my birthday cake,
She lets me lick the dish.
I eat the batter, oh so sweet,
But never all I wish.
Danny and I say,
When we are grown and learn to bake,
We'll make all kinds of cakes.
But never wait till they are done,
We'll eat them 'fore they bake."

"That's dumb, Anne," Dan says, reaching over to poke me with chocolate-covered fingers. "We're too old for silly rhymes like that."

"So don't listen if you don't like it," I snap, jumping over to poke him back. I marvel at how lithe and quick my body is back then.

My nine-year-old self can hardly wait for the party we're having at my grandparents' ranch later. We lived there with them while Daddy was overseas during WWII. Dan and I were seven when Mama and Daddy bought this house in town. Dan and I ride, hike, and fish for brown, rainbow and brook trout in the creek at the ranch. We love it there.

Our party is going to be a cookout with hotdogs roasted over an open fire, marshmallows to toast, and games like water balloon toss and three-legged races. We each got to invite five friends and Mama

*and Daddy and Martha's parents will drive everybody out to the ranch.*
*Today is going to be the best birthday and the most perfect day ever!*
*The sweet warmth of that kitchen, the joy of seeing Mama again,*
*and the intense birthday anticipation you only get when you're a kid*
*surges through me. I want to stay here for a long time.*

But I couldn't stay in 1950. The time I had set for my ME session was over. Blackness descended and I awoke in my seventy-three-year-old body lying on the couch in my office. As I got up, the heaviness and stiffness of my aging body was a shocking contrast to the nine-year-old one I had just left.

But most of all, the sharp image of my exquisite young mother engrossed me. Mama who never got old, who was only forty-five when she died. I was now so much older than my mother ever lived to be. With sadness I wondered—as I often had in recent years—what she would have been like if she had lived to be old, and what our family life would have been like if we'd had her for thirty or forty years longer.

Mama was amazing at creating festive family times for holidays and birthdays and such. Nothing was too much trouble when it came to making celebrations special with seasonal decorations, elegant dishes, delicious food, and familiar family traditions that brought back wonderful memories.

Christmas was never the same after she died. In a way we tried, but in other ways we didn't. We went though the motions like actors in a bad play—hanging the same decorations, cooking the same food, baking the same cookies—but the joy dissipated more and more as we tired of performing our parts.

In the next few years, Daddy and Dan and Meadow and Sandra and I all began to drift away from family times. It was easier than trying to pull everyone together with forced cheer. Mama had been the heart of the family, the spark that ignited the family flame.

A few years later, when I tried to talk to Meadow about my sense of loss around the holidays, she said, "Christmas is just another day, Anne. We don't have to make a big deal about it. Some people just get Chinese takeout and go to a movie." I knew she had a point, but to me special days actually were special. I wanted moments in the present like I had just seen on my ME trip to my ninth birthday.

Jerry was still sleeping on the couch when I got back to the living room. I roused him and got him to the bathroom. Then he said he was hungry—not surprising since he'd last eaten at 4:30 a.m. and it was now nearly 11:00. He sat at the kitchen table while I fixed him a grilled cheese sandwich and some applesauce—not what Debbie wants him to eat, but he likes soft food.

While he was eating, I got out Ned's first letter—the one that said, "Read after you've used the Memory Enhancer several times" on the envelope.

*Dear Anne,*

*If you're following my instructions, which I trust you are, you have used the Memory Enhancer (ME) to make a few trips back to your past. I expect you're amazed, as I was, at the detailed memories that come up. As I said in my earlier letter, it is like the ME uncorks a bottle containing your memories with their original intensity, and those memories envelop you. You're back there, you see, hear, taste, smell and touch what's around you.*

*I also expect you are wondering how and why the ME works. It may look like magic, but I have a more scientific explanation. I think the ME taps into an ability all humans possess, but few have found a way to use. In their studies of memory, researchers have found some people—called hyperthymestics—who can clearly recall every day of their lives since early childhood. In fact these people have no choice about remembering the details about their pasts. Name any date in their lives and they are flooded with details just like that date was yesterday. They can tell you what they were doing that day, what they wore, the day of the week, even the weather, all within seconds.*

*You may have seen some of these people on the television news program, Sixty Minutes. Interviewers ask them what happened on a specific date and they not only remember it, they completely relive the events and their emotions. As one of them said, "You say the date and I'm there as if it happened moments ago rather than twenty-*

*eight years ago. You can almost feel the clothes you were wearing."*
*What about the rest of us who don't remember this way? We*
*can recall recent details as well as they do. Our memories of what*
*happened yesterday are as good as their memories. A couple of days*
*further back, our memories are still good. After that it changes. Their*
*rate of forgetting is very small and ours is very large. By the time we*
*get to a month later, we have forgotten most of what happened*
*while they have forgotten very little. They are very poor forgetters.*

*Most of us can remember details when we are prompted with*
*clues, but we can't retrieve the memories like they do. Nevertheless,*
*I believe we have all those memories. In 1961, neurosurgeon Walter*
*Penfield reported that his specific stimulation of patients' temporal*
*lobes resulted in their vividly recalling memories. He concluded that*
*our brains make continuous, effortless, video-like recordings of our*
*experiences, but that these records are not consciously accessible to us.*

*I believe these unusual rememberers have in their brains retrieval*
*mechanisms that we don't have. We have the memories, but we don't*
*have the hooks to get those memories out. That suggested to me that*
*we could create a hook.*

*I wanted to find a way to recall what really happened using a*
*reliable method. I came to think of individual memory as a personal*
*memory chip that permanently stores all the data we experience in*
*our lives. How to access the data became my quest. Hence—after*
*years of experimentation and development—I created the ME. Now,*
*using the ME, I view my memories in what seems like real time. I go*
*back to a specific date and time and "play" the next few hours like*
*a YouTube video.*

*I expect you've enjoyed the trips you've taken back to your past so*
*far. Now I challenge you to do more with it, to discover its potential.*
*Go back to answer questions about your life. Go back to fill in gaps.*
*Go back to learn from your past.*

For the rest of the day I contemplated Ned's challenge to do more
with the ME by using it to go back to answer questions about my
life, to fill in gaps, and to learn from my past. On the one hand, I

was having a great time going back to relive favorite joyous occasions, but on the other hand, I took his point. Using the ME solely for fun was like using a powerful computer for nothing but games. The ME had much more to offer than entertainment.

By evening, it came to me that I might be able to use my ME trips to repair family discord. If I could re-experience the past—both good and bad times—I might be able to discover patterns that led us to this place. I knew it would be a huge challenge to find the right dates and scenes to relive, but I was eager to begin.

I thought I would learn more from times after Mama died than from earlier times. Before her accident we had our ups and downs like any family, but afterward we were in bleak uncharted territory. Looking back, I've always believed we did the best we could. But how good was our best? What seeds of anger and discontent did we sow in those dark days? I dreaded reliving those times, but it would be worth it if I could find a way to bring our family closer.

# Chapter 10

## Anne

Like most Alzheimer's patients, Jerry likes to go to bed early. After I got him settled in at about 7:30 that evening, I pulled up a 1964 calendar on my computer. Mama died on December 24, Christmas Eve, which was a Thursday. I remembered that the funeral was on Monday, which would have been the 28th. I also remembered that the Air Force required Dan to leave the day after the funeral to go back to Thailand.

I wanted to go back to a time while we were all still there, but not to the day of the funeral and not to Christmas Day because those days had so much going on that it might be hard to focus on our immediate interactions. Beyond that, I couldn't recall any specific events. I went into my office, got out the ME, and set it for Saturday, December 26, 1964, at noon, hoping we'd all have been home having lunch.

*When I come out of the tunnel, I find myself not in the kitchen or the dining room as I had hoped, but in Daddy's study. Daddy slouches in an overstuffed brown leather armchair next to the fireplace where logs blaze and crackle. Dan and I are sitting on a matching leather couch facing him and the fireplace. Sweat trickles down my chest under my green mohair sweater, which is way too warm to be wearing so close to the fire. The deer head over the mantel—one of Daddy's prize trophies—turns my stomach. I want to scream at him to take it down, to never again glorify hunting or have anything to do with hunting, but Daddy and Dan are in the midst of an argument.*

"You should have known better than to take a couple of inexperienced kids hunting in a snowstorm," Dan says, his voice harsh. "After all your preaching about hunting safety, you go and do that? What were you thinking?"

"I promised Sandra." Daddy speaks languidly, slurring his words. He's been drinking pretty much nonstop since the accident. He looks frightful—hair sticking up, shoulders hunched, face blank. "She'd been looking forward…." His voice fades off.

"That's no excuse for bad judgment," Dan's voice rises. "Sandra is a ten-year-old. You were in charge."

My pulse is racing and my face flushing from the combination of frustration and the overheated room. I can't stand much more of this. What could Dan hope to accomplish with his accusations? The only use I could see for getting Daddy to take some of the blame would be to take some of the burden off Ned and I knew that wasn't Dan's intention.

I put my hand lightly on Dan's arm. "Stop it," I say. "There's no point. What's done is done."

Dan shakes off my hand and pulls away from me. "You stop it, Anne," he says pounding his fist on the arm of the sofa. "This isn't something you can smooth over. If you don't want to hear it, go somewhere else."

I want to hit him, to somehow make him shut up, but I also want to escape the fiery supercharged atmosphere. Avoidance wins. I jump up and head for the door. When I open it, I find Sandra huddled in the hall, tears running down her face. I lean down and put my arms around her.

"Don't cry. It will be okay," I say. "They'll get over it." She pulls away, her body rigid.

"No it won't be okay. Nothing will ever be okay again."

Now with my perspective of so many years later, I know she's right. But back then I thought I needed to be strong and capable, to somehow make things okay.

"I need her. I need Mama," Sandra shrieks, her face bright red.

I hold her, rub her back, and murmur, "Shhhh" into her ear. "Mama

*is watching over us from heaven now," I say. "We need to show her
we can go on without her."*

*"But I don't want to go on without her," Sandra wails. "I need her
here, not in heaven."*

*"I know it's hard, Sandra," my twenty-three-year-old self says,
"but this is what God has chosen for us. We need to be strong."*

*I can hardly bear to watch my former self. Was that all the com-
fort I offered Sandra in her deepest grief? Did I really believe what I
was saying to her? Poor Sandra. No wonder she withdrew from us
all. Watching from today, I weep with regret that I hadn't shown my
own grief to Sandra. Shared aguish could have brought us together.
Hiding my vulnerability distanced us.*

I woke up still in tears. I could see that things back then were
much worse than I'd remembered. Grief didn't bring us together to
share our sorrow, it sent us to our own corners to lick our wounds
in private. I wished we had been like some primitive tribe, wailing,
mourning, taking time off for ritual farewells. But that wasn't our way.
We didn't show our sadness to each other. When we were together
we forged ahead and moved on, rising above the yawning hole in
our lives. But underneath, the grief was working, eating away at our
souls, transforming a formerly happy family system into a collection
of unhappy individuals unable to help ourselves or each other.

Had I pushed those bad times out of my memory because they
were too painful to recall? And if I had, was that a useful survival
technique or just a way of putting my head in the sand?

## Jerry

Jerry woke up in the dark, sick to his stomach. "I'm sick," he
moaned. "Anne, I'm sick."

No answer.

He reached out for Anne's arm, but he didn't find her next to
him. He rolled over farther to her side of the bed. It was empty. He
was sweaty and shaky. "Anne," he called." I need you, sweetie. Where

are you?"

No answer.

"Anne?" he called again. "I'm sick. Please help me."

Still no answer. His stomach rolled and lurched. He moved back to his side of the bed and slowly sat up and put his feet over the side. He started to stand up, but his gut spasmed and vomit surged out all over him. He sank back onto the bed. "Anne, please, please come help me. I need you." He wept, tears mixing with vomit.


## Anne

I was still submerged in the desolate family atmosphere of 1964 when I opened the door to our bedroom to check on Jerry. The putrid odor of vomit and the raspy sound of Jerry's sobs jerked me back to current time.

I turned on the light and dashed over to the bed. "Oh, Jerry, sweetie, I'm so sorry I wasn't here when you needed me."

Then I heard myself saying the same thing I had said to Sandra way back in 1964. "Don't cry. It will be okay." But as I soothed him, cleaned him up, changed the sheets and got him settled back in bed, I thought to myself that just like for Sandra, things would never be okay again for Jerry—or for me either now that I had lost so much of him. Our life together, sharing our daily thoughts, insights and observations was gone. But I still loved him and I could still be there for him, and I needed to be. There was no excuse for letting him wake up alone and sick. I could and would do better.

It was only 9:30 p.m. I put the soiled sheets in the washer, and then went to the kitchen and fixed myself a strong "ditch"—which is Montana-speak for bourbon with water. I had some thinking to do.

I could see Ned was right that the ME trips can fill in gaps in our memories. Back in 1964 Daddy had told Dan they went on the hunting trip in the snowstorm because he had promised Sandra. I was there when he said it, but I had never remembered him saying it until my ME trip today. Had he ever said that to Sandra? Was that one of the reasons she pulled away from the family? Did she think the accident was her fault or that we thought it was her fault?

And why had I told Sandra "it will be okay" when she was sobbing in the hall two days after Mama died? Why had I told her she needed to be strong? Why hadn't I encouraged her to talk to me about how she was feeling? If I had listened more, been more empathetic, maybe we would have stayed close and she wouldn't have left the family.

My phone rang. Meadow. I knew I couldn't put her off forever, so I picked up.

"Hey, what's up?"

She sounded exasperated. "I've called three times and you haven't picked up or answered my voice mails. Are you and Jerry okay?"

"Jerry has some bug or something—just threw up all over the bed," I answered, hoping that would justify my ignoring her calls.

"Poor guy. Give him a hug from me. So what are you doing?"

"Sitting here on the couch drinking Jack Daniels while the yucky sheets are in the washer."

Meadow laughed. "Glad to know you're doing something to cheer yourself up. So how was San Diego? And what was in the mysterious storage locker?"

I tried to divert her with a long description of Ned and Keith's house, and with the little information I had about Keith and his relationship with Ned, but Meadow knew me too well to fall for that.

"That's all very interesting, Anne, but quit teasing me and get to the juicy part. Did you go to the storage locker?"

I told her how Keith had given me the key and how he said Ned had wanted me to go by myself and that I did.

"Since you're back here, presumably in one piece, I gather the locker didn't blow up when you opened it, so what did you find? Was it full of treasure?"

I didn't want to lie to her, nor was I ready to tell her the truth, so I phrased my reply in true lawyerly form. "No, no treasure. Nothing like that. Just a table with stuff from his scientific research."

"So......It must be important research if he left it to you so secretively and you had to go all that way to get it. You said even Keith didn't know what it was?"

"Yes, but Keith is a musician. He's not interested in science. They didn't talk about Ned's work."

"Come on, Anne. You're running me around the mulberry bush here. What was Ned up to and why did he leave it to you?"

"It's a lot of complicated stuff about memory," I said. "I don't understand it all yet. But his death has gotten me thinking about the past and what I remember and don't. Do you remember Daddy saying the reason they went on that hunting trip when it was snowing so hard was because he had promised Sandra?"

"I don't know. He might have. It was all so long ago."

"Do you think he said that in front of Sandra? Could that be why she had so many problems?"

"More likely she had problems because her mother died when she was only ten and her father was an alcoholic. Why are you dredging up all this stuff from the bad old days?"

"Not sure. It's kind of a shock knowing I'll never see Ned again and I'm trying to figure out how our family ended up this way."

"Lots of families end up this way, Anne. You know that."

She was right. As a lawyer and a judge for so many years, I had seen plenty of instances of family members hurting each other, stealing from each other, even destroying each other. But I thought of them as families gone wrong. Dysfunctional. I didn't put our family in that category.

I needed to get off the phone. I was running out of diversions and half-truths and in any case she wasn't buying them. So in the end I did have to lie. "Oops, got to go I hear Jerry calling. I'll tell you more in a few days."

I hung up realizing I was going to have to come up with a better story.

# Chapter 11

## Sandra (aka Sister Mary Margaret)

On Sunday morning, Sister Mary Margaret rejoiced as she sang Divine Office with the nuns of the Abbey. Her voice echoed the voices of countless nuns who had sung the same words for over thirteen centuries. She basked in wonder, gratitude and love for the thousands upon thousands who had lived under the Rule of St. Benedict. The Benedictines, most notably the nuns at the Abbey, had become her family over the forty years she had been there.

Sandra rarely thought about her original family, but since Ned's death, her thoughts had turned back to them. In her memory, the years following her mother's death were a gray gloomy blur. None of the family had paid much attention to her except Grandma Clara, who often added to her misery. Daddy was either busy at the law firm, drinking in his study, or passed out in his bedroom. Nicole was a rebellious teenager who went off to the California College of the Arts in Oakland in 1966, only two years after Mama died, got swept up in the hippie movement, moved into a commune, and changed her name to Meadow. The first time she came home for a visit, she had a huge argument with Daddy, left early and didn't come back for years.

The same year that Nicole left, Anne finished her law degree, returned to Helena and joined the family firm. She moved in with the family, but was busy with work and a rekindled romance with Jerry, her high school sweetheart. Anne was kind to Sandra and would often ask how she was doing, but she was too preoccupied to notice the suffering her twelve-year-old sister hid behind her noncommittal answers. Anne accepted Sandra's "I'm fine," with no further probing and went on with her life. After Anne and Jerry got married and moved into a tiny duplex on the other side of town, Sandra saw Anne infrequently.

As soon as Dan got out of the Air Force in 1967, he enrolled at Stanford Law School. By the time he moved back to Helena in 1970, Sandra was sixteen. He was outgoing and friendly with her but either couldn't or didn't see her for the person she was. She was just some generic little sister. He wanted to take her fishing, but she was a vegetarian who was horrified at the idea of killing any living creature. He pushed her to exercise and lose weight, but she wasn't athletic or outdoorsy, preferring to read in her room.

Grandma Clara stayed seven years with Sandra and Daddy, until she died suddenly of a heart attack at age seventy-eight. Sandra had never been close to her. Looking back from her new identity as Sister Mary Margaret, Sandra acknowledged that Grandma Clara must have been overwhelmed. First her husband had died leaving her a seventy-one-year-old widow alone on the ranch; then a year later her daughter-in-law was killed in a tragic accident. She had done what she had to do, moved in with her son and grandchildren to help however she could. But she was a somber woman by nature, no replacement for the vibrant Viv. As Sandra, Sister Mary Margaret had usually heard Grandma Clara's words as judging and criticizing her, so she had kept her distance.

The move from her chilly family life to the warm community at the Abbey was like coming into a cozy kitchen on a cold gray day. She fit in and was accepted there the way she never had been at home. Nevertheless, in her years as a nun she prayed to have an open heart filled with love and compassion, and not to be judgmental and intolerant. This morning she prayed again that the light of God would shine into and through the lives of her family members. She wanted God's grace for them, but she didn't want to spend time with them.

## Anne

On Sunday morning I faced the issue straight on. I'd been back from San Diego for four days without telling anyone anything about what Ned had left me, but that couldn't last, especially with Debby and Meadow. I still wasn't ready to tell them about the ME—both because of my sense of obligation to Ned, and because I wanted the ME to be my secret for at least a while.

So I had to come up with a solid story they'd accept about the inheritance. I decided that staying as close to the truth as possible without telling them about the ME would be my best strategy. In my experience lies eventually come to light, and when they are uncovered, trust is shattered.

I decided to tell them Ned had been doing some research on memory that he considered cutting edge (true), but that he had conducted his research outside the university system (true), without getting Institutional Review Board approval for the use of human subjects (true), which violated his agreements with the university (true). I would say that when Ned realized he was dying he became worried about what would happen to his research after he died (true). He thought his findings were important, but he was concerned that if he left his work to other scientists at a university or scientific institute, it would be embroiled for years if not decades in regulations and red tape (probably true). He knew he didn't have time to explore the best way to disseminate the results of his work, and he thought that as a judge I could consider the legal ramifications (partly true) and find a way to use his research to benefit mankind (could be true).

I would also tell them Ned didn't want me to tell anyone the specific details of his research until I had figured out how to best disseminate it (true) and that I was obligated to respect his wishes about that.

Now that I had that figured out, I was ready for another ME trip. But not such a bleak one as last night's. Going back to the middle of the crisis had shaken me, and I couldn't face any more gloom and despair. I wanted to return to the happy family story I'd been seeing in the old movies, with all of us together having fun.

Holidays would be the easiest to choose because their dates were fixed. I chose Christmas 1958, when Dan and I were 17, Ned was 12, Nicole (Meadow) was 10, and Sandra was 4. I set the ME for 12:30 p.m., thinking we'd be done with stocking gifts and brunch, back from church, and all sitting around the tree opening gifts—and I was right.

*I whisk through the tunnel and there we all are dressed in our fancy church clothes sitting around a Christmas tree jam-packed with piles of brightly wrapped gifts. I bask in the strains of Bing Crosby's "I'm Dreaming of a White Christmas," and my mouth waters at the aroma of roasting turkey.*

*I'm wearing what was my favorite outfit back then—-a gray felt swing skirt appliquéd with pink French poodles, a pink cashmere sweater, and a cinch belt. I feel fashionable and so much more grownup than Nicole, who is dressed in a little-girl purple velvet dress with a white lace panel down the front.*

*Sandra looks adorable in a blue ruffly dress, and a blue bow in her dark curls. She's sitting on a red and white wooden rocking horse, holding her new Tiny Tears doll, and laughing as she rocks.*

*Mama is dazzling as always in a red plaid wool dress with a circle skirt and a ruched black belt that accents her tiny waist. "Look, Sandra is rocking her baby," she says, laughing along with Sandra. She tries to hand Sandra another wrapped gift, but Sandra is too busy rocking, so Mama hands it to Nicole. "Here, open this for Sandra," she says.*

*I reach out and grab the gift before Nicole can get it and begin undoing the ribbon." Mama said for me to do it, Anne," Nicole says, pulling the box out of my hands.*

*Mama turns to me. "Anne, what are you doing? I asked Nicole to open it."*

*I shove the gift at Nicole. "Take it," I say, and she does. I sulk, and notice that instead of the warm family feeling I came here to find, I'm cross because I think Mama always favors the younger kids over me. Dan chuckles and smirks, making me even more irritated. I poke him and he pokes me back. We still have that twin push-pull thing* going on, but at seventeen Dan is a tall, broad-shouldered athlete, who could handily overpower me if he chose to. I am fit but tiny at my full adult height of 5'4," weighing only 115 pounds. Dan would never use his physical strength against me, but he does love to tease.

Nicole opens Sandra's gift, a white furry muff, and holds it in front of Sandra's face. Sandra leans her face down and sniffs it. Nicole giggles. "It's not a pet, Sandra," she says. "It's to keep your hands warm." She tries to put one of Sandra's hands in it, but Sandra pulls back.

"She probably thinks it will bite her," Dan says. We all laugh. Sandra pays no attention, just keeps on rocking.

I think to myself what an impractical gift a white muff is for a four-year-old, which reminds me how Mama loved to dress Sandra up like a doll and curl her hair in long ringlets. Mama was thirty-five when Sandra was born and I'm pretty sure she thought of her as her last baby—which, of course, she was.

We move on, opening gifts. I get a small phonograph, two sweaters, and a silver bracelet. Dan gets a fancy fishing rod and a radio. Daddy gets new golf clubs. Mama gets a gauzy red bathrobe, decorated with intricate gold designs, which I think is the most beautiful thing I've ever seen. She tries it on and twirls around showing off. I'm impressed that Daddy picked out this gorgeous robe for her, but later Mama tells me she bought it herself and wrapped it as if it was from him.

The most exciting gift is Nicole's new black-and-white kitten, which she instantly names Pretty Kitty, and romps with delightedly, looking back and forth from the kitten to Daddy pointing the movie camera at her.

Then comes the shocker. In an eerie twist, Ned's main gift turns out to be a new shotgun and a warm quilted hunting jacket. "But I wanted a chemistry set," he said. "I'm not ready for a gun."

"You're twelve, son. You're ready," Daddy says. "Anne and Dan got their first shotguns when they were ten." He is right about Dan and me. He did give us shotguns on our tenth birthday. But we wanted them. We'd lived on our grandparents' ranch until Mama and Daddy bought the Helena house when we were seven. We loved the rough-

*and-tumble ranch life. The cowboys who worked for our grandfather taught us to ride when we were tiny and we wanted to be part of everything they did, including shooting.*

*But it was different for Ned. He was only two when we moved into town, and he grew up a clever and cautious child who would rather read a book than run around outside. Now, at twelve, he is slender, pale and blinky-eyed, as if he's just emerged from a cave. He does not look like a kid who will take readily to hunting.*

*Dan leans over to take a look at Ned's shotgun. "It's a beauty," he says. "I'll teach you how to use it and soon you'll love hunting as much as the rest of us do.*

*Of course Dan is right. Ned does later learn to shoot and enjoys hunting with the family.*

*I shudder, thinking this must be the very gun he shot Mama with six years later. I want to grab the gun, throw it in the trash, and make them all promise never to go hunting again. But of course my 1958 self has no premonition of the tragedy to come.*

*Suddenly Nicole shrieks. "Pretty Kitty peed on my dress."*

*"Yuk, you stink," Ned says, jumping away from Nicole. "Don't get it on me."*

*Nicole starts to cry. "It's not my fault. She's just a baby kitten," she says, clutching Pretty Kitty to her chest and running out of the room.*

*"Enough," Daddy says. "It's Christmas. Don't fight. We need to clean up this mess before dinner." He waves his arm at the floor littered with wrapping paper, boxes and ribbon.*

*Mama runs after Nicole. "Lets get Pretty Kitty to her litter box and find you some clean clothes," she says.*

*I head to the kitchen to help with cooking Christmas dinner, already looking ahead to the evening and savoring the anticipation of the Christmas formal dance I'm going to with Jerry at The Montana Club.*

Then I was back. I had only set the ME for an hour because I wanted to be sure to return before Jerry woke up from his afternoon nap. I put everything away quickly and went to check on him. He was still sleeping.

I sat next to him on the bed, thinking about my ME trip. It was fun but not as warm and fuzzy as I'd expected from the old home movies. I realized that while those movies keep our memories alive and tell a happy family story, they don't tell the whole story or even most of it. Could I be longing for a past that only existed through the rose-colored glasses of my memory?

# Chapter 12

## Anne

Jerry always wakes up hungry. He was enjoying an after-nap snack of ice cream with hot fudge sauce on Sunday afternoon when Debby stopped by. Of course. It never seemed to fail that she showed up when Jerry was eating something she considered bad for him.

"More sugar?" she said, looking at me like I was feeding him worms.

"Never mind," I said. "This is his treat—isn't it, Jerry?" I rubbed his back lightly. "Look how he's gobbling it up."

Apparently Debby decided to let the sugar thing go for once so she could pursue her own agenda. "So, I'm getting very curious," she said. "You said on Wednesday that you'd tell me more later about your inheritance, but you haven't answered my calls or my messages."

Oops. I knew ignoring her calls wouldn't go down well and I had no acceptable excuse. I didn't want to use the one about Jerry vomiting because she'd be all over me for feeding him junk. So I punted. "Sorry," I said. "I've been kind of busy." Then I got up, took Jerry's empty bowl over to the sink, and came back with a damp paper towel to wipe his mouth.

"Hey Dad, want to walk around with me?" Debby asked, helping Jerry up from his chair.

"We can sit on the couch," Jerry said.

"How about we walk around the room a couple of times and then we sit on the couch?" Debby said.

"No," Jerry said, heading for the living room.

Ha, I thought, now she sees it's not so easy to get him to make the healthy choice.

Debby sighed as we followed Jerry into the living room. He sat on the couch and Debby sat next to him, snuggling close. I sat in a chair next to the couch.

"So, Mom, come clean. What was the big inheritance? You said a scientific thing. What kind of scientific thing and why did he leave it to you?"

I was just about to give Debby my strategically planned explanation when Clint showed up for his afternoon time to stay with Jerry. So we all sat in the living room and I ended up telling them both how Ned had conducted his research on memory without following the university's required internal review system, and that he wanted me to explore the legal ramifications of disseminating his findings.

Debby listened without interrupting or reacting. Like any skilled lawyer, she is skilled at maintaining a poker face. Clint, on the other hand, made faces and cryptic comments like "Awesome!" and "Fucked up."

When I finished, Debby said, "That's odd. I Googled Uncle Ned and from what I read he was quite a distinguished neuroscientist. He didn't sound like the type to skirt the rules."

Clint rolled his eyes. "A corrupt system creates more corruption," he said. "Sounds like he didn't have much choice if he wanted to get anywhere with his research in his lifetime."

Debby pursed her lips at him. "The problem is that he didn't get anywhere," she said. "Since his research was done without going through the university's procedures to protect human subjects, his results can't be published in a reputable academic journal, which means other scientists won't accept his work."

Clint leaned forward, his chin jutting out. "So you think he should have sold out to the establishment and let bureaucrats make decisions about his work? I'd say good for him that he didn't blindly follow stupid rules."

Debby shook her head as if to clear away a fog. "Good grief, Clint! Society has to have some standards. Otherwise there's no way for people to separate scams from beneficial discoveries."

I left them to continue their discussion and keep Jerry company while I headed out to buy groceries.

That evening after I got Jerry settled in bed, I made two more ME trips. The first was to Meadow's tropical birthday party back in 1956. I'd been thinking about it ever since we bought up different memories when we talked about it a little over a week ago at Jerry's birthday party. I did not revisit Meadow's memory of Daddy setting the tablecloth on fire, which may have been because the time I had set on the ME got me there too early in the day, but I did see him flirting with the woman giving hula lessons. That was a detail I had not remembered and it kind of surprised me.

For my next trip, I chose a day I thought Dan would remember, our high school graduation day in June, 1959. I didn't want to relive the boring ceremony, so I picked a time around dinner when I thought we'd all be celebrating. Instead, I landed right in the middle of a big argument Dan and I were having with our parents about a late-night party we wanted to go to at a friend's family cabin at Canyon Ferry Lake. They thought there would be alcohol—of course they were right, but we denied it vehemently—and they did not want us in cars driving after drinking, or with other drivers who had been drinking. Despite our pleas and promises of good behavior, they stood firm. I had forgotten that argument, but I do have a memory of being at the party, so I vowed to ask Dan how we got away with that.

I wanted to compare my ME memories with Dan and Meadow's memories of the same events—without telling them about the ME, of course. So I invited them for dinner Monday night. They both agreed to come.

I made mac and cheese to go along with our grilled fish and salad, because Jerry won't eat fish anymore and he loves mac and cheese. After I softened them up with a crisp New Zealand Sauvignon Blanc, I gave them my story about Ned.

Dan narrowed his eyes. "So he didn't follow the rules and now he wants you to clean up the mess?" he said. "Why bother?"

I took another forkful of salad and considered my answer as I chewed. "I'd like to do something for him," I said, sympathetically. "I'm sorry about the way the family treated him back then."

"And whose fault was that?" Dan asked, jutting his chin forward.

I didn't want to have that conversation, so I didn't reply. Most likely Meadow didn't either, because she gracefully changed the subject. "What do you think of his research?" she asked, helping herself to more salad. "Is it really cutting edge?"

"I think it might be, but I need more time to understand it. It has gotten me thinking a lot about memories, though," I said as a clumsy segue into exploring their memories of old times. "I was thinking about our high school graduation, Dan, and a party we went to that night out at Canyon Ferry Lake. Do you remember that?"

Dan grinned and leaned back in his chair. "I'm stuffed," he said. "You make the best mac and cheese, Anne, and I always eat too much."

Jerry smiled at him. "Mac and cheese. I like mac and cheese," he said.

"Me too," Meadow said, touching Jerry's shoulder. "Aren't we lucky to have Anne to make it for us?"

I wasn't going to let Dan get away with his familiar changing-the-subject behavior. "Thanks," I said. "Glad you all like it. But what do you remember about that graduation party, Dan?"

Let's see, graduation night…wasn't that the party at The Montana Club where Martha's boyfriend dumped her? I remember she was a total wreck and you spent half the night taking care of her."

"No, it was prom night that he dumped her," I said. "It was at an after-the-prom party at Sarah Jean's house. Don't you remember Sarah Jean's mother was so mad when Martha threw up on the couch in their rec room?"

"I thought the time she threw up was at Sarah Jean's birthday party," Dan said.

Meadow burst out laughing. "You two! You never remember anything the same way. It's hard to believe you're twins. Let's see if more wine will help your memories," she said, refilling our glasses.

I could have laughed along with her and let it go, but stubbornly

I still wanted Dan's memory of graduation day to match my newly discovered vivid ME memory. So I took a big swallow of wine and pushed on. "But Dan, don't you remember we had a big argument with Mama and Daddy on graduation day about that party we wanted to go to at Canyon Ferry?" I noticed my voice rising in annoyance. "I'm trying to remember why they let us go—or whether we went without permission and lied to them."

Dan shrugged. "I don't remember, but I had so many arguments with them back then, why would that one stand out? Even so, it was all so long ago, why do you care what I remember?"

I didn't have a good answer, so I turned my attention to Meadow to see if her memories of that 1958 Christmas I had just visited matched mine.

"Meadow, do you remember that Christmas when you got Pretty Kitty and she peed on your dress?"

Meadow laughed again. "I do remember. Pretty Kitty! What a great cat. I loved her right away, even though she did pee on my dress and I had to wear a red and white dress that I hated."

"Do you remember what Ned got that Christmas?"

Long pause. "A fishing rod?"

"No, Dan got a fishing rod. Ned got a shotgun, which was probably the one he shot Mama with."

"No that can't be right. We all got guns for our tenth birthdays, not for Christmas."

"She's right," Dan said. "Dad gave us all our guns on our tenth birthdays."

"Well Ned got a shotgun that Christmas. And he didn't want it. He wanted a chemistry set."

"What year was that? Was Ned ten?" Dan asked.

"No, he was twelve. It was 1958."

"No…no…Now I remember." Meadow said, excitedly. "That was the Christmas Ned got the electric train set. I remember Daddy set it up in the basement the night before and they surprised him on Christmas morning. It was a great train set. It had lots of track, switches, and bridges, and even had a coal car that would dump coal."

"No, that must have been the year before," I said. "In 1958 he got a shotgun."

"How come you're so sure?" Meadow asked. "Is it in one of those old movies?"

I considered saying yes, but then they might want to see the movie, and the film of Christmas 1958 was unwatchable. Back in the 1940s and 50s when the family home movies were made, Mama had to package up the film and send it off to Kodak for developing. When the developed film showed up in the mail, the whole family gathered for the much anticipated viewing. Sometimes the results were a glorious re-creation of a holiday, a special time or a visit from relatives. But other times the results were disappointing—too dark, too light, out of focus or jumpy. Christmas 1958 was one of those times.

"No," I said. "It's not in a movie. I just remember."

"Well, I remember it another way and so does Dan. So who's to say which one of us is right?"

"Dan never remembers family stuff, so why would I believe his memory?" I said. My voice was getting shrill and Jerry was squirming in his chair. I needed to drop it.

"Well anyway, what's the point?" Meadow said. "What difference does it make whether Ned got a shotgun or a train set in 1958? The past is over. All we can do is move forward."

But I wasn't about to concede that truth about the past was irrelevant. Uncovering that truth was the essence of Ned's work. I couldn't resist one parting shot. "Don't you always say we can learn from our pasts so we don't repeat destructive patterns or make the same mistakes again as we move forward?"

"I think my past has lessons to teach me about relationships and career choices and important decisions," she said, "but what's to learn if Daddy gave Ned a shotgun for Christmas. They're both gone and so is Mama and there's nothing we can do about it now. So why dwell on it?"

She had me there.

# Chapter 13

## Anne

I became obsessed with the accuracy of my memories. If Dan and Meadow's memories were so faulty, why would mine be better? Without the ME trips, I wouldn't have remembered the argument about the graduation party or Ned getting the shotgun for Christmas any better than they did.

To test myself, I made as many trips as I could. I used the ME when Jerry was sleeping at night and during his naps. When Clint came over, I told him I needed a nap because I hadn't been getting much sleep, and then I locked myself in my office and used the ME.

I made lists of events to go back to and did my best to pinpoint exact dates and times with the help of online calendars, home movies, and family photo books. I made notes of what I remembered before I went back to an event and later compared those with what I had experienced with the ME.

I wasn't prepared to find so many discrepancies. I was shocked at how much of what I remembered differed from what I saw on my ME trips, and at how little memory I had of so much of what had happened. It was hard for me to accept, but my memories weren't any more accurate than Dan and Meadow's.

Some of what I saw contradicted my rosy memories. For example I chose from a family photo book a trip Jerry and I and the kids took to Yellowstone National Park in 1985. In the photos and in my memory it was a marvelous vacation where we were a happy family together. Bill was sixteen, Debby was fourteen, and Clint was six. We had planned the trip far ahead so we could get rooms at the rustic Old Faithful Inn, a national historic landmark, built in 1903 from local logs and stone.

I set the ME for 10:00 a.m., thinking we'd be out on a hike or walking around some of the park's attractions like the mud pots.

*But when I come out of the tunnel, we're in our hotel room, which is two connecting rooms that open up to be one big room with four queen beds. The decor is knotty pine paneling, simple wooden furniture, and no television or radio. The room does have a phone that I'm using to talk with a client who has a hearing the week we get back.*

*Debby is sitting on the floor glaring at Bill. "I just tripped over your shoes in the middle of the floor, Bill," she says. "You're such a slob. Your stuff is all over the room."*

*Bill laughs at her. "Cool it, Debby, If you looked where you were going, you wouldn'* Chapter 13 *t trip."*

*Jerry and Clint are in the corner building a Lego airplane. They don't even look up.*

*Debby turns her anger at me. "Are you ever going to get off the phone so we can go? This is supposed to be a family vacation. Why are you working?"*

*"Hold on, Laura," I say into the phone as I cover the receiver with one hand and shush them with the other. "Jerry, why don't you go on to the geyser basins. I'll catch up with you as soon as I'm done."*

*"Sure. Let's get ready to go, kids," Jerry says. "Your mom will finish sooner if we leave her in peace."*

*"No," Clint says, flying his plane through the air with his hand. "I want to wait for Mom."*

*I don't have time to argue. I want them out of there so I can get my work done on this important case." No, Clint," I snap. "Go on with Dad. I'll be along soon."*

*Watching now from these many years later, I see Bill shrug in disbelief and Debby shake her head in annoyance, as they grab their jackets and head for the door. I also notice Clint's shoulders are drooping, and Jerry is avoiding eye contact with me.*

*I want to jump in and force my long-ago self to hang up the
phone to go with my family to enjoy this precious time together. But
of course I can't.*

When I woke up, I knew the ME was right. I had forgotten what
happened that day, but after seeing it on the ME I unmistakably
remembered my misguided priorities. I also remembered I worked
all day and never did catch up with Jerry and the kids. They saw the
geyser basins without me.

Other ME trips showed me events that surprised me so much,
it was like looking at an alternate reality. Did I really tell Martha
the year after Bill was born that I thought I wasn't cut out to be a
mother? I heard myself say it to her when the ME took me back to
her birthday lunch that year, but I had no memory of thinking I
wasn't a good mother.

Did Jerry and I really fight over how late Debby should be allowed
to stay out when she was in high school? I'd always remembered us
as a united front when it came to the kids, but the ME showed me
being much stricter than he was. If I was the "bad cop" parent to his
"good cop," does that explain some of her protectiveness of Jerry and
her impatience with me?

Overall, I was inclined to believe the ME over my memories
because the events were so real when I went back with the ME. I saw,
heard and felt what was going on. Nevertheless, I had to consider that
the ME could be wrong. After all, my task here was to evaluate its
usefulness. What if what it showed was some fictional version of the
past constructed by my unconscious?

Now my big question was how I could know whether the events
I saw on my ME trips were what truly happened. It was time to read
Ned's second letter—the one that said "Read when your trips raise
questions about the ME's accuracy" on the envelope.

*Dear Anne,*
*By now I expect you've discovered that events in some of your
ME trips conflict with the memories you had before the ME trip. And*

*if you ask other people who were part of that event, their memories may also differ from what you observed on your ME trip.*

*We neuroscientists know memory is unreliable. People's recollections of actual events are often riddled with errors. Why? When we remember past events, it's less like replaying a film, and more like reconstructing an event from bits and pieces of information. We believe the reconstruction process changes the original bits of stored memory, and the more often someone reconstructs a memory, the more it is likely to change. It's like that game where people whisper a sentence around in a circle and the sentence that comes out in the end is completely different.*

*You know that problems with eyewitness testimony have been uncovered when DNA testing revealed false convictions based on unreliable eyewitness testimony. You probably also know the U.S. National Research Council has recommended that the criminal justice system exert tighter control over the use of eyewitness testimony in court and come up with a more scientific approach to the identification of suspects in police lineups.*

*Even worse, false memories can be created by giving people misinformation about their pasts. Hundreds of studies, most notably those of Elizabeth Loftus, have demonstrated this. The research shows that the more people imagine an event happening in the past (that did not actually happen), the more people will be convinced that the event actually took place.*

*So why am I convinced the memories I experience with the ME are accurate? As a scientist I conducted carefully controlled research to test the ME's accuracy. First, I recruited twenty pairs of subjects who had spent a lot of time together growing up—either siblings or close childhood friends. I interviewed them separately about times they remembered strongly, both good and bad times. As is almost always the case, their memories of some events differed considerably.*

*For each pair, I chose three of those disputed events and had them each write their memory of it. Then I used the ME to separately take each of them back to the three times they had written about. After each ME trip, I had them, again write about the event.*

*In every case their original descriptions of the events, written before the ME trips, differed substantially from each other. But after their ME trips both members of the pair described the event the same way. Furthermore, the subjects who described the event differently after their ME trip than they had before now agreed their original memory had been faulty and the ME memory was what had actually happened.*

*Then I did a second set of tests with another twenty pairs of subjects, one of whom was a young adult in their twenties and the other a parent of that young adult. The parents were in their late forties or early fifties. I interviewed the parents to discover three specific happy or unhappy events when their adult child was younger than two years of age. Then I used the ME to take each parent back to relive that event. After their ME trips, each parent wrote about the event.*

*I then took the young adults back to those dates and times using the ME. They saw themselves as babies in situations they were much too young to remember as adults on their own. When they got back, they wrote abut those events. In every case, the young adults' accounts matched those of their parents.*

*This research supports the accuracy of the ME at a high confidence level. My own experiences with it as well as the accounts of my volunteers reinforce that. Of course I would like to have more testing done at some point if you are able to arrange that, but right now I am satisfied the ME shows events as they truly happened. What the ME shows you is the actual experience before your memory recreates it as a story.*

# Chapter 14

## Anne

By the end of the week my trips had become more of an indulgence than an evaluation of the ME. I had tested the ME enough to know how it worked, and after reading Ned's letter, I was by and large convinced of its accuracy. Now I just wanted to have fun reliving my past.I let myself go and dived in. I relived times I had reason to believe I would enjoy, and when I found an exceptional one, I returned more than once. I spent delicious hours with Jerry back before Alzheimer's got him. Returning to lively family times when our kids were little, as well as intimate, romantic times with just us two, nourished my soul. And going back to conversations Jerry and I had about books, music, movies, politics, and the meaning of life refreshed my view of him when I returned to the present.

I spent time with Martha during our high school years and later as professional women and moms in Helena, sharing everything until her death. Having her back, hanging out together, was as satisfying as comfort food without the extra calories.

I visited days as a kid with my parents and brothers and sisters, days in school, days enjoying the outdoors when I was young and energetic, relishing the physical sensations of occupying my youthful body again. Not all of the times I revisited were highlights, but they were all interesting and some were spectacular.

I drifted so effortlessly into times gone by that my present and my past began to run together like pools of spilled paint. I was lost in time and loving it. I got so accustomed to being my younger self that I rejected the wrinkled face I saw in the mirror and the physical restraints imposed by my aging body. My current world began to look so strange and unfamiliar that I sometimes became disoriented walking around the house, expecting to be in the house where I had grown up.

Occasionally, in a moment of clarity, I asked myself whether I should stop and scrape the remnants of my past off my feet before I got hopelessly mired in familiar former times. But each time, I chose to stay in yesteryear. I chose not to give recent events priority over joyous bygone days. I chose to cruise through time, letting it take me where I wanted to be.

Over the weekend, I had asked Meadow and Debby to each come over and spend a few hours with Jerry while I took a nap. My excuse to them was Jerry was waking me up so much at night that I was sleep deprived—which was true. Like most Alzheimer's patients, Jerry was often awake and restless at night. But of course I had another agenda.

I didn't often ask for help so Meadow and Debby were both solicitous of my health and pleased to oblige. I had a little guilt about going off on my ME trips, but not much. I rationalized that the ME trips improved my mental health, which translated into better care for Jerry.

When I emerged from my office Saturday afternoon, Debby had Jerry at the kitchen table playing with tiles that looked like dominoes, except instead of different numbers of dots the tiles had various colors and shapes to match up. I sat down at the table with them and watched Jerry painstakingly create a design, matching some tiles by color and others by shape.

"Debby, do you remember that Schwinn bike we got you when you were ten? You looked so cute riding it and you rode it everywhere," I said.

"Sure. I remember that bike," Debby said. "Maybe I looked cute, but I wanted to look cool. Bill had a red and yellow Schwinn Sting-Ray with the cool high-rise handlebars and the banana seat, but the one you got me was called a Fair Lady. It was pink and the basket was white wicker trimmed with flowers. I was always so jealous of his bike."

Disillusion pierced me as I realized this didn't fit my shiny memory. Should I have known she wanted a different bike? But wait—maybe that's just her memory looking back. Maybe she did really love her bike when she was ten. I tried to win her over. "I think you liked that bike more than you remember. You always had a big smile when you were riding it."

"I liked riding a bike. In fact I still do." She paused, and gave me a questioning look. "Why are you thinking about my old bike now?"

I straightened in my chair as I summoned my prepared answer to her question. "I had a dream about you riding that bike."

"Oh," she said, turning back to Jerry and his clumsy design.

I couldn't see any harm in reminiscing with family members about old times. It's not as though they would ever guess I was using the Memory Enhancer. They'd never even consider the existence of such a device. What I didn't realize was what they might think instead.

On Sunday afternoon Meadow encouraged me to take as long a nap as I needed. "I love spending time here with Jerry," she said, putting her arm around his shoulders. "It's a gorgeous warm sunny day, so I brought ice cream for us to take out to the back garden." She gave his shoulders a squeeze. "Chocolate ice cream, Jerry—no nuts or chewy stuff. Does that sound yummy?"

Jerry smiled. "I like chocolate," he said.

When I came out a couple of hours later, they were on the living room couch, listening to relaxing instrumental music, probably one of Meadow's meditation mixes. Jerry was dozing against her shoulder, looking relaxed and peaceful. Her caring and effort brought tears to my eyes. She delicately extricated herself, slipping pillows under Jerry's head.

We took some lemonade out to the back garden, leaving the door open so we could hear Jerry if he stirred. It was still warm at 5:00 p.m., which we never take for granted in Montana, even in June. We chatted about nothing much until one of my ME memories bubbled over.

"Do you remember the time I took you to Lady and the Tramp when you were seven?" I asked. "You were so upset when the Aunt Sarah character locked Lady in the basement and Tramp in the closet, that I thought I was going to have to take you out to the lobby."

Meadow gave me a quizzical look. "No. I don't remember that at all," she said. "I'm not even sure it ever happened."

Of course I knew my memory was true, so I couldn't let her mistrustful remark go by. "Oh, it happened all right." I said. "You cried and cried."

"Okay, maybe so, but how do you remember little details like that after all these years, Anne? And why? Why do so many of your sentences now start with 'Do you remember?' Are you worried about losing your memory like Jerry has?"

I answered her questions too quickly, missing the concern behind them. "Of course not," I said. "I just like to remember the times we shared so long ago."

# Chapter 15

## Anne

Monday afternoon Clint was there, but I had to shop for groceries and do a couple of errands while he was with Jerry, so I didn't have time to use the ME. But it was all I thought about. After Clint left at 6:00, I fixed Jerry some tomato soup, and hustled him into his pajamas. I had no guilt about getting him to bed early because he was usually drowsy after he ate and wanted to sleep. I knew he'd be more wakeful later as a result, but I was so addicted to the ME, I couldn't stop myself. I set off on another ME trip, with no thought at all that there was somewhere else I was supposed to be.

## Bill

"Daddy, can we eat in front of the TV since Mommy's not home?" Miranda asked. "We could watch *Phineas and Ferb.*"

Bill was tired after a long day and he found the quick-witted kids' show entertaining, so he decided to say yes, even though he knew Amelia would prefer they had a family dinner at the table. "Okay," he said, "as long as you and Vicky eat all your spaghetti and salad. But if you're not eating, we'll have to turn it off and go back to the table."

"Yay!" Miranda squealed. "We'll eat all our dinner, won't we, Vicky?"

"I will," said Vicky, "but I don't want any lettuce in my salad."

"Duh!" Miranda said. "It's not salad if you don't have lettuce."

"Well I just want carrots and tomatoes in mine, okay Daddy?" Vicky said.

"Fine," Bill said, "help me carry stuff into the rec room. Vicky, you take the silverware and napkins, and Miranda you take the parmesan cheese and salad dressing. I'll bring the rest."

They had almost finished dinner but were still watching TV when Amelia called. She sounded distressed. "Your Mom hasn't showed up for the Evan's Place Foundation Board meeting, and we should have started twenty minutes ago. Everyone else is here."

"Have you called her?" Bill asked, even though he was sure Amelia would have already done that.

"Of course. I've tried calling her several times and it just goes to voicemail. That's not like her. Have you heard from her? What do you think is going on?"

Tonight's meeting was important, and Bill couldn't imagine Anne forgetting about it. This was the first meeting of the foundation board. Amelia had worked nonstop recruiting members, getting up to speed on laws and regulations, and filing government paperwork. Her enthusiasm for the project had done a lot to lift her out of her grief over Evan.

Worry pushed Bill out of his comfortable-family-evening space. It wasn't like his mom not to show up when she had promised to be there and when she knew how much her involvement meant to Amelia. "No, I haven't talked to her in days, and I have no idea why she isn't there," he said. "I agree it's not like her. Mom isn't one to be late or forget a commitment, especially when it involves family."

Amelia sighed. "I don't think I can wait any longer for her," she said. "I'm just going to tell the others Anne's not feeling well and we should go on with the meeting. If somehow she does show up, I'll figure out some explanation."

"Sure, go ahead with your meeting," Bill said, working to keep his voice calm as his concern about Anne grew. "Meanwhile I'll try to reach her, and if I can't I'll give Clint a call. He's there a lot, so he may know something. Oh—and if she does show up, call me."

Vicky and Miranda were done with dinner by then and their TV show was over, so Bill got them each a juice bar to take out on the deck, where he could watch them from the kitchen window. Then he called his mom and got voicemail. Next he called Clint, who said he had been over there earlier but their mom hadn't mentioned anything about a meeting tonight. "Which is weird," Clint said, "because if she was going to a meeting she would have needed me to stay with Dad."

"She's not answering her phone," Bill said. "I'm worried. Could you go by and check on her?"

"No, you'll have to go. I'm on my way to a meeting."

Probably a meeting of the strange cult he belongs to that believes our planet is going to be recycled, Bill thought. Surely Clint could be a little late to that meeting to check on their mother. It wasn't as if the world would be ending this week. "I'm here alone with Miranda and Vicky so I'd have to take them," Bill said. "Couldn't you just stop by on your way?"

"Sorry bro," I can't be late to this meeting, but I'll check in with you later about Mom."

Exasperated, Bill tried Anne again. Still voicemail. He headed out to the deck. "Hey, girls. We need to jump in the car and make a quick trip over to Gramma and Granddad's house."

## Anne

*I'm back in 1968, when Jerry and I had just found out I was pregnant with Bill. That was before home pregnancy tests, so you had to go to the doctor, get lab work done, and wait for the office to call with the results. We just got the call and we're ecstatic, jumping up and down, kissing, hugging.*

*Suddenly a loud banging interrupts us—or not "us" exactly. My current self hears the banging, but Jerry and my former newly-pregnant self pay no attention. This is the first time anything like this has happened. I am my former self, but my current self is distracted by something my former self apparently doesn't hear. The banging gets louder and I hear a voice yelling "Mom. Mom. Are you in there?" I reach up and pull off the ME headset.*

I jolted into the present in a flash, my stomach lurching. The voice and the banging continued. Bill. The voice was Bill and the banging was him knocking on the locked door of my office. "Hang on. I'll be right there," I yelled back to him, as I gathered the ME paraphernalia and shoved it into the closet.

"We were worried about you when you didn't show up for Amelia's foundation board meeting tonight," Bill said. "And you weren't answering your phone."

My heart sank with a thud. How could I have forgotten this meeting that was so important to Amelia? My voice cracked as I spoke. "Oh, no. Was that tonight? I completely forgot. I've been so tired lately and when Jerry got sleepy after his supper, I just grabbed a chance for a quick nap. I'm so sorry."

"It's okay, Mom. We know you have a lot going on. Amelia can fill you in and you can make the next meeting. I just wanted to be sure you and Dad were all right."

Lucky for me, it was Bill—my easiest child—who found me sleeping. He rarely gets ruffled or makes a big deal out of anything. I was also fortunate that Jerry was still sound asleep in bed, and that Vicky and Miranda were easily distracted by TV and cookies and didn't ask any questions.

Still, I recognized a close call when I saw one and I resolved to be much more careful. My resolution lasted a couple of days, but each day the pull to revisit my past grew stronger until I slid back again.

# Chapter 16

## Jerry

Jerry woke up early from his after-lunch nap on Wednesday. He had to pee, so he made his way to the bathroom. Then he looked for Anne. He didn't see her, so he shouted, "Anne? Where are you?" She didn't answer. He went to the kitchen. She wasn't there. He was dizzy, so he sat down at the table and waited. She didn't come. His legs were restless, so he got up and went to the living room. His eyes darted around the room. She wasn't there. He paced back and forth calling, "Anne? Anne?" No answer. He wanted to find her, wanted to be with her. He stopped pacing and stood at the window. It was sunny out. Maybe she was outside. He shuffled to the front door, opened it and went out, oblivious to the fact that he was wearing only a tee shirt and briefs.

## Debby

Debby was sitting in her Weller & Associates, LLC office mulling over the long call she had just finished with the social worker from the Teen Rehab Institute. Josh was making progress, but it would still be a while before she could visit. Even though the news was positive, her mood was melancholy. Despite Josh's belligerence and their frequent blowups before he went to rehab, his absence left a hole in her life.

Her phone buzzed again.

"Deborah Barnes?"

"Yes."

"Officer Joe Mitchell from Helena PD."

Debby's mind flashed to Josh, then she remembered it couldn't be about him. Must be one of the firm's clients. "What can I do for you Officer?"

"We picked up an elderly gentleman wandering on Montana Avenue wearing only a tee shirt and briefs. He's confused and anxious. Very upset. Didn't want to go with us. We called the numbers from his MedicAlert Safe Return bracelet. His name is Jerry Barnes and you're the second listed contact. We weren't able to reach the first contact, Anne Barnes."

"Oh my god, he's my dad! I'll be right there. Where is he?" Debby was out of her chair heading for the door, phone at her ear.

"He's in our patrol car, so we can take him home if you want."

Debby thought for a minute. If the officer hadn't been able to reach Anne, where was she and what was going on? She told the officer to bring her dad to the law office and she would take him home from there.

## Anne

When my ME session ended, I was savoring a joyful glow from reliving a romantic night out with Jerry about fifteen years ago. I went to our bedroom to check on him and give him a big hug. I had only done a forty-five-minute session, so I figured he'd still be asleep. He wasn't in bed, so I ran to look in the bathroom. Not there either. Uh-oh. I was sweating by then and my legs were shaky.

I should have been hearing Jerry call me the way he usually does when he can't find me. But the house was silent. Maybe he'd wandered into the living room and fallen asleep on the couch.

I dashed into the living room, my heart racing. I didn't see him anywhere and to my horror I saw that the front door was ajar. I stared slack-jawed at the open front door. Good grief! Had I forgotten to lock it? I gasped, eyes wide. How could I have left it unlocked? That's a major "no no" from Alzheimer's care 101. Everybody knows Alzheimer's patients wander off.

I ran outside, but saw no sign of Jerry in the yard or the street. My stomach churned. I ran back in to get my purse and keys to go look for him in the car.

Just as I was about to back out of the driveway, Debby pulled in behind me with—to my utter relief—Jerry sitting next to her. I knew I was in for it from Debby, but my first concern was Jerry.

I jumped out, ran to the passenger side of Debby's car and tried to open Jerry's door. It was locked. Debby clicked the doors unlocked and got out on her side. She looked grim—face tight, eyes narrow.

I opened Jerry's door and embraced him, then helped him out. "Were you looking for me, sweetie? I'm so sorry you couldn't find me." I held him tight, kissing his face and neck. His breathing was regular, his body relaxed, and he looked happy to see me.

Debby stood next to us, arms crossed. Her silence said it all. I pulled back and turned toward her. "How did he find you?" I asked, dreading the details I was about to get.

"He didn't find me. The police found him wandering on Montana Street. They called the number on his bracelet to find out who he is. They couldn't reach you, so they called me. Then they brought him to my office. What happened, Mom? Where were you?"

I had screwed up big time, but Jerry was safe, so my primary concern was damage control with Debby. All I could do was be apologetic and not defensive. "I'm so sorry. I just fell asleep for a minute while he was napping and when I woke up he was gone. I have no idea how I left the front door unlocked. Thank goodness he's safe. I'll be much more careful about the door from now on."

Debby gave me a forced smile. "Well, I need to get back to the office," she said in a flat tone. Then she hugged Jerry, said "Bye, Dad," and got in her car and left.

## Bill

Bill had been flying high finishing the paperwork on a big sale when Debby called and wrecked his mood. After she filled him in on their dad's escapade that afternoon, she insisted on an immediate family meeting—without Anne—to discuss what she called "issues we need to confront as a family."

At first Bill had thought Debby was overreacting, but he did have a lingering concern about the way his mom had slept through Amelia's meeting a couple of nights ago, and how hard he'd had to bang on the door to rouse her. So when Debby told him Dan and Meadow had agreed to come to the meeting, he decided it might be a good idea to find out what they were thinking. He agreed to the meeting and called Amelia, who was also on board. Debby said she was still trying to reach Clint.

"Let's have the meeting at our house tonight instead of at the law office," Amelia said. "That way I can be there and we won't need a babysitter. The girls will be in bed by 8:00. That should be early enough."

By 8:00 p.m. everyone was there, and the little girls were settled in upstairs. Amelia put out lemonade, wine, and some salty pretzel crisps on the coffee table in their rec room, and then joined Bill and Debby on the sectional sofa. Dan had claimed the sand-colored Barcalounger next to the sofa, where he leaned back, eyes closed, feet resting on the raised footrest. Meadow rocked back and forth in Amelia's favorite white rocking chair next to Dan. Clint was on the other side of the room, perched on a small lime-green stool in front of Vicky and Miranda's Lego table, laboriously constructing an elaborate spaceship.

Even though it was his house, Bill waited for Debby to start things off. The meeting was her idea after all and he was slightly uncomfortable meeting like this behind his mom's back.

"Clint, how about joining us over here," Debby said. "We're ready to start."

"Clint didn't look up. "I'm fine over here," he said. "I can hear you and you can hear me."

Debby paused and took a deep breath. Bill noticed tension in her neck and shoulders. He hoped she wasn't going to push Clint to move. If she did, Clint would probably blow up and leave. Not a strong beginning for a difficult family conversation.

Debby bit her lip and turned her attention to the rest of them. "Okay," she said, "you all know Dad wandered off this afternoon and the police found him and brought him to my office. It was bad enough that he was meandering along a busy street in his underwear, but when I got him home, Mom seemed to think it was no big deal. She said she had dozed off and somehow left the door unlocked. I know she's been tired. She had me over there on Saturday to stay with Dad so she could take a nap."

Meadow stopped rocking and leaned forward. "She says she's not getting much sleep at night." She had me there on Sunday and she took a nap then too. I think taking care of Jerry is wearing her out."

Bill looked at Amelia. They hadn't told anyone except Clint about Anne missing Amelia's foundation meeting, but maybe they should now. He kept his tone casual. "Mom did miss a meeting Monday night that she had promised Amelia she'd be at. We got worried when we couldn't reach her by phone, so I took the girls and went over. She'd fallen asleep and Dad was asleep too. It's not like her to forget a meeting, but she did seem tired." He turned toward Clint. "You're there a lot, Clint. How does Mom seem to you?"

Clint answered without looking up from his Lego creation. "If she doesn't have errands to do, Mom does sleep a lot when I'm there. Dad can be very stubborn and he wants her with him all the time. It's no wonder she's tired."

Debby cleared her throat and rubbed the side of her face. "This is why I'm worried about Mom. It sounds like she's sleeping way too much. She might be depressed or sick. I wonder if she needs to see a doctor and get a complete evaluation."

"I haven't seen any sign that she's depressed," Meadow said. "And if she's sick, I think she would have told me. I think she's just worn out. Maybe we could all help her more."

Debby was shaking her head. "I think there's more going on with her than being tired. She's so focused on the past, she's not paying attention to the present. Forgetting a meeting or leaving the front door unlocked isn't like her at all. I'm a little bit afraid that—heaven forbid—she might be starting to have memory problems of her own." She raised her eyebrows and waited for a response.

Bill groaned silently to himself. Just as he'd feared, Debby was overreacting, jumping to the worst possible conclusions. But then Amelia spoke up. "Anne is still sharp as a tack," she insisted. "She's grieving, that's all. Her lifelong best friend just died. She loses Jerry a little more every day. Then her brother died and that brought back all the grief connected to her mother's death and Ned leaving the family. I've learned a lot about grief in the last year since Evan died. It can be overpowering. It can make you think you're crazy. A grief support group could help her cope."

Meadow nodded several times. "You're right about the grief, Amelia. Anne misses Jerry—the Jerry he used to be. She's lost so much—Jerry, her career. This is not the way she thought her life would go. That's why she's so focused on the past."

Bill chimed in. "It's true Mom talks about the past a lot, but lots of older people do that," he said. "She likes to think about the good times in her past—possibly it helps to drown out some of the bad stuff in her present. But Vicky and Miranda give her a way to focus on the future, and she's great with them. I think it's just hard for her being with Dad so much. No exercise, no intellectual stimulation."

Debby was shaking her head. "Then there's the elephant in the room," she said. "None of us has even mentioned Mom's quick trip to San Diego and her strange secrecy about what our Uncle Ned left her. Every time I ask her about it, she dodges my questions. What's up with that?"

Bill saw Debby going way off the track at this point, so he jumped in. "I think we all know Mom's good at ducking questions she doesn't want to answer, but she'll tell us when she's ready." He looked inquiringly at his Uncle Dan, who continued to lean back in the recliner, as if this family drama didn't directly involve him. "What do you think, Uncle Dan? Do you think there's something wrong with Mom? You've known her longer than any of us."

Dan took a moment, then answered with calm deliberation. "Anne likes to be in control so she doesn't always tell everything she knows. If she's hiding something about Ned, it's most likely connected to the guilt she's always had about him. She may think the details of his research on memory portray him in a bad light. As for her focus on the past, she is slightly obsessed with being right about her memories. But so what? As likely as not she is right about most of that stuff. I don't remember much about old times."

Bill couldn't tell which side of the fence Dan was on. "So you don't think any of this is a problem we should take seriously?' he asked.

"No, I am concerned about her," Dan said. "I agree she's wasting her time and energy focusing so much on the past, I don't want her living in her memories. She needs a good future, too. I've been trying to entice her to work at Weller and Associates a day or two a week. She'd be so great at mentoring new associates, and they'd love the chance to learn from her."

Debby turned to him. "But you've talked to her about that, right, Dan?"

"I have."

"And she wasn't interested. Isn't that right?"

"True. She said she retired to be with Jerry."

"What about something not work-related to get her out of the house?" Bill suggested. "Maybe she could take a yoga class with you, Meadow. I could stay with Dad."

Meadow nodded. "Great idea, Bill," she said. "I do think Anne needs new activities and a new focus. If she wants to think about the past, maybe we could interest her in writing a memoir about her life and career."

"It's her life, you know." Clint finally looked up from his Lego. "You all can't plan it for her. She gets to decide for herself what she wants to do and you all don't get a vote." His voice rose and its intensity increased. "Mom's being pushed to give up her attachments sooner than the rest of you, but everyone who wants to go on living will have to do that soon enough. This corrupt world is going to be recycled. The only beings who will survive will be those who are willing to give up their attachments and leave."

Bill was taken aback at Clint's going off into la-la land. But there was no way he was going to follow up on Clint's crazy predictions. Seemingly no one else was either.

There was silence, thick and uncomfortably sticky, until Debby stepped in. "Clint does have a point. We can't plan Mom's life for her. She makes her own choices, always has and presumably always will. Anyway, I don't think new activities are the answer. We need to find out what's going on with her."

Dan jerked the recliner to an upright position and leaned forward to face Debby. "You said you think Anne needs a complete medical examination. Is that your main goal?"

"Yes," Debby replied.

"On what basis can we convince her to do that?"

"We can talk to her about her exhaustion and her sleeping so much. Remind her that if she falls asleep again, something really bad could happen to Dad. He could burn himself on the stove, or start a fire, or go outside again and get hit by a car. And we should point out that she may have some physical problem that may be getting worse. Tell her it might be something that could be fixed easily now, but would be hard to fix later."

"Okay," Dan said. "It certainly wouldn't hurt for her to have a checkup. I'll help you try to persuade her. How about you, Bill?"

Bill was stuck—unable to find a good reason not to go along. "Sure," Bill said, "but I also think we need to help her find more time for herself. She needs more help taking care of Dad, whether from Clint or the rest of us. We all need to step up."

# Chapter 17

## Debby

In the end Bill, Meadow and Dan agreed to go with Debby to talk to Anne late Friday afternoon. Amelia would stay home with Vicky and Miranda, and Clint would hang out with Jerry while they talked. It had taken all of Debby's persuasive skills to convince Dan to be the one who would begin the conversation, but she had gotten him to agree, albeit reluctantly. Her mom would be much more open to having this talk if the prime impetus came from her twin brother.

Debby saw this discussion as only an opening move. She had more concerns than she had voiced at the family meeting. Maybe being the mother of an addict made her extra suspicious, but she couldn't help wondering whether her mom might be drinking or taking drugs to deal with stress. Her secrecy about the inheritance from Uncle Ned wasn't a good sign. Anne's problems had gotten much worse after her trip to San Diego. Could whatever her mom had found in Uncle Ned's storage unit have upset her in some major way that was too much to cope with on top of taking care of Dad?

## Anne

When Dan called Friday morning to say he wanted to stop by for a TGIF drink after work, I didn't expect anything out of the ordinary. He occasionally came over for drinks on a Friday afternoon, and I always enjoyed sharing that relaxed space with him. I had his favorite Knob Creek bourbon ready to pour over ice, and had fixed a gin and tonic for myself.

But he showed up with an entourage. Their faces looked more like Monday morning misery than Friday afternoon fun. Putting two and two together, I figured they were worried about Jerry's Wednesday escapade, but I didn't appreciate their showing up unannounced to share their concerns. I knew I had messed up and I didn't want to hear dire predictions of disasters awaiting Jerry if I didn't pay better attention to his whereabouts in the future.

Although I was wary of their intentions, I invited them all in with a smile and offered them drinks. Mama always said, "You catch more flies with honey than you do with vinegar." I'd followed that advice all my life with good results.

Once we were all settled with our drinks, Dan leaned in toward me with the eyeball-to-eyeball look I knew meant he had something serious to say. "You may be wondering why I brought my sidekicks along," he said. "We all came because we're worried about you, Anne. From where we sit, it looks like you've taken on more than you can comfortably handle. We see you forging full-steam ahead, maybe not noticing what's happening on the sidelines. Remember how Garth, that cowboy at the ranch, used to say, 'If you're ridin' ahead of the herd, take a look back every now and then to make sure it's still there with you'? We're thinking you need to stop and take that look."

Dan has a habit of lapsing into cowboy folksiness when he's trying to be endearingly persuasive. It works pretty well with juries, but not so much on judges—at least not this judge. I stared into the depths of his crinkly brown eyes, and forced a smile. "Thanks for your concern Dan, but I'm well aware of what's going on in my life." I kept my voice as steady and sweet as a knife slicing through cake. "And I'm quite capable of handling all of it."

Then the rest of them came at me with gentle firmness. They were worried about me. Why was I spending so much time sleeping? Why was I so focused on the past? I should be moving forward. Maybe Jerry's care was too much for me. Maybe I had medical problems of my own. They wanted me to get a medical evaluation, to get more help with Jerry, and to get out more on my own.

I listened in silence with my inscrutable judge face and my open-minded judge attitude. While they had some points about my sleeping, with my missing Amelia's meeting and with Jerry wandering off, they were turning a couple of tiny mistakes into a problematic pattern.

Of course what was really going on with my "sleeping" wasn't me just carelessly nodding off. It was me going on ME trips, but I wasn't ready to tell them that, so I had to answer circumspectly.

I worked hard in my reply not to be defensive. "I do appreciate your concern," I said—which in a way I did. "I know you all want the best for me and for Jerry, but you should remember I retired to take care of him, not to take yoga classes, write my memoirs, or mentor law students. I've done plenty of interesting things in my life, but now I want to be there for Jerry like he's always been there for me."

Meadow nodded, "Of course you do, Anne," she said. "We understand that. But you don't have to do it all by yourself. There's an Adult Day Care program I've seen at the Senior Center when I've been there teaching pottery. I've noticed a lot of music and laughing, and the staff are sweet and enthusiastic. I think Jerry might enjoy going there a couple of days a week, which would give you a little time to yourself."

I shook my head. "Jerry wouldn't like strangers helping him, and anyhow I have a part-time caregiver—Clint. He almost always has enough time for us, and when he doesn't I do appreciate the help the rest of you have given us. But that's all I need."

Debby had been frowning for a while. "Mom, if you have enough help, I wonder why you're falling asleep so often. Like we said, we want you to get a complete physical exam. What if there's some problem you don't know about? How can you take care of Dad if you don't take care of yourself?"

"I've been a little tired lately," I said, "but it's no big deal. I don't think I need to see a doctor."

Bill gave me his sweetest look as he spoke up softly. "Mom, you've gone through a lot of loss recently, with Martha dying, and then with Uncle Ned dying, on top of Dad's decline and your retirement. Do you think a grief group might help? It's done a lot for Amelia."

He could have a point there. But I didn't want to get involved in a group in a town where everyone knew me. Even with confidentiality rules, there might be gossip. "Maybe, Bill," I said. "But I don't think I'm ready for that right now."

"Well, Amelia and I want to help. You've helped us so much with the kids and I know you love having Vicky here on Thursdays, but we also know how much energy it can take to keep up with her. With all you have going on, we're thinking you could use a little break from that schedule. We can add an extra day to her preschool schedule—no problem—while you get your energy back."

I wondered whether the subtext here was they were afraid I wasn't capable of keeping up with Vicky, but I decided to just respond to his surface statement. "Thanks Bill, but I look forward to her Thursday visits and having Vicky here perks Jerry up," I said. "We would miss her if she stopped coming."

I didn't offer to refill their drinks, hoping that now they'd had their say, they'd be on their way. But Debby wasn't ready to quit. "We're also concerned about your state of mind," she said. "It seems to us like you're living too much in your memories, not seeing a positive future for yourself."

I wanted to strangle her, but forced myself to give a measured reply. "It's true that my memories are important to me," I said, evenly. "Of course they are. More of my life is in the past than in the future, and most of my memories are happy ones." I took a minute to gaze at each of them in turn. "Don't any of you ever think about good times in your past? Haven't you had a warm glow come over you when you remember a special time?"

"Of course we have, Anne," Meadow said in the soothing voice she uses with Jerry. That voice annoyed me. I didn't want to be managed.

"Look," I said. "I'm not sick and I'm not crazy. Remembering the past makes me feel like my life has roots and continuity, it makes me see myself positively, it shows me my life has been worthwhile, and it gives me strength to move forward. And when I remember joyful times with Jerry, I feel closer to him, which makes it easier for me to do all I need to do to take care of him."

"That's all fine, Anne," Dan said, "I can see why you want to focus on your past with Jerry, but why so much interest in our childhood? Lately you seem to find the past more appealing than the present."

I stood firm. "It's not that I think the past was better, it's that I'm seeing how it all fits together. It's about the meaning of my life. I can learn from my past. I can't go back and erase my mistakes, but I can gain wisdom that will help me moving forward."

Debby looked at me with a wide-eyed earnest expression as if I were confused or dim-witted. "Here's the thing, Mom," she said. "You're not moving forward. We've talked about it and we all agree that you need to do something different. It can't be all about what you want. You have to think about Dad's safety."

"Don't you think I know that, Debby?" I struggled to keep my anger in check so it didn't show in my face or my voice. "You have to know I want the best care for your dad. If I didn't think my taking care of him was the best, I would make another choice."

"It's not always so easy to know what is best," Debby said. "I was doing my best for Josh and I thought it was what he needed, but it wasn't enough. I had to face that and send him to rehab."

Good grief! Could she be equating Alzheimer's Disease with drug addiction? "I don't see the analogy there, Debby," I said. "Are you suggesting that sending your father away would make him get better?"

"Of course not," Debby said. "But hanging around here watching TV, eating junk food, and getting into who-knows-what-kind of trouble when you fall asleep isn't good for him. Spending some time at the Adult Day Care program with activities run by trained staff, meals planned by a nutritionist, and other people like him to socialize with could have benefits."

"You've made your points," I said, "and I've listened. I know your intentions are good, but I need to follow my heart and do what I think is best."

"We can't just sit back and let you and Dad go downhill," Debby said. If you're not willing to take any of our suggestions, what are you willing to do?"

Before I could frame a reply, Clint and Jerry walked in from the backyard. "If you guys are done telling Mom how to live her life, could you go now?" he said. "Dad wants to watch some TV."

"Clint's right," I said. "It's time for you all to go. Jerry needs his supper and I need to think about your concerns. If you'll all come back on Sunday, I'll give you my answers."

That night I didn't use the ME after I got Jerry settled in bed. Instead I put on Beethoven's *Ninth Symphony* and sat back in my comfortable wing chair to think. Dan's memory of Garth and his cowboy sayings made me recollect another Garth favorite, "If you find yourself in a hole, the first thing to do is stop diggin'." Maybe it was time for me to put my shovel away.

I didn't want them pushing me to get medical or psychiatric evaluations I didn't need, especially because I didn't want to have to lie to professionals to explain my recent behavior. I didn't want family intruding into Jerry's and my life, despite their good intentions. I didn't want them watching everything I did and drawing negative conclusions. I didn't want to lose visits from my grandchildren.

I could ignore their concerns, stand firm and tell them all to back off. But I didn't want to be creating rifts in the family when I was trying to repair family discord. I needed to find a way to bring them along gracefully.

In order for them to realize I wasn't sick or depressed or mentally incompetent, they needed to know what was going on. I needed to tell them about the ME. But I am an honorable person and I didn't want to break my commitment to Ned.

How could I keep it all—my family relationships, my honor and my independence? I could destroy the ME and go on with my life the way it was before. That would put an end to my "excess sleeping," and no doubt to my focus on the past. But I was far too enchanted with the ME to give it up.

I began to rethink my commitment to Ned. He had written, "*I'm asking you to keep it to yourself until you've made a decision about its value.*" While I loved the ME, I hadn't made a decision about its value to society. I could see some issues with spending so much time in the past, with seeing ugly interactions I had let myself forget over the years, and with discovering inaccuracies in memories I had stead-fastly believed in. I had no idea what further complications might arise with continued trips, or how other users might react. I couldn't make a decision yet.

I needed to see how other people responded to the ME. Leaving aside Ned and his volunteers—who I couldn't discuss the ME with—I was a sample of one. I came to the conclusion that it was time to invite the family to try the ME. I would start by telling them Ned had left me something that had changed my life and if they agreed to back off on their concerns about me I would share it with them. I would also insist they agree to keep Ned's secret. Then I would do my best to explain the ME and its attraction for me.

I was apprehensive, but resolute. I wanted so much from them. I wanted them to understand the value of the ME and why I'd been spending so much time using it. I wanted them to stop watching over me and let me take care of Jerry on my own. I wanted them to try the ME so they would see how amazing it could be to go back and see the past as if they were living it. I wanted them to join me in redeeming Ned.

# Chapter 18

### Anne

I invited the family for Sunday afternoon when Jerry would be napping. They all came. Bill and Amelia even got a sitter for the girls so they could both be there. We gathered in the living room, Bill and Amelia on the couch, Clint on a couple of big floor pillows he had dragged to the end of the room under the bay windows, and the rest of us in comfortable chairs I had moved around to create a cozy group. The coffee table in the middle held iced tea, raspberry lemonade and a big plate of chocolate chip cookies I had made to sweeten their moods.

I began by asking them to hear me out before they asked questions. Then after I swore them to secrecy, I told them the whole story— about what I found in Ned's San Diego storage locker, about the ME and how it works, about the information and requests Ned left, and about my ME trips.

I definitely had their attention. I was determined to make my case in a way that persuaded them to see the ME as something positive for our family, and to see me as healthy, sane and in control of my life. It was like a closing argument to the most challenging jury I'd ever faced.

### Dan

Dan leaned back in his chair, arms folded, listening to Anne go on and on about the genius of Ned's invention. Possibly Ned was a genius, but so what. What did he ever do for this country or for Montana or for Helena or for his family? Ned was a monumental screw-up. Why believe he somehow all of a sudden came up with something great?

No matter what Anne said, Dan couldn't see himself strapping something to his head that would send electric signals to his brain. His brain for god's sake! Knowing Ned, it was his one last strike against the family—a way to fry their brains so they'd all end up like Jerry.

Dan smiled as he looked around at the others. Debbie had her attorney poker face, showing no reaction. Meadow looked all "far out" enthusiastic as usual, ready to jump off any cliff she saw. Clint was lost in space somewhere. Bill had a man-you-can't-be-serious kind of expression, and Amelia was whispering in his ear, probably telling him not to be rude.

If Ned wanted this device to make a difference in the world, why would he leave it to this group? All the more reason, Dan thought, to believe Ned had other motives in mind.

## Meadow

Meadow was so breathless with excitement she nearly swallowed her cookie whole. She was instantly drawn to this invention called the ME, which she saw as a sign from the universe that she needed to go back and examine her previous relationships. She agreed with Anne that we can all learn from seeing the truth about our pasts, and using our observations to examine patterns and discover ineffective tendencies we can change.

Meditation and other practices had helped Meadow open her heart and mind, but she still found certain issues surfacing again and again — crummy relationships that never worked out, questions about her life goals, and difficulty letting go of old grievances. Lately these weaknesses had been in her face more than ever as she pursued her quest to find a soulmate with whom she could share true love.

Trying the ME did not intimidate her at all. Meadow was always open to new ways of experiencing the world and was committed to healing and awakening. She had had exhilarating out-of-body experiences when she was on the verge of falling asleep or when she was meditating, where her soul had left her body and visited other locations.

Meadow was thrilled that something new could enrich her experience and move her further toward enlightenment. That her brother Ned of all people had given her this chance made it all the more significant. She struggled to sit still as she waited for Anne to finish.

## Amelia

Amelia sipped her lemonade and listened with interest to everything Anne was saying. At first she thought Anne's grief had made her delusional, that she was engaging in magical thinking. But the information Ned had left and Anne's description of the device were so scientific and rational that she began to believe. She had always known Anne to be a meticulous researcher who evaluated evidence wisely.

Amelia was especially struck by Anne's recounting of her ME trips. The way Anne told it, she wasn't only seeing the past, she was touching it, smelling it, tasting it, and hearing it. She was experiencing herself in her former body and she was in the middle of scenes with people long dead, but who seemed vividly alive.

Tears ran down Amelia's face. To be with someone again who was no longer on this earth was a gift everyone could enjoy. Evan! She could go back and be with Evan—hold him, hug him, kiss him, touch him, smell him. She would do anything to do that.

She put down her glass, pulled Bill close and whispered in his ear, "I want to go back and be with Evan. Can you imagine?"

## Bill

After gobbling two cookies, Bill was trying to resist a third when Amelia whispered in his ear. He didn't know what to think about her enthusiasm for this invention. What his mom had been telling them had sounded like it came from The Twilight Zone. How could it possibly be real? But apparently Amelia thought it was.

Bill didn't want to go back to be with Evan. He'd spent much of the last year trying to put Evan's tragic death behind him and move on. The loss of his son was a great sorrow to Bill. He had had so many dreams for Evan and loved him so much. Focusing on him the way Amelia did would keep Bill in a terrible dark place.

Bill had little interest in trying this device his mom liked so much. He was more of a moving-forward than a thinking-back sort of guy. But Bill loved Amelia passionately, and her suffering had been hard for him. He would support her in trying anything that might help her move through her grief.

## Clint

Clint lay back on his pillows. He had only come to this gathering to support his mom when he saw the rest of them trying to take over her life. Sure she was strong and tough and had her experience as a judge to draw on to stand up to them, but they were powerful too, especially his Uncle Dan, who could effortlessly dominate a room like a lion in a flock of antelope.

His connection to his family was thin now that he was working on giving up his earthly attachments. He didn't really care what had happened in their past or even who actually shot the grandmother he'd never met. But as he listened to his mom's story, he began to respect this Uncle Ned—another relative he'd never met. The guy had ditched his family when they dumped all over him, and went on to become a neuroscientist who invented something he cared passionately about, and he did it totally outside the system.

Clint could see why Ned would want to find a way to go back to the worst day of his life to see what happened during a tragedy he couldn't remember. Clint himself lived with memory loss about the day his platoon was blown up in Iraq. It would be a horrible day to relive but maybe remembering it would put an end to the terrifying nightmares that tormented him. Sometimes he went days or even weeks without a good night's sleep. If the ME could help, he might give it a try.

## Debby

Debby drank iced tea and watched their reactions, keeping her face impassive while she listened and thought. This was her M.O. as an attorney. See where the others are coming from. Don't declare yourself. Of course this was family, not clients. They had different expectations. All the more reason to bide her time.

The past is better left in the past, she thought. This family's past, my past. Debbie couldn't see how good could come from plowing up events and conflicts long buried. She shivered at the thought of going back to see herself as the awkward teenager who was never popular the way Bill was. Reliving law school would be worse—cutthroat atmosphere, always watching her back.

She had no interest in summoning up her relationship with Josh's dad. She was done with that. Josh was the only good that came from it. She hated remembering how she fell for Fletcher's promises year after year, believing he would leave his wife for her. No way did she want to look back and listen to his lies again.

The future was what mattered to her. Her main goal was to do whatever she needed to do so Josh would get his life together.

Furthermore, she didn't think the ME was doing her mother any good. From where Debby sat, it looked like her mom was addicted to this device. Anne had all the signs of addiction—obsession with spending more and more time going back on these virtual trips; neglecting Dad and taking risks with his safety to get her "fix" from the past; missing important appointments; giving up other activities; ignoring her family's concerns; and refusing to acknowledge she had a problem.

## Anne

When I got to the end, I took a deep breath and mentally crossed my fingers. I was prepared for skepticism but I figured if I could get one or two of them to try it, they'd like it and others might follow." What do you think?" I asked. "Would you like to try the ME?"

Meadow—bless her— jumped up, ran over and grabbed me in a huge hug. "Thank you Anne for believing in Ned and bringing the ME back, and for doing the research. I can't wait to try it." Her words tumbled over each other. "It sounds like the invention of the century."

I was thrilled that the first response was so positive. But then Dan took the edge off, scowling, arms crossed across his chest. "I'm not doing it today or any other day," he said. "And I recommend the rest of you stay away from it, too. It sounds dangerous."

Meadow darted over to Dan, gave him a quick hug and then pulled back. "Don't be a wet blanket, Dan," she said. "Just because you don't like to take chances, don't try to talk the rest of us out of a great new experience."

"Fine, Meadow," Dan said, pushing her away gently. "If you want to fry your brain, don't let me stop you."

I noticed Amelia weeping in Bill's arms. Did family conflict bother her this much? "Amelia," I said, "don't let Dan and Meadow upset you. Like any brother and sister, they just like to poke at each other sometimes. It doesn't mean anything."

Amelia raised her head, pulled away from Bill's arms, and wiped her face with a tissue. "I don't care about them arguing," she said. "I'm thinking about Evan, about using the ME to go back to when I can hold him and kiss him and smell his sweet baby smell. Oh Anne, I really want to do this."

"We trust you, Mom, and I'm all for Amelia trying this ME," Bill said. "How would it work? "How long does it take? Would we have to use it here? Should we set up some sort of schedule?"

"Whoa, Bill," Debby said. "You're all in on this already? Don't you at least want to think about the risks?"

Bill glared at her. "Didn't you hear me say I trust Mom, Debby?" he said. "And I actually know a lot about risk assessment. In this case, given all Ned's research and Mom's experience with the ME, the probability of harmful effects looks to be low. Amelia wants to try it and that's fine with me."

"But you never knew Ned," Dan said. "He was a monumental screw-up. I wouldn't trust him and I suggest you shouldn't either."

I couldn't let that stand. "That's not fair at all, Dan," I said. "None of us knows what happened that day. And Ned went on to have a distinguished scientific career. I think we can trust him. Plus, I've used the ME more than twenty times and here I am, good as ever."

"But Mom," Debby said, leaning forward toward me. "You took a big chance trying the ME. Uncle Ned didn't use the university's required review procedures, so his work wasn't peer reviewed. All you have is his word. It seems like a big leap of faith to me. I'm with Dan. I don't think any of us should be using that thing." She sat back with a smug look on her face.

Clint had sat up and was shaking his head and muttering to himself. He turned to Debby, hands outstretched like a traffic cop. "Hang on a minute Debby," he said. Why are you trying to tell everyone what to do? How about you and Uncle Dan make your own decisions and let the rest of us think for ourselves?"

Just then Jerry wandered in, up from his nap. "You're all here," he said, looking around at us as he headed for the plate of cookies. "Is it a party? Where's the ice cream?"

But it was more like a truce than a party. The lines were drawn. Dan and Debby left, repeating their dire warnings. Meadow, Amelia and Clint were eager to try the ME. Meadow offered to spend the next week at our house to give me some relief with the household tasks so I could arrange ME trips, and so there could always be one of us awake with Jerry. I had plenty of room for her—the whole upstairs Jerry and I weren't using—so I accepted gratefully and we set up times for her, Amelia, and Clint to travel back to their pasts.

# Chapter 19

## Meadow

Meadow hustled home, grabbed some clothes, toiletries and her computer, and dashed back to Anne's, anxious to try the ME. She knew precisely the time she wanted to revisit—her twentieth birthday, August 17, 1968. That was the day she connected so intensely with Rafe, soul-to-soul, when they briefly became one spirit.

In 1968, Meadow was an art student in San Francisco, where it was the year after The Summer of Love in Haight-Asbury: free love, free food, and free drugs in Golden Gate Park; peace marches, flower children, and rainbow-colored clothes. She had dropped acid and had a spiritual experience in which she realized there's a whole bigger context out there and we're a tiny little piece of the great web of life. She had been sure she knew where her mind was at, what great art was all about and how to create it. It was a time in her life she continued to be nostalgic about and she couldn't wait to return.

Meadow settled in easily once Anne gave her the instructions and connected her to the ME. She took deep breaths and let her body and mind relax into the trip.

*When Meadow emerges from the dark tunnel her twenty-year-old self is barefoot, wearing a red and brown paisley maxi skirt and a gauzy white top embroidered with multicolored flowers. Her hair is long and loose held back by a purple beaded headband. She's sitting crosslegged, facing Rafe, on a sagging couch covered with a blue flowered spread in the old house they share with eight housemates.*

*Her body is light and lithe. Her soul is calm. Her life is blissful.*

*Rafe is wearing a red, green and orange tie-dyed tee shirt and frayed cutoffs. His long bushy brown hair blends together with his frizzy brown beard to encircle his face. His eyes are filled with love, joy and giving.*

*The spicy pungent odor of marijuana smoke hangs in the air along with the scent of patchouli musk incense from sticks burning on a nearby table. The only sound is the splashing of water in a fountain made of balanced rocks.*

*Meadow's current self is astonished by the psychedelic colors of the floor pillows, woven wall hangings, candles, and lava lamps. A couple of straggly plants in macramé hangers hang from the ceiling. This decor they had thought was so cutting-edge and freeing looks contrived and dated to her now.*

*She and Rafe are soul gazing—silently staring deeply into each other's eyes and holding intimate eye contact to create an open heart space and harmonize their energies. Their breathing is synchronized. They allow all their love to pour out into each other's eyes. Meadow is completely at one with Rafe.*

*When a timer dings to signal the end of five minutes, they break eye contact, bow, and say "Namaste" to each other. They continue to sit silently letting their emotions wash over themselves freely. Meadow profoundly understands that it isn't things that are important, it's the people you love and the people who love you. For her those people aren't her broken family back in Montana, they are Rafe and the others in this young artistic community who have come together to create and celebrate their own loving family.*

*Rafe breaks the silence and the spell as he reaches for her hand. "Let's go upstairs," he says. They run up to Meadow's tiny room, which is barely big enough for the mattress on the floor and her belongings stashed in multi-colored stacked cardboard boxes. They fall onto the mattress gazing into each other's eyes once again as they begin to kiss softly, breathe deeply, and touch each other slowly and gently. As they make love, she gets that they are absolutely attuned to each other, allowing spirit to flow through themselves and into each other in a continuous loop of energy. She believes they truly see, feel, celebrate and honor each other as they merge into one.*

*Revisiting this scene, Meadow marvels at her former self's energy, expanded consciousness, and emotional attunement. This rapturous intimacy is what she's been unsuccessfully looking for over many years since that time.*

*But then she sees something she hadn't remembered. As she lies there savoring the glow, Rafe jumps up, pulls on his pants, and darts out the door. She hears him dash down the stairs, figures he has to pee, and assumes he'll be right back. She waits, but he doesn't return to her room. She gets dressed and goes downstairs where she finds him in the kitchen eating ice cream while in a deep discussion with Sheena. He looks up when Meadow comes in. "Hey Babe, want some? It's chocolate." She shakes her head, wondering how he can change spaces so quickly.*

*From the perspective of her more-experienced current self, she sees that her connection with Rafe was transitory. The process, not the person created the magic.*

Meadow woke up blown away. Despite all her New Age background, the ME was way more powerful than any experiences she'd had or ever thought she could have. She put the ME away, carefully following the instructions Anne had given her before the session. Then she opened the door and went to find Anne, who was lying on the living room couch, eyes closed, listening to a Mozart piano concerto.

Meadow sat on the edge of the couch and gently touched Anne's shoulder. "That was incredible," she said. "I can't wait to do it again."

Anne sat up and hugged her. "I'm delighted you liked it," she said. "Jerry's asleep. Let's have a glass of wine and you can tell me all about it. Did you go back to when we were kids?"

Meadow followed Anne to the kitchen, where they collected a bottle of Merlot, a couple of glasses, a hunk of cheese and some crackers. "No, I didn't go back to childhood," she said. "I went to my twentieth birthday when I was in San Francisco with a guy I thought was a soulmate."

"Sounds intense."

"It was. The whole ME experience is so different from my usual remembering. It was in my face—like eating a juicy ripe peach—instead of in my head—like reading about a peach," Meadow said as they settled back on the couch with their wine and cheese. She spoke slowly as if recalling a distant time or place. "When I have remembered in the past, it was me thinking back, trying to reconstruct events. But the ME was the past—relived with understanding from the present. I completely saw and was who I was at twenty, while at the same time knowing what would come after that."

"I know. Being right there and at the same time knowing the future—that's the strange part. Was the time different than you had remembered it, or was it the same?"

"The same and different," Meadow said. "I had forgotten a lot about the way we lived back then. But with the ME it all came back just like you said—very vivid. I could smell the pot and the candles and the incense and hear the fountain splashing." She laughed. "We thought we were so highly evolved, but mostly we were just stoned and doing whatever turned us on."

"And how about the boyfriend?" Anne asked. "Was he as great in person as in your memory?"

"Some of what I remembered was the same, but not all. And my understanding of it was different. As I circled back deeper inside my former self, I realized there was nothing magic about Rafe. It was all a game to him, and to me as well. We loved new experiences, loved sex, and loved the free life we were living, but our love for each other wasn't exclusive or significant. It was casual and momentary. We loved each other in the way we loved and were loved by everybody around us. We loved the times, but the people were interchangeable."

"Great insight," Anne said, "especially if you've been wanting to find love today like you thought you had with him back then."

"Exactly."

"So what happened to Rafe? Why didn't you stay together?"

Meadow savored her wine and let her mind drift back, trying to remember a breakup or saying goodbye to Rafe. But nothing came to mind. "I don't even know," she said. It's odd but all I can recall is that he moved out of the house soon after that birthday experience and I never saw him again. I don't remember missing him, so his leaving must not have been traumatic."

"Does this change your concept of a soulmate?" Anne asked.

Good question, Meadow thought—and as she answered she was talking as much to herself as to Anne. "You know, it actually does," she said. "There's an intriguing guy I met a couple of weeks ago on Match.com. I like him, but I've been sort of standing back because he didn't quite fit my image of a soulmate."

Anne smiled and curled into a more comfortable position on the couch. "Sounds interesting. Tell me more."

"Sure. His name is Jimmy, he's an architect and he lives in Calgary." Meadow grimaced. "But what kind of guy in his sixties still goes by 'Jimmy'? Sounds like he's ten."

"Duh—Jimmy Carter," Anne said, shaking her head. "He was president, remember? And he's way past sixty, still goes by Jimmy, and is one of the most admired men in this country."

Meadow shrugged. "Okay, you're right. Anyway, I like Jimmy. His wife died of cancer five years ago, but he just joined Match.com a few months ago when he decided it was time for a new relationship."

"So he hasn't dated since his wife died?"

"Oh, he has, but sounds sort of like me. No one really rang his bell."

"Is he still working?"

"He has his own architectural firm, but he's mostly retired. Spends most of his time on art now. He's a painter—spends a lot of time working on technique, takes classes. He's emailed me photos of some of his paintings. They're pretty good. I respect his work and his approach to art. Plus he has a good sense of humor and a mellow outlook on life. Maybe we could be soulmates."

"Maybe you could. Anyway, Calgary is only a short plane flight from here. Maybe you should meet him and see how it goes."

Meadow had been thinking the same thing to herself as the conversation had gone on. "I might," she said. "I'm definitely going to consider it."

She was still lost in thought when Anne straightened, took a deep breath, and changed the subject. "You said you can't wait to take another ME trip. Where—or I should say when—do you plan to go back to next?"

Meadow took a minute to change lanes and consider. "I'm not sure. Maybe I'll go back to the late seventies when I was married to Hayden, and Harmony was a baby. I'd like to see if there was any reason I stayed with him besides my believing Harmony needed a father. Not that he was ever a good father, even before he took all our money and disappeared. Harmony always blamed me for his leaving, us having to go on food stamps, everything." She put down her glass. "Hey, maybe I should get her to fly in and use the ME to go back and see what a complete jerk he truly was."

"Do you think she'd come all the way from London to do that?"

"Probably not."

"Don't you want to go back to when we were growing up, to see Mama and Daddy again, to see us all as a happy family, to see Ned and Sandra again?"

Meadow leaned back and closed her eyes. "Not really," she said sadly. "I don't think we were all that happy and I don't think I have much to learn from those days. Mostly I just want to forget it."

## Anne

It was late, so Meadow and I both went to bed, but I couldn't sleep. I kept thinking about Meadow saying she didn't have good memories of our childhood. How could she believe we weren't happy? How could she want to forget? She was sixteen when Mama died, so she'd had many years of our happy growing up time. Why didn't she want to remember?

To distract myself, I went back to the living room and turned on the TV to a recording of one of my guilty pleasures—the reality show *Survivor*, where contestants compete to be the last member of a group marooned on an island where they face challenges and vote each other off until the lone survivor wins a million dollars. A lot of people see reality TV as schlocky junk, but I find Survivor fascinating. As the players interact, they build and destroy relationships, and I try to predict which ones will outlast the others through their plots, schemes and alliances. It's an amazing picture of the tension between self-interest and being part of a group. Much like being a family member.

This episode was one that expanded the focus from the players' artificial island-family to include members of their real family back home. There is always an episode like this at a point where contestants, who have been on the island for many weeks, are tired, hungry and homesick. The show flies in a relative for each remaining contestant, and they compete amongst each other to be able to spend time with their loved one. It is an emotional teary time.

As usual, I was impressed by how much the players had missed their family members and how thrilled they were to see them. It was heartwarming. It was the way family should be. So much of what people do in life is about family. It's what keeps us motivated, gets us up in the morning. We care about them, they care about us.

Family first. That's how Mama brought us up. Just the other day on one of my ME trips, I heard her say to my younger self, "Family comes first, Anne. Family is everything. Without family you are alone in the world."

I wanted the family to be together the way Mama would have wanted. I wanted us all to have good memories of family traditions that linked the generations and strengthened family bonds. I wanted us all to be happier and more resilient, which I was sure we would be if we had more family closeness. I vowed once again to use the ME to make that happen.

# Chapter 20

## Amelia

Amelia was busy all day Monday with web-design clients, writing a new blog post for her Evan's Place website, and taking care of the girls after they got home from their summer gymnastics day camp. But she couldn't keep her mind off the ME. Bill insisted she should go over to his parents' house after dinner to try it. "The girls and I will have some fun Daddy time, watch a movie and eat popcorn," he said. "I'll make sure they have baths before they go to bed." He was sweet that way, which was one of the things she loved most about him.

Amelia could hardly sit still through dinner. The idea that she could see Evan tonight, touch him and hold him was so breathtaking she could barely eat or pay attention to anything else. As soon as dinner was over, she gave the girls goodnight kisses and dashed off.

The instant Anne hooked her up to the ME, Amelia was on her way to her past.

*When Amelia comes out of the ME tunnel, she is rocking Evan in the white rocking chair in the rec room of their house. He's one month old. Miranda, age five is building at the Lego table and Vicky, age three is pushing her baby doll around the room in a tiny stroller. Evan is wide awake, looking up at Amelia, gurgling and cooing to her. She smiles at him. "Hi, sweet baby," she says, leaning down and kissing his face. "Hi sweet baby Evan."*

*Her current self revels in his delicious baby smell, taking long deep sniffs as she strokes his soft arms. For the first time since he died, she no longer has the sharp ache of yearning for him.*

*Vicky pushes her baby doll over next to the rocking chair and sticks her face in Evan's face. "Hi, Evan," she says. "Hi baby Evan."*

*Amelia frees one arm to give Vicky a hug. "Look, Vicky," she says. "I think Evan is smiling at you."*

*Miranda runs over to them. "I want to see him smile," she says. "Will he smile at me?"*

*"Come closer," Amelia says. "Stand here with Vicky." Amelia pulls Miranda in and they all lean over Evan babbling at him. He smiles, waves his arms around, and hits himself in the face with his fist.*

*"Look," Miranda says, "he punched himself." She giggles.*

*"Babies do that," Amelia says. "They haven't learned to make their hands go where they want them to."*

*"Did I do that, Mommy," Vicky asks.*

*Before Amelia can answer, her phone rings. She grabs it from the table next to her. Caller ID shows a client from her web-design business. She's supposed to be on maternity leave until Evan is three months old, but some clients still call with problems they think only she can fix. She should let the call go to voicemail, but she answers.*

*Current-day Amelia is aghast that her former self is wasting even a few minutes of her time with Evan to talk to a client. She wants to scream at herself, "No, don't talk on the phone. Don't give up any precious minutes of your brief time with him." But that was impossible. She couldn't change the past. If only she had known Evan would barely live to be two months old, she would have treasured every second like gold.*

Amelia woke up suffused with love and happiness. Evan's presence remained with her as if he were lying next to her on the bed. Despite her regrets at having taken the business call, she was at peace for the first time since his death.

When she came out to the living room, Anne was waiting expectantly. "You look different," Anne said. "How was it?"

"Amazing," Amelia said, running over to squeeze her mother-in-law in a huge hug. "I can never thank you enough—and of course

I can't thank your brother Ned, much as I wish I could. Being with Evan was incredible. I want to do it again and again. The ME can change my life. If I can do a short ME trip back to Evan every day, or even every other day, I think I can stop grieving and be my old self again, because Evan will always be my baby there for me to visit and I can be with him just like when he was alive."

## Bill

When Amelia got home, she told Bill about her ME trip, and insisted he try it, too. "You can go back and be with Evan just like when he was here," she said. "You'll be amazed how real it is."

Bill was too sad about losing Evan to want to go back and be with him. But the more he listened to Amelia talk about the ME, and the more he thought about what his mom had said about it, the more intrigued he became. Why not give it a try? There were plenty of great times in his past that would be fun to revisit. He set up a time to try it the next day after work, and chose to revisit a perfect ski day back in his championship skiing training days.

*Bill is skiing run after run on one of the best fresh powder days ever at the Big Sky Resort. It's one of those amazing March snows that dropped nearly eighteen inches of powder overnight. Perfect turns on long double black diamond runs, epic views, and the experience of bottomless freedom. It's every bit as exciting as he remembered it.*

*Bill is only sixteen, but he doesn't mess around. He is in the zone—focused and confident. He skis aggressively, jumping cliffs, floating through soft powder, bouncing off moguls. His body is strong, and relaxed, his mind is sharp.*

*His present-day self is exhilarated by reliving his body's peak fitness and performance and his skill speeding down the mountain. His current self notes that it's great to remember there is nothing like doing what you love when you're doing it well. You get into a groove where you can do your best with almost no effort and nothing fazes you.*

Bill woke up refreshed, renewed, and ready to move forward

with a strong spirit. "Wow, Mom," he said when he came out. "This thing is better than a virtual reality game. I was sixteen again, skiing totally in the zone, one of my best ski days ever. I'd forgotten how fantastic that can be."

His mom cocked her head to one side and narrowed her eyes the way she used to do when he was a kid and she thought he was putting her on. "Come on Bill," she said, smiling. "You didn't seriously pick a ski day to go back to. Tell me the truth. You could choose anything in your past life. Where did you go?"

Duh! Bill suddenly got that she had expected him to choose some significant time like Amelia had. She would think a ski day was a bad selection—sort of like goofing off. Maybe he could reframe it in a way that she'd realize its importance to him. "No, Mom, I really did go back to the ski day, but it wasn't just fun, I learned a lot from it. I realized I need to make more time for skiing next winter, and especially for taking Vicky and Miranda skiing. I want to share this with them. There is so much I can teach them, so much fun we can have together."

## Clint

Clint ignored his mom's advice to begin by going back to a happy time in his life. Instead, he chose to revisit the day in 2007 when his platoon was blown up in Iraq. It was a scary choice, but he thought he needed to see what truly happened that day. He never wanted to forget his friends who died there.

*Clint's unit is headed back to the base mid-morning after completing a mission where they had successfully followed up on tips from an informant about the location of a weapons cache. They're on a dirt road—three Humvees, four soldiers in each. He's joking with the guys in his vehicle about who did the most pushups and pull-ups the day before. They're all feeling good about the mission, not expecting trouble.*

*Clint's present-day self enjoys reliving the camaraderie he had with his buddies, but is sick at the thought that they will all be dead a few minutes from now. They mean more to him than anyone. They are like a big family each doing their best to make sure the others don't die. But did he do his best for them? That's what he came back to find out.*

*Their vehicle is the third in the convoy when it hits an explosive. There is a deafening boom, Clint is thrown out of the vehicle and slams into the ground several feet away. His ears ring and thick smoke fills his eyes. His pulse races, and every breath he takes is like a stab in the chest. Sharp suffocating odors from the explosive and the engine fuel fill the air.*

*When he looks up, he can see his vehicle but he can't see his men. The Humvee is on fire and spare ammo is starting to explode. He tries to get up and run to the vehicle to help them but he can't move. He howls at the shooting pain in his legs when he tries to stand up. His right arm is bleeding profusely, and scalding pain engulfs his whole body . He can't move his legs. Can't move his arms. He screams for help over and over again. Everything goes black.*

## Anne

It was horrible. Clint was screaming in my office as if someone was strangling him. I ran in and found him writhing as if his body was wracked with pain. I yanked the ME headset off his head, sat next to him on the couch and cradled him in my arms. "Shhh, Clint. It's a dream. You're OK. It's just a dream." I said over and over, stroking his face softly.

He gradually calmed, opened his eyes, gave me a dazed look, and began to weep. "They all died," he sobbed. "I couldn't help them. Why them and not me? Why did I survive?"

I hugged him tighter. "There's no answer to that question," I said. "It's just what happened. It wasn't your fault."

He struggled free from my arms, sat up and shook his head as though to clear a fog. "It was so strange, Mom," he said. "I was right there in Iraq with everyone from my platoon. I was excited to see my friends, but so sad because I knew they would die soon. Inside my head I was who I am now, but I couldn't change what I did or said in the dream or vision or whatever it was. I couldn't warn them or say goodbye or tell them how much I cared about them."

He looked inquiringly at me.

"Yes," I said. "Your experience sounds like mine so far. I watch myself in the past, but I can't change anything."

"That's harsh," he said. "It's the gut-wrenching guilt I live with every day. My buddies are gone and I'm here."

"Is that why you were screaming?" I asked

"No," he said. "The screaming was when our vehicle blew up and I was on the ground bleeding and watching it burn. The pain was brutal and I couldn't move to help anyone. All I could do was scream."

We sat in silence for a few minutes. I wanted to hug him again, but he had stiffened and backed away. "I think you should stay here overnight," I said. I don't want you to be alone."

"No, Mom," he said in a tense voice. "I don't need you to take care of me."

"But you might have terrible flashbacks. You might need someone to talk to."

"I'll be fine by myself, Mom. I've dealt with this before."

"I'll be worrying about you all night. Can't you just stay so I'll know you're all right?"

"No, Mom. You have to face reality here. You can't fix this. You can't fix me. War is shit, our government is shit, and there's nothing you can say or do to change that."

# Chapter 21

## Anne

At first I had thought of the ME as kind of enhanced 3D family movies, where we could revel in joyous times from the past. But as we continued to explore, my understanding of the ME's potential impact grew more complex.

It wasn't all fun and games—except maybe for Bill. Clint's grueling trip was horrible for me. I also knew from my own experiences that re-visiting the past could be painful. On one of my trips I went back to the day Jerry and I got the terrible news of his Alzheimer's diagnosis. Like Clint, I knew it would be agonizingly harsh, and yet I wanted to relive it because it was a profound time in my life, a time when Jerry and I connected intensely—soul-to-soul—in sorrow, knowing our lives would be forever changed. I figured Clint revisited his life-changing day for similar reasons.

In the next few days, Meadow and Amelia each faced frustration and heartache at being unable to affect the past. Meadow went back to a passionate gathering of friends in the late sixties when they believed they could change the world. She emerged in tears. "It was awful," she said. "I knew we would be going to a protest later and it would be a disaster." She gasped as if the memory was choking her. "I wanted to tell them not to go, that it was dangerous." Meadow's voice rose. "I wanted to tell Brook not to go there, that she would be hurt there, that her life would be ruined." Now she sobbed. "But all I could do was be there and watch her decide to go with no idea of what lay ahead."

Amelia also came out of my office weeping after one of her trips.

"I went back to when Evan was first getting sick in his last few weeks," she sobbed. "I had looked back so many times in my mind wishing I had done something different, wishing I had taken Evan to the doctor sooner, wishing I had recognized earlier how sick he was. When I looked back with the ME I could see I should have taken him to the ER sooner. But I realized I am the same woman, so I would be likely to miss the signs again and make the same choices again and get the same horrible outcome again in that situation. Maybe seeing it again should give me peace of mind that I did my best, but instead it feels hopeless, like there was no chance I could have saved Evan."

What could be more frustrating than watching, knowing what would happen, knowing other possibilities, but not being able to do anything to change the outcome? I echoed their grief as the three of us comforted each other and confronted the unyielding reality of days gone by.

Bill continued to go back only to good times. He was irate over Amelia's distressing trip and suggested she shouldn't use the ME anymore. But she prevailed. "I won't second-guess myself again," she said. "I'll just go back to times when Evan was healthy and I can enjoy him. If I can see him every day, my life will be on track again."

Jerry sat woodenly though all the ME trips and discussion, like a solitary passenger on a boring bus trip. I so wished he could be the lively, loving Jerry I'd been seeing in our past. I wanted us to remember our old times together. Then it hit me. Now could be the time to give Jerry a try with the ME. Why not? What if he could go back and remember clearly? I could set it for a scene I'd visited. Let him go there and re-live it like I did. Maybe it would awaken something in him.

I didn't worry much about the risk. Realistically Jerry didn't have much brain power left anyway, so how much could it hurt him? Also I'd done it more than twenty times now with no ill effects. Meadow agreed it was worth a try.

I didn't think Jerry would let me put the ME headset on him if he could see it, so we waited to hook him up until after he fell asleep for his nap. Then I sent him back to the time of my first ME visit, the day he proposed to me in the mountain meadow. I sat next to him as he lay there and I didn't notice any changes. He didn't toss and turn or moan or speak or anything. He just slept. I had no idea what he was experiencing, but he woke up smiling.

"Where are we? Where's the picnic?" he asked. He sat right up and gave me a big hug and a long lingering kiss.

"It was a dream about the past," I said. "We were hiking in the mountains, the day you proposed and gave me this ring." I held out my hand.

He touched the ring gently and beamed at me. The vacant look I'd grown used to was gone. Jerry's soft brown eyes and the whole look of his face were like he used to be. "I love you, Anne" he said. "We have been happy sharing our lives together."

I hugged him with tears in my eyes and joy in my heart. "Oh, Jerry, you're back! You've come back to me." But he slipped into dementia again while I was hugging him, slumping backward and staring blankly into space.

Tears ran down my face. Losing him again after our brief reconnection broke my heart.

I looked over at Meadow, who had been watching from across the room the whole time. She shook her head. "Unbelievable," she said. "Do you think we found the cure for Alzheimer's?"

"I wish," I said. "but you can see his recovery was only momentary. For him it must have been like a door opened for a few minutes but then slammed shut again."

Still, the ME had given me an incredible gift with his brief moment of clarity. Jerry was still in there and at some level he could remember our past. And who knows how he might do with more ME trips?

So I chose another special time for Jerry to visit—again one I would visit first to be sure it was a good choice before I sent him back. I settled on the trip Jerry and I had taken to Hawaii in 1997 to celebrate our thirtieth anniversary. Clint had just graduated from high school and Bill and Debby were in their twenties and living in town, so it was finally easy for us to have a romantic getaway. We stayed in an oceanfront room at the historic Moana Surfrider on

Waikiki Beach, alternating relaxing on the beach with driving around the island of Oahu visiting tourist attractions. We climbed Diamond Head, snorkeled at the Hanauma Bay Nature Preserve, toured the Pearl Harbor historic sites, and soaked up sunshine, ukulele music, and tropical drinks. It was a perfect trip.

I wanted to revisit the early evening of our actual anniversary, a magical time Jerry and I spent watching the sunset from the Surfrider's Beach Bar, sipping Mai Tais, and listening to live music. I looked up the dates on a calendar and the sunset time on the internet and was able to precisely pinpoint the time to set the ME for. Then I was off.

*I sweep through the tunnel into a soft blanket of sultry tropical air. An ocean breeze whispers across my face wafting with it the sweet scent from the fragrant white tuberose lei around my neck. I take a deep relaxed breath. Heavenly.*

*Jerry and I are sitting at a glass-topped table surrounded by lush foliage and shaded by an enormous banyan tree. We fit right in with my lavender sundress and Jerry's dark blue linen shirt. Jerry looks fit and alert, and my current-day self soaks up this former him who I miss so dearly in my present life.*

*"Dreams really do come true," croons the soft voice of the ukulele player strumming chords and singing "Somewhere Over the Rainbow." A hula dancer in a soft pink flowered dress moves gracefully to the music.*

*The ocean is almost in our faces, waves breaking on the sandy beach in front of the patio. I am entranced by the surfers sliding and bobbing across the waves. I lick my lips, savoring the pineapple, dark rum and curaçao in my drink.*

*"The song is right," I say. "Dreams do really come true. Our life together with our kids has been better than I ever dreamed—and it still is. We are so lucky. Sometimes I almost have to pinch myself to believe it. Happy anniversary, Jerry."*

*Jerry's face lights up and his eyes shine. "We are lucky," he said, "but we have also created a lot of our good fortune. I think we made the best decision right after we got engaged when we chose to stay in Helena and build our lives there even though you had attractive opportunities in other places. You don't have any regrets about that, do you?"*

*"No. No regrets," I say. "Turning down the job in San Francisco didn't hurt my career one bit, and bringing up our kids in Helena where they've had family and roots has been priceless. And for you, being able to continue your dad's real estate business and now to bring Bill into it has been invaluable."*

*He grinned. "I love working with Bill. Who knew our ski champion would go into real estate? And he's so good at it."*

*"I know," I say. "Bill inherited your sociability gene for sure. You've never met a stranger and neither has he."*

*Jerry reaches for my hand across the table as the sun begins to set over the ocean, a brilliant yellow ball sinking toward the horizon, flanked by pink streaks stretching across the sky and reflected in the blue water below. "Our family—you and our children are everything to me," he says. "I enjoy my job, but it comes in second. Happy anniversary, Anne."*

*"Mama always said 'family is everything,' I say. And she was right." Tears sting my eyes as I think of her. "I only wish she could have lived to know our children. She would have loved them so much."*

*My current self wants to tell my former self to focus on Jerry, to stop thinking and talking about Mama who was long gone by then. I should enjoy every crumb of him while I can, before he begins to fade away. But I don't have that foresight, so I go on into old heartaches. "If only we could bring Ned and Sandra back into the family," I say, "it would be even more perfect."*

*Fortunately Jerry wouldn't let me spoil the mood. "We are perfect, Anne" he says, squeezing my hand. "Be here and enjoy us."*

I wake up relaxed, still basking in the tropical glow and relishing the intimate connection I had with Jerry in Hawaii. Yes, I thought to myself, this would be a good experience for Jerry to revisit.

## Jerry

After Jerry ate his favorite supper of tomato soup and a grilled cheese sandwich, Anne helped him get ready for bed. He was tired and fell asleep almost as soon as he settled in.

*Suddenly Jerry finds himself on a tropical patio, having a drink with Anne. He is elated at the beauty around him and filled with love for Anne. This gorgeous beach is the perfect place to celebrate their thirtieth anniversary. When Anne begins to talk about how lucky they are, he completely agrees. Anne and their children are the best things that have ever happened to him, they are everything to him. He tells her that as he holds her hand during the sunset and wishes her happy anniversary.*

*Jerry's current self is transfixed by the scene—the romantic music, the pungent drink, the lush foliage are so vivid. In the back of his mind he senses an awakening of consciousness, of experiencing sensations as richly as he did in the past. It is as if he has turned on windshield wipers to clear a muddy film from his mind. Intoxicated by his newfound mental clarity, Jerry wants to stay in this place forever.*

When he woke up in his Helena bedroom with Anne sitting on the bed next to him, Jerry brought with him his awareness of the marvelous life they have had together. "I love you so much, Anne," he said. "I am so lucky to have you in my life." He sat up and kissed her—a sweet loving kiss. Then he leaned back, put his hands on her shoulders and gazed into her eyes. "I had a dream about Hawaii," he said, "about the time we went there to celebrate our anniversary. I loved being there."

"Yes," Anne said. "It was a special time."

"Let's go there again," he said, his voice full of enthusiasm. "I want to go there again with you and sit by the beach and watch the sunset again."

"Maybe we can," Anne said. "Let's talk about it tomorrow."

Urgency grabbed Jerry. "No," he said, stomping his foot, "not tomorrow. Now. Let's make plans right now."

"Okay," Anne said. "How soon do you want to go and how long shall we stay?"

"Stay where? Where are we going?" Jerry asked, as the familiar fog came over him again. He clenched his fist in a futile attempt to hang on to an important thought that was slipping away.

## Anne

I was blown away. Jerry's recovery—if that's what it was—had lasted several moments longer and been more complete than the last time he used the ME. And both times he woke up remembering at least part of the scene he had revisited.

Somehow Jerry was still in there. Could the ME be his ticket back to rationality?

# Chapter 22

## Debby

Debby left work early on Wednesday for her first visit to Josh at the Teen Rehab Institute. Dread battled with anticipation during the hour-long drive, as she rushed to make her 3:00 appointment with Josh's counselor. The meeting with the counselor, required before she could visit Josh, could be good news or bad news. Debby knew better than to expect a major turnaround so soon, but she was hoping for some improvement.

She got there on time but ended up spending half an hour in a windowless waiting room. Typical bureaucracy. In her haste to arrive on time, she'd forgotten to charge her cell phone, so she was reduced to examining pamphlets and posters entitled "5 Myths About Drug Abuse and Addiction," "Definitions of Recovery," and "Heroin Addiction Cycle" while she waited.

Debby was pondering a poster that warned against believing overcoming addiction is simply a matter of willpower, when Josh's counselor, Nina Balshaw, came to escort Debby back to her tiny office. Nina was a round-bodied girl, young, sweet-faced and amiable. "It's so nice to see you again, Ms. Barnes," she said. "I'm so sorry you had to wait."

Nina's office was a long skinny room with a large window behind a wide desk, which barely fit between the side walls. Nina squeezed past the desk and into her chair behind it, motioning Debby to the molded plastic chair facing the desk. After a few minutes of small talk, Nina's smile disappeared and her tone turned regretful as she gave Debby some bad news. "Unfortunately Josh isn't yet doing the work he needs to do to get well," she said. "He continues to deny having a problem. He does admit he "messed up," as he puts it, but he insists that now he will be fine without help."

Debby's heart sank when she heard this, but annoyance quickly obscured her sadness. *Good grief,* she thought. *Isn't it supposed to be your job to get him to do the work he needs to do? Isn't that why I'm paying the big bucks?* But she didn't say any of that, just nodded, kept her face impassive and listened.

"I know this is difficult," Nina said. "We have a good family group that meets here every week. You might find it helpful in dealing with your feelings about Josh's recovery."

*No way,* Debby thought to herself. *I don't want to sit in a group and listen to other families' horrible addiction stories.* "Thanks, but I'm so busy at work that I don't have time for a support group," she said. "But what can I do to move Josh along to doing the work he needs to do?"

"Use your influence to motivate him toward change. Support and encourage him, keep the lines of communication open. He needs that. But at the same time you need to stand firm with him. Let him know what you expect. Set boundaries."

*Standard stuff,* Debby thought. *Do they think parents of addicts don't read the advice that's out there in all those books, blogs and websites?* But she kept these thoughts to herself as the session continued. She'd done her research before she sent Josh here and The Teen Rehab Institute had the best reputation and success rate in the region. She had to believe they knew what they were doing.

When the time to see Josh finally came, Debby was nervous but resolute. She knew she was through with letting Josh take advantage of her and lie to her. She had sent him to rehab so he could recover and he needed to get with the program.

When she walked in to his room, Josh was slumped on his bed reading a *Lord of the Rings* book he'd in all likelihood read fifteen times before. He closed the book and glowered at her. "I hate it here, Mom. I can't believe you stuck me here. The people here are beyond strange and they totally don't get me. Why do I have to be here?"

He was skinnier than ever and his eyes looked like he'd been crying. Deep inside, Debby wanted to sit on his bed, hold him in her arms like when he was a little boy, pat his back and tell him everything was going to be okay. But that wasn't going to help him now, so she chose the one chair in his room, scooted it closer to his bed and sat down. "I think you know the answer to that question, Josh."

He sighed loudly. "Okay, you've made your point, Mom. Now I'm clean and ready to go home. I've learned my lesson."

"Your counselor doesn't think you're ready yet, Josh, and I agree with her."

"Mom, please. You have no idea what it's like here. The people are weird, the food sucks, and I don't even have a computer. You have to let me go home. I promise I'll stay clean."

"I wish I could believe you, but you've lied to me too many times."

"Come on Mom. Remember all the fun we used to have, biking, hiking at the ranch, playing games with Vicky and Miranda? Can't we just go home and be happy again?"

"We haven't been happy for a long time, Josh. Biking and hiking and playing with your cousins were all a long time ago before you started taking drugs and hanging out with addicts."

"We could do all that again, Mom. Just get me out of here."

"When the staff here thinks you're ready to come home, I'll do that. And before you go we'll all meet together and set up a plan for how life at home will work for both of us."

Josh turned his back on her and re-opened his book. "If that's the way you're going to be, you can go now," he said. "I don't want to talk to you."

Debby swallowed her anger and spoke calmly. "Okay Josh, I'll see you next week. Meanwhile you need to cooperate with the program here. That's what will get you home."

Debby drove home with tears blurring her vision like a rainstorm. She was sad, angry, guilty, and scared about Josh's addiction. She had thought a lot about what she could have done differently to have prevented this nightmare. She knew she had trusted Josh too much, let him get away with too much. He had lied about where he was, who he was with and what he was doing. He had skipped school and his grades had suffered. At first she had seen this as typical teenage acting-out behavior. But then he had become a thief as well as a liar. He had stolen money from her billfold, and stuff from their house, and used her credit cards to buy things he resold. All to get money for drugs. By the time she had forced him to get help, his life had become all about how to get money for drugs and how to hide his habit.

Now that she had finally grown a backbone, she was going to keep it. It was hard to turn her back on him when he was begging to come home, but she knew she had to if she wanted him to get clean and stay clean. She would try to think of Josh as a difficult client in her law practice, and continue to remind him as she did them that actions have consequences.

By the time Debby got home, it was nearly 6:30 and she was aching for a long bike ride. Time outside would nurture her soul. In June the sun doesn't set in Helena until nearly 9:30 p.m. and it was a beautiful evening, so she changed her clothes and went to the garage to get her bike. She thought about calling her friend Luke who she'd been biking with lately on weekends, but decided she'd rather be alone to think.

She headed west on Lyndale, then North to Centennial Park and on to Spring Meadow Lake State Park, where she sat by the lake for a while watching kids swimming and playing on the beach, and families picnicking. They looked so cheerful and carefree. She envied their free and easy enjoyment of the summer evening.

Debby thought about what Josh had said about wanting to come home and be happy again. She wanted that too, but she doubted Josh would keep his promises. Like father, like son, she thought, remembering all the times Fletcher had promised to leave his wife and marry her. He was separated when they got involved and said he was getting a divorce. He said he loved her and wanted a future with her. But when she found out she was pregnant, she checked on the status of his divorce and found out he had never filed divorce papers.

She remembered the day they broke up as vividly as if it was yesterday. She didn't need any memory enhancing device like her uncle Ned had created to call it up in her mind. When she looked back, she saw herself standing in the kitchen of her old apartment. Her belly was swollen and the baby stirred inside her.. The smells of Chinese takeout hovered in the air—a smell that nauseates her to this day.

Fletcher stood in the doorway, his arms crossed over his chest.

"You need to tell her," she said to him, tears dripping down her face. "Now. Right now. This baby will be here soon."

He stepped into the kitchen and took her in his arms. "I will," he said, rubbing her back. "But I have to wait until she recovers from her shoulder surgery."

Debby shook free of his embrace so she could see his face. "We don't have time to wait," she said, grabbing his arm and shaking it. Her voice rose in frustration. "You need to file for divorce now, so we can be together after the baby is born."

He shook her hand away. "It's not the right time," he said. "We're not ready for this, Debby. It was your decision to keep this baby. I thought I could go along. But I can't. We aren't in a position to raise a child together. I'll help support it, give you whatever I owe, but I don't want to have it be part of my life."

"I don't need your money," she said. In a sudden rush of anger, she shoved him back toward the door. "What I need and what this baby needs is your love. If you can't give us that, then it's time for us to call it quits."

That was it. Fletcher never met Josh, and Josh doesn't know who his father is. She's thought about telling him now that he's older, but has been afraid he wouldn't be able to deal with the rejection he'd surely get if he approached Fletcher.

Bottom line, she had trusted Fletcher and he betrayed her trust. She wouldn't be so naive with Josh. She would make sure any agreements between them had fail-safe oversight provisions.

Her mood was darkening. Sitting by the lake wasn't having the restorative effect she had been hoping for, so she decided to ride back to town. Maybe she would stop by and visit her dad. Although he couldn't have much of a conversation with her, she took comfort in being with him, hugging him and feeling his love.

But when she got there, Jerry was already in bed asleep. Duh! She should have known he would be. And now she was stuck having a conversation with her mom, who of course took the opportunity to try to convince her to try Uncle Ned's Memory Enhancer.

"Meadow and Amelia both love it," her mom said. "It's so amazing for Amelia to be able to go back and spend time with Evan when he was healthy and happy. She says if she can see him every day, that will put her life back on track."

Debby didn't think this kind of denying reality was very healthy for Amelia, nor did she think it would last as a remedy for her grief. "How long do you think she'll want to do that?" she asked. "Don't you think she'll get tired of him always being the same age, not growing and changing the way babies do when they're alive?"

"I don't know," her mom said. "That's up to her. Maybe by the time she gets tired of it, her grief will be healed. But wouldn't you like to go back to when Josh was a sweet innocent baby, before all his problems?"

There was a part of Debby that found that possibility appealing, but her rational mind squashed it. "What would be the point?" she said. "I couldn't change anything. I need to be focused on Josh's future, not his past. And I need to keep my brain in good shape so I can support him and myself in the present time, so I certainly don't want to hook myself up to some untested electrical device."

"It's perfectly safe," Anne said. "We even let your dad try it and he came back to himself for several minutes remembering happy times."

Debby gasped in horror. "I can't believe you hooked Dad up to that thing! Mom, you're a lawyer, you're a judge, you know about putting vulnerable older adults at risk. This more than anything tells me you've gone off the deep end."

# Chapter 23

## Anne

Despite Debby's ill-tempered outrage every time I mentioned the DE, I was becoming more and more convinced of its value, especially after seeing what it had done for Jerry and Amelia. As various family members and I dove into our pasts, I continued to weigh the pros and cons. So far, pro was winning. In spite of some difficult trips, everyone who had tried it—even Clint—had given the ME a thumbs up.

I had pretty much given up trying to convince Debby to try it, but I still desperately wanted Dan to give the ME a shot. He's my twin and he's always been an important part of my life. He's smart and honorable—a man of integrity, who prides himself on standing firm in his beliefs. But when new evidence comes along, he will incorporate it and revise his opinion. I hoped that once he heard about the others' experiences with the ME, he'd let go of his conviction that it was dangerous.

I longed for him to use the ME to go back and relive the good times we had as children. So often the intimacy I want with Dan is missing. We joke and have fun, but our interactions sometimes seem superficial. His sardonic view of the world puts a wall between us. I hoped that going back and re-experiencing the close family relationships we had as kids would thaw his feelings and he would drop his guard and let me in.

So the next evening I left Jerry with Meadow, and met Dan after work at The Hawthorn, a wine bar downtown on Last Chance Gulch.

Neutral territory. The dark candlelit room was quite a contrast with the daylight outside, but it had a cozy ambience, and was the sort of place where, even though we know half the town, we would be left alone to talk privately. We sat at a thick wooden table in a back corner sharing a bottle of spicy Argentinian Malbec, accompanied by a cheese plate with chunks of manchego, stilton, and camembert, and a basket of house-made breadsticks..

I tried to tell Dan what he was missing by not trying the ME. I told him about Amelia and Evan, about Bill's skiing, and about Meadow's experiences going back to her hippie days. I explained how Clint relieved some of his guilt by recovering the lost memory of his worst day at war, and finally I recounted Jerry's remarkable brief awakening.

He listened quietly, sipping his wine and nibbling on cheese. When I stopped, he waited a minute, then said, "What do you want from me Anne?"

"I want you to think about their experiences, Dan. They found their ME trips added a lot to their lives, healed wounds and gave them new perspective, and they're all fine. No bad effects from using the device. Does that change your mind about the danger of it?"

"Not really. Six of you have tried it, and one of those has Alzheimer's so can't report. That's not a big enough sample to be meaningful. And as for the value of the experience, I only know what you're telling me, which is hearsay or your opinions. Furthermore, the benefits you describe vary from person to person."

"More like it varies depending on the part of your life you choose to revisit," I said. "None of them have gone back to when they were kids, but I have done it several times and found it amazing. It's so wonderful to go back to our childhood, see the fun we had, and see Mama and Daddy alive and young again. And it's surprising. There's a lot you've forgotten and a lot turns out to be different from what you remember."

"You'd be surprised what I remember, Anne," he said. "I remember plenty about when we were kids."

"Like what?" I took a substantial sip of my wine and sat back to listen to his recollections.

"Well let's see," he said, grinning, "I remember that time in third grade when you got sick and threw up all over your desk. You got to go home, but the rest of our class had to stay in the stinky room while Sister Agnes Louise cleaned up the mess. Or the time when we were five and you swallowed a penny. You had to poop in a pot for days so Mama could dig through it until she found the penny and knew it had passed through you. If I'm not mistaken, that penny is taped in the back of your baby book."

I was laughing so hard by then that I almost couldn't answer him, "Okay. Okay. You remember all the times I came out looking ridiculous. What else? How about stuff you did?"

"Sure. How about when we were little kids and I begged Grandma and Granddad to take out their false teeth and let me hold them? It was years before I understood why they wouldn't do it. Or—thinking of teeth—what about the time my tooth went down the drain and I wrote a note to the tooth fairy explaining why I should get my money even though the tooth was gone. I think of that as my first legal pleading."

"Okay, okay, Dan. Enough."

"No, wait," he said. "What about the time Mama went off and left eggs boiling on the stove and they exploded and Ned started screaming because he thought someone was shooting at us and Dad came running in and tripped over a toy car and lay sprawled on the floor. Ned thought he'd been shot and killed?" Dan leaned back and gave a deep belly laugh.

I glared at him, irritated at his lack of empathy. "That isn't one bit funny, Dan. Nothing about Ned and shooting can ever be funny."

"Sorry," he said. But he didn't look sorry.

## Dan

Dan wasn't actually sorry for his comment. What was true was true. Why pretend it wasn't? Sometimes Dan thought his twin sister had no sense of humor anymore, especially when it came to the family. She was all about being politically correct in family discussions. No one should say anything negative or anything that could possibly be offensive to anyone else. Her memories had always been rose colored nostalgia, and this device of Ned's had made that worse.

"Anyway you have to admit I remember our childhood," he said. "Maybe not the way you want me to remember it, but I do remember. I remember enough, so why go back and see it again?"

"Remembering is one thing," Anne said, "but the ME is way beyond that. It's reliving the time, being there just like you were when it happened. I think you'd find it fascinating. If you don't want to go back to when we were kids, you could start by going back to when Charlene was little. Wouldn't you like to see your daughter as a little girl again?"

Dan recoiled at the thought of revisiting the years when he was married to Charlene's mother. "Those times would include my witchy ex-wife," he said, "so I definitely don't want to go there."

"What about times when you were in the Air Force or in law school? Meadow has learned a lot from going back to times when she was in her twenties."

Dan chuckled. "That's the difference between me and Meadow. She's always trying to get insights and improve herself. I think I'm just fine the way I am. I like my life—work I enjoy, lots of friends, and family that only hassles me some of the time." He smirked. "Unfortunately this is one of the times."

"Come on, Dan," Anne said. "I'm not hassling you. I'm inviting you to open your mind to an amazing opportunity. Can't you move out of your comfort zone for once and take a chance on something new?"

Dan swallowed his annoyance at her unfair judgment. Maybe he was comfortable now, but all those years working with his father at the family law firm were far from easy. Nor was the hell his ex-wife put him through before their divorce was final. And, as for risk, putting himself out there by running for the state legislature and serving the eight years the Montana Constitution allows, he'd had his share of treacherous times.

"Look, Anne," he said. "I remember what I want to remember and I don't need to hook up my brain to some experimental device to do it. Can't we just leave it at that?"

## Anne

His words came through loud and clear, but I wasn't ready to let go without one more try. "I wish you'd reconsider," I said. "Going back to those early days in the family, seeing Mama and Daddy alive again, can transform you. It's an amazing gift, which you're refusing to take advantage of for reasons I can't accept."

"Here's the thing, Anne," he said. "It's not all as rosy for me as it is for you. Some things I don't remember because I don't want to remember. I don't even like to think about Dad, much less return to the past and see him."

"Damn it, Dan, you just can't bear the thought that you could be wrong about Daddy. That's why you won't try the ME. You're afraid to go back and see that your carefully constructed—and I do mean 'constructed'—list of wrongs he did you is nothing but a figment of your imagination."

Dan sat back, arms crossed over his chest, staring at me steely-eyed. "No, Anne," he said, "I just don't want to see the old bastard again. He's gone, I'm not. Let's keep it that way."

I've learned to step back, take a breath and think before I react. But this time my training failed me. I glared at him and pounded my fist on the table. "Stop for a minute. Listen to yourself. You're shutting down a possibility that could bring this family together in a new stronger way. I'm not just using the ME for myself, I'm using it for all of us. Every time I go back, I see ways we were close and ways we let our closeness slip away instead of building on it."

I left in a huff and as soon as I got home, I told Meadow all about it. "I can't believe how negative his view of our childhood is," I said. "He has no interest in even thinking about it, much less revisiting it."

She sighed. "I keep telling you our childhood wasn't as golden as you remember it. I think when you use the ME you are looking at a different past than Dan and I remember."

"That sounds unlikely. The past is the past."

"But there were good times and bad times. If you only go back to times you recall fondly, you're only seeing one side of our family interaction."

Was I cherry-picking the times I re-visited to fit my sunny view of our family past? No. I had seen some negative times, especially with Daddy drinking. Still, I had to admit I had seen many more pleasant than unpleasant times. As a person who prides herself on being fair, that was not acceptable.

"Okay, you have a point," I said. "How about you choose a time for me that you think I should see, and I'll go back to that time?"

Meadow clapped her hands together and jumped up. "Sure. Give me a few minutes to double check the date and time and I'll set you up."

She hooked me up without letting me see the date or time, and I was off to a day that wasn't a horrible, terrible day, but was a day I had no wish to relive.

*It's Easter Sunday. The scent of sugar and chocolate wafts from our Easter baskets, which are stuffed with Cadbury crème eggs, yellow marshmallow chickens, multi-colored jelly beans, and the most prized confection for each of us—a hollow chocolate rabbit with our names in sugar icing.*

*I think it's 1954, because Meadow (who was Nicole then) looks to be about six. That means Dan and I are almost thirteen, and Ned is eight. Sandra is an infant. We're still wearing our new Easter finery from church. I love my full-skirted lavender and white floral dress with its wide purple sash, and Nicole looks adorable in her ruffly pale blue dress trimmed with white lace.*

*Daddy is sitting off to the side of the room with a drink and a cigarette, scowling, while Mama tries to get everything set up for us to hunt for the colored eggs the Easter Bunny left. Dan and I don't care much about the egg hunt at our age and we know enough to stay quiet when Daddy is irritable, but Ned and Nicole are eager and restless.*

*"Okay, take the candy out of your baskets so you can use them for the eggs you find," Mama says. Ned grabs his basket and starts*

*chomping on his chocolate rabbit.*

*"Don't eat that now, Ned," Mama says. "Just leave your candy on the table."*

*Ned takes one last bite before he puts down the chocolate rabbit. "Ned, if you eat one more bit of that candy, it's going in the trash," Daddy yells. Ned starts to cry.*

*Nicole tries to cheer him up with a tiny stuffed rabbit from her basket. "Hoppity, hoppity, Ned," she says, running her bunny up his arm. "Happy Easter, hoppity, hoppity."*

*"Enough, Nicole," Daddy yells.*

*Nicole runs over to him. "My bunny just want to say Happy Easter, hoppity, hoppity," she said poking him with the bunny.*

*Daddy grabs the bunny. "That bunny is going away," he says, stuffing it behind him in the chair.*

*"Noooo," Nicole screams. "My bunny. Give it back."*

*"Give her back the bunny, Will," Mama says, and quit being so grouchy.*

*"I'm sick and tired of all this noise and nonsense," Daddy snarls. "Get them settled down, Viv, or I'm going to throw all this Easter stuff in the trash."*

*Both Nicole and Ned are bawling loudly now, Mama is trying to quiet them and Dan and I are laying low taking it all in.*

When I woke up, I realized there was a good reason I had never taken a ME trip back to Easter. I never liked Easter as a kid. As good Catholics, my parents and their friends gave up alcohol for Lent. To celebrate the end of this deprivation they all went to a big party the Saturday night before Easter when Lent was officially over, and drank enough to make up for their weeks of sacrifice. On Easter Sunday they were hung over and grumpy and we paid for it.

Meadow was waiting for me in the living room. I joined her on the couch. "Okay. You got me," I said. "Easter was always yucky and I'm sure other times were too. But I still think the happy times outweighed the unhappy ones by a lot."

"Maybe for you," she said, "but not for Dan and me. Certainly not for Ned, and I seriously doubt Sandra has a lot of happy memories."

Somewhere deep inside I suspected she was right, but it was hard to let go of my hope of pulling them all into my warm-fuzzy-family-movie past.

# Chapter 24

## Anne

My talk with Meadow had gotten me thinking about Sandra. She should know about the ME too and have a chance to try it. She was so young when Mama died that her happy family memories must be dim. The horror of Mama's death and the miserable years that followed may have blocked out positive family memories. Sandra might welcome a chance to go back before it all happened to see Mama and Daddy and the whole family when we were all happy.

The more I thought about this, the more eager I got. This could be a game changer for Sandra and the rest of us. If she could go back and see how Mama doted on her, see how much she was loved, see the good times we all had, maybe she would see us all in a new light. Maybe she would want to be part of the family again, to spend time with us, to be our sister as well as a sister of God. I had to go see Sandra to tell her about the ME and encourage her to try it.

The next day, when Meadow and I were fixing our lunch, I ran the idea past her as she toasted a bagel to go along with her salad. "You could call her and see if she's interested," Meadow said, as she artfully spread cream cheese on her bagel and topped it with a tiny dollop of apricot jam.

She put her food on the table, sat down across from me, took a bite and chewed slowly. Then she asked "When was the last time you talked to her?"

I dipped an apple slice in my salted caramel yogurt. "I haven't talked to her in years," I said. "Most of the times I called her whoever answered said she couldn't come to the phone but they would give her a message and she would call me back. But she never did." I popped the apple slice in my mouth, savoring the combination of tart apple and sweet-salty yogurt.

I waited for Meadow to respond, but she kept eating, so after I finished chewing I went on. "A few times when I was in Denver for work, I left a message saying I'd like to drive up to see her," I said, "but she only called me back one of those times and that was to say she was very busy rehearsing new music and couldn't take time for a visit. So this time I'm not going to call. I'm just going to show up. I think that will make it harder for her to refuse."

Meadow looked up from her lunch. "It's a ten-hour drive from here to the Abbey in Colorado," she said. "That's a long way to go when Sandra might not be willing to talk to you. But if you want to do it, I'll take care of Jerry while you're gone."

"Thanks," I said. "I won't drive from here. I'll fly in to Denver, rent a car and drive to the Abbey. It's only about a hundred miles from the airport. If I get an early flight in and a late flight out, I can do it all in one day."

## Sandra (aka Sister Mary Margaret)

Wednesday night Sister Mary Margaret dreamed about Mama. Her dream was a disturbing one she had had many times, but it had been years since she last dreamed it.

*She and Ned are lost in a dense forest. The temperature is bone-chilling and the air is so thick with snow they can only see inches in front of their faces. Sandra is scared, starving and freezing. Picking up her feet is harder with each step as she stumbles blindly after Ned. She has an overwhelming urge to lie down in the snow and sleep, but somehow she knows she must keep going.*

*Suddenly they come upon a clearing with a tiny house in the middle. Golden light shining from its windows streaks across the snowy path. They run to the door and knock. When the door opens, there is Mama wearing her favorite bathrobe—the gauzy red one decorated with intricate gold designs. She smiles and welcomes them in. It's warm inside from a fire blazing in the fireplace. The room smells of pine mixed with the scent of chocolate and gingerbread, wafting over from mugs of hot cocoa and a plate of cookies on the table.*

*Sandra gasps at her overwhelming sense of joy and relief. She runs to Mama to hug her, but some invisible wall stops her before she can get there. "Mama," she shrieks. "What are you doing here? We thought you were dead."*

*Mama walks closer, bends forward, and grasps Sandra's hands. Sandra smells her Chanel No. 5 perfume and feels her soft warm hands. As Mama tries to draw Sandra into her arms, Sandra wants to go but something seems to pull her away.*

*Suddenly Mama drops Sandra's hands, moans and collapses on the floor. Sandra screams. She tries to help Mama but can't get close enough to touch her. She looks for Ned but can't see him. "Oh, no. Ned, where are you? We have to help Mama."*

*Sandra runs around the room and then to the door, searching frantically for Ned. When she opens the door to look for him, a frigid wind sucks her out into a furious swirl of snow. She can't see, can't get her breath, feels herself suffocating.*

She woke up trembling and gasping for breath.

Every time Sandra had the dream it ended the same way—with a crushing sense of loss and regret that she had not been able to save Mama.

By Friday Sister Mary Margaret's memory of the dream had faded, but an unsettled feeling still lingered in the back of her mind, pulling her from her tranquil Sister Mary Margaret identity back to being troubled Sandra. She knew better than to resist or try to control or figure out this disquietude. As Sister Mary Margaret, she had learned to stand back and accept her past as it was, to let go of the anger and frustration that were so much a part of Sandra, and to be in the present through work and prayer. Her prayers flowed most smoothly when she was gardening as she was today.

Weeding in silence freed her mind until a nun rushing toward her interrupted the quiet. "Your sister Anne is here to visit you." Sister

Georgetta said, slightly out-of-breath. "She's waiting in the lounge at the Retreat Center where the Abbess said you can meet with her privately."

Sister Mary Margaret wiped the sweat from her brow with a grubby hand and looked up. Thinking of Anne jolted her back to being Sandra again. Seeing Anne and talking with her would make that even worse.

"I have no wish to see Anne," Sister Mary Margaret said. "Please tell the Abbess I would prefer to continue my gardening."

"Are you sure?" Sister Georgetta asked. "Wouldn't you like to spend at least a few minutes with your sister?"

"No thank you, Sister, I would rather not." Sister Mary Margaret replied softly as she went back to weeding.

Sister Georgetta walked back to the Abbey, but returned a few minutes later. This time she spoke gently but firmly. "The Abbess said this is a time to have an open heart and to offer your sister Anne compassion rather than condemnation. The Abbess would like you to show generosity of spirit and visit with your sister who has come a long way to speak with you about your brother who died recently."

Sister Mary Margaret stood up and walked toward the Abbey. "I will do as the Abbess wishes," she said. She knew compassion could not co-exist with anger in her heart, so as she went to her room, washed up, and walked over to the Retreat Center, she focused on Anne's strengths and on positive memories of their times together.

She sat with Anne in the Retreat Center lounge, a large quiet room furnished with comfortable stuffed armchairs and small couches arranged in conversational groupings. Anne looked the same, only older, but she was like a character from another life. Why would Anne visit her to talk about Ned's death? What did she want? Sister Mary Margaret's insides quivered. She tried to calm herself by looking at the soft pastel murals depicting saints, choirs of angels, and other religious images that adorned the walls.

She struggled to pay attention as Anne went on and on about how Ned had left her something secret that she had to travel to San

Diego to get. Anne talked about her trip and how she went to Ned's house and met his partner, Keith. She treaded carefully when talking about Keith, doubtless thinking Sister Mary Margaret would be shocked that Ned was gay. But Sister Mary Margaret had no reaction. In her mind, Ned's life choices were between him and God and did not involve her.

What did shock her was Anne's description of how she and Meadow and other family members had been using this thing called the Memory Enhancer, which she said was Ned's life's work. As near as Sister Mary Margaret could understand it, they were plugging themselves into a computer, shocking their brains with electricity, and reliving events in their past lives. Why would they take such a chance with their God-given bodies and brains?

Anne raved about the warm family scenes she had revisited using Ned's invention, how wonderful it was to see Mama and Daddy when they were young, and to see all of us as children. "And what's so amazing is that when you go back, you are really there—seeing, hearing, touching, smelling, and tasting everything as your former self—and at the same time you are aware of yourself as you are today. It's like a dream, only much more real and vivid."

Sister Mary Margaret said nothing. She had no wish to dream of Mama again or of any of her past. She focused on listening to Anne with the open heart The Abbess had requested.

Then Anne leaned in toward her, gazing earnestly into her eyes. "And so, I was thinking," Anne said, "that the Memory Enhancer could give you the opportunity to go back and see Mama again, see how much she loved you, and see what a wonderful childhood you had before the accident. You were so young, I can't imagine you remember much of it. Of course I can't bring the Memory Enhancer here to the Abbey, but maybe you could come home to Helena for a few days so you could try it."

A massive wave of dizziness engulfed Sister Mary Margaret. In her mind's eye she saw herself teetering on a high cliff overlooking a massive rocky canyon. Her stomach lurched, and her hands trembled as the fear of falling into the dark pit of her past overwhelmed her.

"No," she managed to eke out. "No, I can't go there. Helena isn't my home, the Abbey is my home."

"You're right, I shouldn't have said 'home,'" Anne said. "But you haven't been back since you came here, even when Daddy died. We love and miss you. Couldn't you come for a short visit?"

Sister Mary Margaret was so nauseous, she was afraid she would throw up all over herself and Anne. "I have to go," she said, as she jumped up and ran for the door.

# Chapter 25

## Anne

I drove back to the Denver airport with a heavy heart, a painful lump in my throat, and tears stinging my eyes. If Sandra wouldn't even consider trying the ME, she must have turned her back on the family completely. Barring some miracle, our baby sister was lost to us as much as if she were dead.

Not only was my failure to interest Sandra in the ME a punch in the gut, but worse news awaited me at home. My plane back to Helena from Denver was delayed almost two hours. When it finally landed and I turned on my phone, I found six missed calls from Meadow and two voicemails assuring me Jerry was fine but asking me to call her ASAP.

She answered on the first ring.

"What's up?" I asked.

"There are some women waiting outside the house to talk to you," she said. "I wanted to give you a heads up so you wouldn't be taken by surprise, and so you can think about how you want to handle it."

I switched quickly into judge/lawyer mode. "Handle what? Who are these people and what do they want?"

Meadow sighed. "They want to use the ME to go back and spend time with their dead children."

"What?" I gasped. "How do they know about the ME?"

Could this day get any worse? I wanted to press rewind and start over.

Another sigh, followed by a long pause. "Apparently Amelia let something slip at her grief support group meeting about how she's been spending time in the past with Evan. When she realized what she'd done, she tried to divert them, but they bombarded her with questions. She says she couldn't lie to them. She finally gave in to their begging and pleading and told them about the ME, swearing them to secrecy. About an hour ago, three of them showed up at your door. I didn't let them in, but they refused to go home, so they're outside in their car."

"How much did she tell them?" I didn't actually want to hear any more, but reality was out there ready to rumble.

"I don't know the details, but Amelia's here if you want to talk to her."

I couldn't see any point of getting into a phone conversation with Amelia about this. What was done was done. Now we had to figure out how to deal with it. "No, I'll wait until I get home," I said.

Sure enough there was a car parked in front of the house. A tall blonde woman wearing a bright blue sweatsuit jumped out and ran toward my car as I pulled into my driveway and opened the garage door with my remote. She got right in front of me, so I would have had to run over her to get into the garage. I had no choice but to stop and get out.

Right behind sweatsuit lady was a heavy woman wearing jeans and a maroon University of Montana Grizzlies hoodie. Following her was a tiny woman in spandex leggings and a long black-and-white-striped tee shirt.

"Please excuse this intrusion, Judge Barnes," sweatsuit lady said. "But what we heard from Amelia tonight is so exciting, we couldn't wait another minute."

I said nothing. Just stood silently and waited for her to continue.

"Like Amelia, we've all lost children," she said. "It would change our lives if we could spend even one minute with them now. We'll gladly pay you anything you ask if you'll let us try this Memory Enhancer that Amelia told us about."

Their grief hung heavy in the air. I absolutely understood their desire to re-experience times with their lost children. But I wasn't ready to share the ME outside the family. Legal and ethical concerns swarmed through my head.

"I am so sorry for your losses," I said, projecting my sincere sympathy to each of them in turn as I looked into their eyes. "And I understand why you want to use the ME. But we're only just testing it now. It's too soon, too risky to let you try it."

The tiny woman in spandex jumped up next to me and grabbed my arm. "We could be part of your testing program," she said. "We wouldn't tell anyone and we'd let you take any measures you want on us to see how the ME affects us."

The other two women nodded enthusiastically.

The mother/grandmother part of me wanted to throw my arms around them, take them into the house, and hook them up to the ME. But the lawyer/judge part of me pulled me back to rationality. "I'm so sorry," I said. "We can't let you try the ME today. I hope there will be a time very soon that you will be able to, but that time isn't now. Please understand that we have to be completely sure of its safety and possible long-term effects before we share it outside the family."

"Please," the woman in the grizzlies hoodie begged, tears streaming down her face. "We're willing to take the risk. We'd do anything to be with our children again."

"I'm sorry," I said, "but I can't let you do that. Now I need to put my car in the garage and go inside." I moved past them and opened the door of my car to get in.

"No," they shouted in perfect unison as they encircled me and pushed my car door shut. "You have to let us try it," tall sweatshirt lady said. "We don't want to threaten you, but it looks like we have to. If you don't let us try it, we'll put up information about the ME all over the social media—Twitter, Facebook, Instagram, wherever— and you'll have thousands of desperate people storming your door by tomorrow."

I learned long ago not to give in to threats. "If you do that, we'll have to destroy the ME and no one else will ever get to try it, including you." I gave them my best steely judge look, firm and unyielding.

"Don't test me on this," I said. "I promise you you'll regret it if you do. Now please move away from my car."

"We'll give you two days to think about it," the tiny woman said. "We'll be back on Sunday evening to talk about the possibilities."

As soon as I got inside, Amelia ran toward me in tears. "I'm so sorry, Anne. I don't know how it happened. I was just so happy about being with Evan…" She broke into sobs and covered her face with her hands. I moved closer, my arms outstretched to hug her, but she raised her hands to stop me and began to pace around the room. "No, Anne. What I did is unforgivable. We all promised to keep the ME secret and I broke that promise. I didn't mean to, but all of a sudden I heard myself talking to my group about how wonderful it was to be holding Evan again." She stopped, wiped her face with a tissue, shook her head, and returned to her frantic pacing. "I tried to cover it up, but they were all over me with questions and I couldn't find a way out without lying and I couldn't lie to them—they've suffered so much, I just couldn't lie to them. But now they want…" Overcome by weeping, she collapsed on the couch, clutching her arms around herself.

I walked over and sat beside her, pulling her into a side hug against my shoulder. "What's done is done," I said. "We all make mistakes. I know you would never break a promise on purpose. I wouldn't have chosen this, but it may not be the disaster you think it is. As Daddy used to say, 'You can't tell the depth of the well by the length of the handle on the pump.' We need to pull ourselves together, take a clear look at the situation, and think about how best to handle it."

Meadow had been sitting silently in a chair next to the couch. Now she leaned in toward us and asked, "What did the women outside say to you?"

I sighed. "They want to use the ME to go back to be with their deceased children. Of course they do. I totally understand that. But I can't let them." I was firm in my position. Besides my implicit contract with Ned to keep the ME a secret, I had many reasons not to hook up other people to the ME yet.

"So after you said no, what did they say" she asked.

"They said if I don't let them try the ME, they'll put up information about it on a bunch of social media sites and we'll have thousands of people at the door. They'll be back Sunday evening for my decision."

Amelia gasped and pulled away from me. "Oh no! I can't believe it! That's the worst thing they could do. We have to stop them." Her eyes were wide, her voice shrill.

"Can't you get some kind of court order to keep them from telling about the ME?" Meadow asked. Then she smacked herself in the forehead. "Duh! Of course you can't. You'd have to tell the court about the ME, and more people would know."

"Yes," I said. "And even if we wanted to go that route, it would take way too long to work through the courts."

"Well, maybe we should consider letting them try the ME," Meadow said. There are only three of them. We could swear them to secrecy."

Leaping to a solution without fully understanding the extent of the problem is always a mistake in my book. "Hold on," I said. "We need a lot more information before we take any action. How many people were at your group today, Amelia?"

"Eight, counting me."

"So it's not just three—there are four others we haven't heard from. And some of them may have told other people."

Amelia shook her head. "No, I don't think they would. At least not yet. Our group has strict confidentiality rules. What is said in the group, stays in the group." She paused. "Of course one of them might slip up like I did."

"True," I said, "and we don't know about that. I think we should meet with all seven group members tomorrow and talk this through. Let's see what we're up against. Amelia, can you get them all here tomorrow afternoon?"

Her face flushed. "I'll try my best. It's the least I can do. What time?"

"Let's try for 3:00 when Clint will be here to stay with Jerry."

# Chapter 26

## Anne

"Some friends of Amelia's from her grief support group are coming over this afternoon," I told Clint. "Jerry gets anxious when strangers come here, so could you maybe take him to the park for a while? It's a little cloudy out, but still warm. I took him over there this morning and he had a great time walking around and hanging out, but he won't remember so he'll be fine to go again."

"Sure," Clint said. "But if having strangers here upsets Dad, why did you invite them?"

"I didn't exactly invite them," I said—and went on to tell him what had happened.

Clint raised his eyebrows. "Wow. That sounds serious. What are you going to do about their demands?"

"I plan to explain why we can't let them try the ME now, and ask them to keep it secret until we can."

"Good luck with that." Clint shook his head, like he thought I was deranged. "I predict it will be a hard sell."

## Meadow

Meadow had cleaned up the lunch dishes, vacuumed Anne's living room, and changed her clothes twice in edgy anticipation of the meeting with Amelia's group members. Still time dragged and her uneasiness grew. The intense longing of those grieving parents to see their lost children again would be a formidable challenge for Anne to combat.

Meadow could understand Anne's objections to letting them try the ME. What if she hooked one of the parents up and something went wrong and injured the woman's brain? What if they couldn't wake up one of them from the ME? What if one of them had an extremely painful experience like Clint's? The possible complications were infinite.

She wanted to support Anne, but this was Anne's show, and Meadow didn't want to be intrusive. "Is there anything you'd like me to do to help during the meeting?" she asked Anne. "Anything you'd like me to say?"

"Not that I can think of," Anne said, "but let's put out some juice and soft drinks and bring in some chairs from the dining room. We can set them up between the couch and the living-room chairs."

Meadow helped Anne arrange the chairs to form a slightly lopsided circle with the cold drinks on a table in the middle. She took a deep breath as she scrutinized the setup. "It's good that we'll all be able to see each other's faces," she said. "That should help them feel included."

Promptly at 3:00, Amelia showed up, followed immediately by six of the seven group members who knew about the ME. "Maria's out of town," Amelia said, "But everyone else is here." After Meadow helped Anne get everyone seated and offered them drinks, she took a seat in the circle. As she looked around at the women, their anticipation hit her like a strong wind. These women knew what they wanted and they didn't want to wait to get it. Meadow couldn't imagine how Anne was going to convince them to step back and wait for what could be a very long time.

## Anne

Once everyone was seated, Amelia said, "They'd like to introduce themselves and tell you a little bit about the children they lost. Can we go around the circle and do that to start?"

I was delighted at her suggestion as that was how I had planned to break the ice. "I think that's a great way to begin," I said, gazing around the circle at each of the women. "I'm Anne, and over there is my sister, Meadow, and you all know my daughter-in-law, Amelia."

I turned to the pale young woman next to me. She looked to be in her late twenties, with black hair tied back in a ponytail, straight thick bangs, sad heavy-lidded eyes and big dangly earrings. "Can we start with you and go around the circle from there?" I asked, softly.

She nodded and began in a shaky voice. "Sure. I'm Carrie," she said, her chin trembling. "We lost our beautiful baby daughter to SIDS when she was four months old. One day she was a happy laughing baby who filled our days with wonder, and the next day she was gone." She covered her face with her hands. "It's been three years and I still can't believe she's not here."

Her grief hit me with a familiar punch. When Bill and Amelia lost Evan, the loss was unimaginable for all of us. We miss that baby terribly.

Next was the heavy woman who wore the Grizzlies hoodie the night before. "I'm Arlene. My son was ten when he drowned on a Cub Scout trip swimming with his friends at the lake. He was so bright and so good, and he made everybody laugh and smile." She closed her eyes briefly before she continued. "I can never forgive myself for letting him go on that trip."

Every mother's dread. I thought of all the things I let my kids do when they were growing up, and other things they did without my permission. How would I have coped with a loss like Arlene's?

A ruddy-faced woman with a mop of crinkly red hair spoke next, her voice strong and slightly loud for the setting. "I'm Tracey. My son died from a drug overdose—oxycontin—when he was seventeen. He had so much promise and so much potential." She ran her hands through her hair and grimaced. "I can't help thinking that if I had said or done something different he would still be with me."

Josh's face popped up in my mind. This could have been him—and it still could if the treatment center Debby chose isn't able to cure his addiction. My stomach turned sour.

Next was the tall, athletic, blonde woman, who I thought of as sweatsuit lady from the other night. "Hi. I'm Marsha," she began, her voice firm and crisp. "My daughter was sixteen when she was killed in a car crash. She was a talented musician and an outstanding student with her whole life in front of her. It was all lost in an instant." Marsha paused and looked down at her feet, then continued in a muted tone. "I was driving and I can't remember any of it. They said it wasn't my fault. The other car went right through a red light and hit the passenger side of my car." Her voice cracked. "I can't stop thinking that somehow I could have saved her. I need to go back and relive that accident, so I can see what really happened."

I of course thought of Ned, who created the ME to see a fatal accident he couldn't remember; and also of Clint, who used the ME to relive the painful accident that killed his platoon members. Like them, Marsha was haunted by her inability to remember details of the tragedy.

The next to speak was a very young moon-faced woman with wide-set blue eyes. Her whispery voice quavered. "I'm Shelley. My baby boy was born eleven weeks too early. He only weighed one pound. He was in the NICU for a month with lots of tubes and wires, so tiny and fragile. He was on a ventilator, so we couldn't hold him, but we were there every day." Tears streamed down her face. "He had surgery and other procedures and then he got an infection and we had to disconnect him from the machines. It's been a year, but I still wake up every morning and think, 'my baby died.'"

I've had friends who delivered premature infants and I've heard them berate themselves for any tiny thing they might have done to cause that. No matter how much their doctors reassured them, they still feared they were somehow inadequate as mothers. I could tell Shelley carried that pain with her.

The tiny woman who wore the spandex leggings the other night fidgeted in her seat, squinting her narrow eyes at whoever was speaking until her turn came. "I'm Laura," she said, "My Mattie died from brain cancer when she was eight. It was glioblastoma. We did everything we could—radiation, chemotherapy, clinical trials, but we lost her. She was wonderful, funny and so smart. A part of me died with her."

To watch your child waste away, consumed with pain. Thankfully I hadn't lived that, but I could imagine it. The hope that would come with each new treatment. The despair when yet another treatment failed.

An icy grief grabbed me and squeezed me in its grip until I could barely breathe. These women had each lived every parent's worst nightmare, the day or night when someone—a doctor, or a policeman, or whoever—had said the tragic words: "I'm sorry, there is nothing more anyone can do." They had absorbed the news and somehow gone on living in a world without their child, a world filled with unthinkable pain and anguish, a world where nothing was as it should be for them.

# Chapter 27

### Clint

Not long after Clint and his dad got to the park, Jerry was hungry. Clint pulled out a banana from his pocket and started to peel it. "No," Jerry said. "Not banana. I want cookies and milk."

"I don't have cookies and milk right now," Clint said. "How about a banana?"

"No." He stomped his foot. "No banana. I want cookies. Let's go home."

They went on this way for several minutes. Jerry kept refusing to walk on until Clint finally gave in and took him home. They went in quietly through the back door and sat in the kitchen with their milk and cookies. Clint put Jerry where he couldn't see into the living room and cued up a puppy video on his iPad for him to watch. Then Clint moved his own chair closer to the living room where he could hear most of the conversation with Amelia's grief support group members.

At first Clint was turned off by their attachments to the past. But their pleas and stories moved him. Everything on this planet would be gone soon anyway, so it didn't matter what his mom did with the ME. If it would give them some peace, why not let these grieving women try it?

### Anne

Listening to the stories, my chest ached. I wanted to hug these women, to share my deep sympathy, to do whatever I could to brighten their lives. But I forced myself to keep my impassive judge face on. I had to stand firm against the pleas I knew were coming. As a judge I have heard more sad stories than Oprah, and I have decided the fate of countless defendants who pleaded for my sympathy. I can apply the rules when that's my job, no matter how much I commiserate with the people who my ruling will impact.

"Your pain and grief touches me deeply," I said, "and I do understand why you want to do what Amelia has done and use the Memory Enhancer to relive a time when your children were alive. Unfortunately, as I said the other night, it's too risky to share the ME with you right now."

"I told you we're willing to take any risk," Arlene, whose son died in a swimming accident, pointed her finger at me. "You have no idea what my life is like. If I hadn't let him go, he'd still be with me. If only I had known when he walked out the door that morning that I would never see him again…All I want is my son back. If you can give me that, how can you refuse?"

How could I? I wanted to let her take the risk, but that would be irresponsible in so many ways. "I'm sorry," I said. "The ME hasn't been tested enough yet. I don't even know all the risks you might be taking. I can't guarantee your safety. I can't let you do it."

"I told you I'm willing to be part of your testing program. You can take whatever measurements you need to on me if you'll just let me try your ME," Laura, the fidgety one, accented her points with sharp hand gestures. "It would change my life to go back and be with Mattie during her good years. By the time she died, her suffering from the cancer and the treatments was so intense that she wasn't herself anymore. Do you know how agonizing it is to watch your child suffer like that? That last year fills my memory of her so much that it erases the good times. Please let me have those good times back again." She looked fixedly at me, her face stark with need.

I was beginning to crack like a tree smothered with wet heavy snow. But I had to stand firm, so I pulled back and regrouped. "I understand"—

Before I could go on, Carrie, whose baby had died from SIDS, leaned forward in my direction and interrupted. "You can't understand." Her voice was shrill. "You can't know the longing I have to hold Tasha in my arms again. The biggest fear of any parent who has lost a child is that they will forget that child. Tasha was only four months old when we lost her. I wish I had more pictures, more videos, but we thought we had plenty of time. I wish I would have known time is so precious. I'm begging you to let me go back the way Amelia has and hold my baby again so I can always remember her."

I sat in silence. I don't think I've ever had so many conflicting yearnings pulling me in different directions. The desperation and longing of these women, the potential risks to them and the liability to me and my family if something went wrong, my implicit contract with Ned to make a carefully considered decision. He had written that some would say the ME is self-indulgent and addictive and could eventually lead to the destruction of humanity. I had certainly experienced the self-indulgent and addictive aspects of it. And I still didn't know if it would be good for humanity.

Meadow was in tears by then, sniffing and wiping her nose every few minutes.

When I didn't respond, the mood turned from sadness to anger. The unfairness of their suffering, the relentless pain. They were talking over each other:

"I don't know how to move on."

"I feel so lost."

"Every birthday, every holiday is one more time of what could have been, who he might be today."

"I feel like I failed her as a mother."

"Some days I don't know if I can go on. I feel my pain will never go away. I'm here just because I'm here."

"Stop." Tracey, the redhead whose son had overdosed, held her hands up firmly, palms out. Her ruddy face was splotchy and she spoke in a booming voice. "I think Anne knows who we are, what we want and why we want it. But I don't hear her moving in our direction. Now we need to talk about where we go from here."

I said nothing, waiting to see what would come next—actually pretty much knowing what would come next. Sure enough Marsha spoke up. "Like I said the other night, we don't want to threaten you, but we will if we have to. If you don't let us try the ME we'll put up information about it all over the social media—Twitter, Facebook, Instagram, wherever—and you'll have thousands of desperate people storming your door."

Amelia, looking increasingly uncomfortable, flushed and sweaty, shifted in her chair. "No, Marsha," she said. "Threats aren't the way to go here. We need to find a solution that works for all of us."

"That's easy for you to say, Amelia. You can go back and hold Evan every day. We just want what you have."

"I know that, Marsha," Amelia said, "but if the whole world finds out about the ME overnight, there won't be any way to manage it. None of us will get what we want that way."

"Amelia's right," I said. "We can't—"

To my surprise Clint burst in from the kitchen and interrupted me. "Wait, Mom," he said loudly stepping into the center of our circle of chairs and facing me. "Why not let them try it?" His tone was intense and challenging. "I don't see why you think it's so risky. It hasn't hurt any of us. I probably had the worst trip, but I'm glad I did it. I sleep better now that I was able to go back and see that I couldn't have saved any of my buddies. You can help these women. Why not stop with the bureaucratic babble and give them a chance."

Clint was a striking figure in the middle of this group—his gaunt skinny body, his spiky black hair sticking out in all directions, his five-o'clock shadow. The women stared wordlessly until Meadow spoke up. "This is Anne's son Clint," she said. "He's a military veteran who knows more than any of us hopefully ever will about risk and taking chances for a greater good." She turned to me. "I'm sorry, Anne," she said, "but I agree with Clint. If the ME can give these women a chance to heal their grief, we should let them try it. They've been through so much."

Et tu, Brute? I thought, stung by her betrayal. Couldn't she have waited until after they left to give me her opinion? The same went for Clint of course, but I didn't expect such considerateness from him.

I had to answer her clearly and firmly so the women would understand that my position was unchanged. "No, Meadow," I said. "You know that's not the way I make decisions. I've listened to their stories, their problems, and their pleas. Now I need time to deliberate. As I've said, I am profoundly touched, but this is a complex issue. Maybe there is a solution that will work for all of us, but a hasty decision won't serve any of us well."

"So where does that leave us?" Marsha asked.

I was done with this discussion. I was getting a headache and needed some time to myself. "You all need to go home now, and I will consider everything you've all said and let you know my decision as soon as I can," I said.

"Why can't you agree now to let us try it?" Marsha said. "Your family is willing to go along. It sounds to me like you're just putting us off."

"I am putting you off," I said, trying not to sound testy, "so I can have time to look carefully at my choices, weigh the pros and cons, and assess what is the right thing to do."

"How long will that take?" Tracy asked, her face even redder than before. "We won't guarantee to keep your secret much longer."

"That will be your decision to make," I said. "We all have to do what we think is best."

# Chapter 28

## Anne

After the women left, fatigue overwhelmed me. I asked Meadow, Clint and Amelia to leave as well. I didn't need or want any more opinions or arguments.

I tossed and turned all night. Every time I woke up, my stomach was in knots. The grieving mothers' demands had me between a rock and a hard place. If I took the risk and let them try it, who knew what might happen? If I refused they would publicize it so extensively that I'd be deluged with more requests and demands than a multi-billion-dollar lottery winner.

What should I do about the ME? Should I give it to the university or some scientific institute who could test it and control its use? But that would violate Ned's wishes not to have the ME become a project of a system where it would be embroiled for years if not decades in regulations and red tape?

Or should I destroy the ME and end all the controversy? The ME trips of the past weeks hadn't helped me decide. Those experiences flooded my mind, running together in a confusing mess.

Amelia was over the moon at being able to be with Evan, and Jerry's return from dementia was exciting, even though brief. Both Meadow and Clint had said the ME helped them, but Clint's painful trip had frightened me. My head pounded as I flashed back to him writhing in pain and shouting.

As for my trips, in all honesty I had to admit to mixed results. It was possible that the family was right about me spending too much time in the past. While I loved going back to when Jerry was his old self, doing that had led me to neglect him in the present time.

Some of my trips back to our childhood were thrilling but others were frightening, like when I went back to the days right after Mama died and found myself in a boiling family caldron where Sandra's grief, Dan's anger, and Daddy's drunken rambling swirled around and through me.

How could I know what results other people would get? At the very least the ME should come with warnings and some pre-screening of people who might use it.

Jerry was snoring away next to me, which made it harder to get back to sleep. I was in a feverish daze, achy and my head pounding. I finally got up and went to the kitchen for some herbal tea.

As I sat there drinking my tea and staring into space, I remembered Ned's final letter in the envelope marked *"Read when you're ready to put it all together and make a decision."* How had I forgotten to read it?

I went and got the envelope and opened it, my hands trembling. This was surely going to be the place where Ned revealed what he found out when he went back to the fateful day that started him on this quest to recover old memories. My chest tightened and my breathing accelerated. Did I want to know?

*Dear Anne,*

*I recognize that it will not be easy to make a decision about the ME. While it may have excellent results for many people much of the time, it may create problems for others.*

*Exactly, I thought. I so wished he was still alive so we could discuss this. But he wasn't, so I read on.*

*Some people will say spending time in the past is wasting time, not evolving, not moving on, not accomplishing anything. It's not reality. It's self-indulgent and addictive. It could even eventually lead to the destruction of humanity if people came to prefer living in the past.*

*Others will say spending time in the past brings enlightenment, insight on how your past affects your present, insight as to how not to make the same mistakes again. It helps the person you were inform the person you are.*

*It's tempting to think the ME can resolve conflicts between people who remember the same event differently. They can go back and see who is right. They can find the truth and agree on it. But doing this may create more conflict than it resolves. No one likes to be wrong, and those who are may simply deny the accuracy of the ME and continue to insist they are right, which is likely to infuriate those who went back and had their memories confirmed. I do not think it will be accepted as a way to prove a legal case in court, but you'd know better than I would about that.*

*While ME trips can be painful when you find out your memories aren't accurate or when you see tragic events repeat and are unable to change them, the trips have a host of positive effects. Users can:*

- *Heal a relationship by looking at where it went off track*
- *Relive great times with friends in school, sports, camp, etc.*
- *Re-experience youthful bodies and athletic skills*
- *Re-experience a grown child as a baby or young child*
- *Re-experience the places and things of childhood*
- *Relive past times with loved ones who have died*
- *Recover memories of events blocked from their memories*
- *Discover the truth about what really happened*
- *Re-evaluate the past, find meaning and understanding*

*As you undoubtedly know by now, the ME can be exciting and fun and also upsetting and depressing, depending on which scenes from your life you choose to revisit. Using it can enrich your life as well as push you to rethink episodes from your past. In my mind, this is reason enough to make the ME widely available.*

*But the more compelling reason is for people like me who have something in their past that they must revisit in order to remember what really happened or to see the event more clearly. In my case I needed to know what happened. All of it. The details. Did I kill my mother? That's what I'd been told. But I had no memory of it.*

*I have spent most of my life trying to recover my memory of what happened on December 24, 1964, the day I supposedly fatally shot Mama in a hunting accident. I say supposedly because I couldn't remember doing it, nor did I have any memory at all of the shooting. I remembered getting to the ranch, walking a long way in the snow until we got to the area where we were going to shoot pheasants. After that there was a blank in my memory until the next thing I remembered—Mama on the ground in a pool of blood and Dad and some other people getting her into an ambulance. They took her to the hospital in town, but she was already dead by then. Afterwards, I stayed in my room trying everything I could think of to remember the shooting. But I couldn't. I tried asking Sandra what she remembered but she just cried and said she couldn't remember anything. I refused to talk to anyone else, not even the priest when he visited.*

*For many years I was drowning in guilt. Everyone said it was an accident. But they treated me like a murderer. And I felt like one. But as time went on there was a glimmer of hope. Maybe Dad was wrong. Maybe I didn't do it. Maybe Dad was the one who shot her, or maybe Sandra. I didn't want to throw Sandra under the bus the way Dad had thrown me. She was only ten when it happened. But I sure was ready to make Dad take responsibility if he was the one.*

*I desperately needed to know what actually went down that day. The ME gave me that opportunity. Finally I had a way to go back and see for myself. You might think that day would have been the first scene I revisited. But it wasn't. I waited until I had experience using the ME, was comfortable with it and completely convinced of its accuracy. Then I set the time for December 24, 1964.*

I froze. Was I going to finally find out what truly happened in that accident that killed Mama more than fifty years ago? I wanted to know and at the same time I was afraid. I took a deep breath and read on.

*I won't repeat the parts of the day you already know or were witness to. Here's what I didn't remember until I was able to see it using the ME:*

*Snow was coming down hard, making it difficult to see very far ahead. Mama had shot a pheasant and went off to get the downed bird. She was gone a while, but was much closer than we thought because she was obscured by brush and by the thick falling snow. When another bird flushed, all three of us fired—Dad, Sandra and me. We heard Mama cry out and we all dropped our guns and ran to her.*

*A shotgun blast had hit Mama in the back of the head, dropping her to the ground. Blood was gushing out of her head and she was unconscious. Of course there were no cell phones then, so Dad had to run for help. He left Sandra and me there with Mama. Mama was gasping for breath, like she was choking or drowning. Sandra was crying and screaming at me to do something. I was frantic, but there was nothing I could do. Mama died before help came.*

*Why Dad blamed it on me is something I can never know. He's gone now and I doubt he ever talked about it with anyone. And even if he did, I couldn't go back and hear that conversation because I can only go back to scenes from my own life.*

*I've gone back to this scene many times and it's always the same. We all fired. There's no way to know who killed Mama.*

*I need the rest of the family to know the truth. But only Dad, Mama, Sandra and I were there. So besides me, Sandra is the only one left who can see it, and I would never ask that of her. Nevertheless, seeing that day for myself has brought me peace. While reliving it has been horrible, seeing that all three of us fired lifted a huge load of guilt off my shoulders.*

*The ME has done what I needed it to do for me. The ME has the potential to help others whose memories of traumatic events are incomplete. Did a soldier do all he could to help his dying buddy? Did a kid taunt his friend into taking a fatal risk? Did a driver cause the crash that killed his friend? The ME can give them answers.*

*But I leave it up to you, Anne, to decide whether, and possibly how, to make the ME available to others.*

My stomach was turning cartwheels. I nearly threw up. So this was the answer to the family mystery? Ned was as much the victim of the shooting as Mamma was. My heart ached for him. Poor Ned. Why would Daddy have done this to him? And how could Daddy have done this to our family? All those years we'd been living with a lie that had divided us and shredded the caring network we could have been.

I wanted to confront Daddy with this discovery. I wanted to accuse him, to hear what justification he would give. I knew I would never think of him the same way again.

Was this what Dan had been trying to show me about Daddy? Could Dan be right? Was Daddy the selfish bully Dan remembered rather than the loving father who lived in my memory?

My headache had gotten so much worse by then that I couldn't think about this or fully process the implications of what Ned had written. I put my head down on the kitchen table and fell into a feverish sleep.

# Chapter 29

## Jerry

Jerry woke up hungry. Daylight. Morning. Time for breakfast. He didn't see Anne, so he got up and went to the kitchen. He saw her sitting at the table with her head down, but she didn't look up when he came in. "Anne? I'm hungry," he said. "Let's eat breakfast."

She didn't move, so he shook her shoulder. She moaned. "Wake up, Anne," he said. "I need breakfast." She didn't get up. Jerry went to the refrigerator, got out some milk and put it on the table. He turned back to the refrigerator, reached for some eggs, but lost his balance, dropped the eggs on the floor and fell on top of them in a pool of squishy glop. He tried to stand up, but he kept slipping. "Help me, Anne," he yelled. "I need help."

## Anne

In the back of my foggy brain, I heard a thud and Jerry yelling for help. Where was I? What was going on? I forced myself to wake up. There I was face down at the kitchen table, my head pounding, and my body shaking with chills. Jerry lay on the floor in a mess of broken eggs. How had this happened? Nothing made sense in my feverish state.

I struggled up, holding on to the table for balance, and stood there swaying slightly. How could I help Jerry up off the floor without falling myself? I pushed a chair toward him. "Hold the chair, Jerry," I moaned. "Hold the chair and stand up."

He reached for it, but couldn't get a grip. I rotated it so the seat faced him, and pushed it closer. I tried to help him get his arms up to the seat, but his body weight kept pulling him down. "Push yourself up with the chair," I implored, but he just lay there wailing, "Help! Help! Help me!"

This was bad. My headache was getting worse by the minute, my body was burning up, and I could barely think. We needed help. Where was my phone? Most likely plugged in to its charger next to my bed where I leave it at night. Could I make it to the bedroom to get it? I had to.

"I'll get help, sweetie," I said. "I'll go call Clint to come help us." Summoning a reserve of energy from somewhere, I staggered out of the kitchen, down the hall and into the bedroom, where I collapsed on the bed. I nearly blacked out, but some part of my mind stayed conscious enough to grab the phone and call Clint. Voicemail. Damn!

Now who? Bill usually got up early, and he was strong enough to get Jerry up off the floor. When he answered, I took a deep breath and got right to the point. "I'm sick. Jerry fell in the kitchen. I can't get him up. We need help."

His no-nonsense reply was a welcome relief. "Of course, Mom. No problem," he said. "I'll be right there."

I lay there stupefied, too weak to go back to the kitchen.

## Bill

Bill had just finished his early morning workout and shower at the gym and was getting dressed when his mom called. She sounded dazed and upset, nothing like her usual self, so he didn't ask questions, just jumped in his car and headed over.

He used his key to get in and went straight to the kitchen where he indeed found his dad on the floor in a mucky mess of broken eggs. "I'm going to find Mom and I'll be right back," Bill said, keeping his voice calm to reassure Jerry before he dashed through the house to look for his mom. She was sound asleep on her bed, so he ran back to the kitchen to help Jerry. "Hey, buddy, let's get you up out of this mess," he said, reaching under Jerry's arms and lifting him up. "And let's get you out of these yucky pjs and clean you up."

His dad didn't show any signs of pain or injury, just anxiety, so Bill helped him to the bathroom, got him undressed, showered, and into some clean clothes. All during that, Jerry kept repeating, "I'm hungry. I need breakfast," so Bill fixed him a bowl of cereal with milk, settled him on the couch away from the messy kitchen, and turned on the TV. Then he went back to the bedroom to check on his mom.

He sat down on the bed next to her and touched her face. She was burning up. "Mom, have you taken any aspirin or anything?" he asked. She groaned, but didn't answer. He hated to wake her, but he needed to know what was wrong and whether she'd taken any medicine. He gently shook her shoulder. "What's wrong? How long have you been sick? Have you taken anything?"

She opened her eyes and looked at him with a bleary gaze. "Headache," she mumbled. "Chills, fever. Didn't take anything. Too much hassle to get it."

Bill brought her some aspirin and a glass of water, which she barely sat up enough to swallow. He was concerned that she might need more than aspirin. He didn't want to overreact, but whatever was wrong with her had sure come on hard and fast. Amelia hadn't said anything about his mom not feeling well after being over here with her group yesterday afternoon.

"You look really sick, Mom. Maybe I should call your doctor. Is it still Dr. Hensley?"

His mom slowly opened her eyes and shook her head from side to side. "No," she said, her voice faint. "Don't call him. It's just a virus. I'll be better tomorrow."

Bill was mindful of her recent strong reaction when the family tried to get her to see a doctor, and he didn't want to make that mistake again. Probably she was right and she just had a virus. "Okay, Mom," he said, "but someone needs to be here with you and Dad until you're well enough to watch him. I have to go meet a client who flew in from California, and Amelia has the kids and we shouldn't expose them to whatever you have, so should I call Clint?"

"Okay," she said, and closed her eyes and nodded off again.

## Anne

Ned's letter haunted my feverish dreams. Ned and Sandra hunting with Mama and Daddy on a snowy day. Shooting. Screaming. Running. Blood on the snow. Crying, everyone crying.

It was me crying, which woke me up. My head still hurt and I was hot and achy. Debby was sitting on a chair next to my bed, typing on her laptop. "Don't cry, Mom," she said. "Dad's all right. He was hungry at 11:00 so I fixed him some lunch and now he's napping on the couch."

Right. Now I remembered. Jerry had fallen in the kitchen and Bill came to get him up. "What time is it?" I asked.

"Almost noon," she said. "How are you doing?"

"I have a bad headache, and probably a fever," I said, "but I can get up. Why are you here? Bill said he would call Clint."

"He tried, but he couldn't reach Clint or Meadow, so he called me and asked if I could work over here until he gets done with his clients. You don't need to get up. Bill said you took aspirin earlier. I'll get you some more and maybe some ginger ale to wash it down."

Suddenly I remembered I had left Ned's letter on the kitchen table. I doubted Bill even noticed it, but Debby was more likely to—if she hadn't already. I wanted to get it before her eagle eyes caught sight of it.

"Thanks, but I have to pee, so I need to get up. I can get the ginger ale." With great effort, I sat up, swung my legs over the side of the bed, stood up, and almost blacked out. I would have fallen if Debby hadn't grabbed me.

"Let me help, Mom," she said, guiding me toward the bathroom. "You're shaky. I'll stay with you to be sure you don't fall."

I didn't want her to stay with me, but I was unsteady and I did have to pee, so I agreed to let her help me to the bathroom. And obviously there was no way she'd let me go to the kitchen by myself, so I accepted her getting the ginger ale, hoping she wouldn't notice the letter.

When I was safely back in bed and had swallowed my aspirin, she sat down in the chair and gave me a stern look. "Mom, I think you need to see a doctor. Bill told me you don't want to, but as sick as you are, I think it would be a good idea."

Her tone was tender, and I appreciated her concern, but I pushed back against her request. Why were they always pushing me to get medical attention? "No," I said. "I know myself and my body, and this feels like a virus that will be gone tomorrow. There's no reason to see a doctor."

"But what if it isn't a virus?" she said. "What if it's a reaction to that ME device you've been hooking yourself up to?"

What? Good grief, how did she come up with that? I lay still for a minute with my eyes closed, trying to collect my thoughts. "I don't have any reason to think my being sick is connected to the ME," I said. "Why would you think it is?"

"Your main symptom is a bad headache and you've been connecting that thing to your brain. Conceivably that could raise your temperature also."

"No one else in the family who used it is sick," I mumbled.

She leaned in closer and looked me directly in the eye. "You used it sooner and you've used it more, so it makes sense that you'd get sick first."

I struggled to answer over the demands of my aching body, but finally got a coherent sentence out. "But Ned tested it on other people," I said, "and he used it a lot himself, and he said none of them had bad effects."

"But he died of cancer and we don't know how the other people are doing."

"I don't see any relationship there, Debby. Headache and fever aren't signs of cancer."

Debby sat back, her palms raised in front of her, in a perfect imitation of Dan when he was dubious. "So, here's the thing, Mom," she said. "I found Uncle Ned's letter to you on the kitchen table. I didn't know what it was when I picked it up, but when I saw it was all about the ME, I couldn't stop myself from reading it. This ME has so taken over your life that I had to know more."

My head throbbed. My exasperation and pain merged into nausea. She had not only found Ned's letter, she had read it. I could barely summon the energy to reply. "You shouldn't have read it. You know that. It's a private communication from Ned to me."

"Okay, you're right, but I did read it and I can't put the genie back in the jar now. Reading what Uncle Ned says he learned about the accident that killed your mother puts a whole new light on everything."

"I know. Poor Ned. What Daddy did to him was unconscionable," I said, glad that at least she could sympathize with Ned.

But that wasn't where she was going. "Yes your father was horrible and that could mean Uncle Ned had a lot of anger directed at the family. It's possible that Uncle Dan is right about the ME being a plot against you all—Uncle Ned's last revenge. Maybe he knew it would mess with your brain and make you sick, and maybe that's the whole point."

"No Debby. Ned wasn't like that. You never met him. Dan's view of him is way off, so don't go by what he says. I'm too tired to talk about this any more. Could you please let me rest now."

# Chapter 30

## Debby

Debby worked, hung out with her dad, and watched over her mom all afternoon. Anne refused to eat anything, slept most of the time, and when she woke up was too weak and shaky to get up on her own. Debby became increasingly concerned to the point that she could no longer focus on her work.

By the time Bill showed up to relieve her at the end of the afternoon, Debby was distraught. Her fear that the ME could be responsible had intensified as the hours went by and Anne got worse. What if the ME had fried her mother's brain like Uncle Dan predicted? And the alternative—that her mother had contacted some serious disease—wasn't any better. Anne needed medical attention, but whenever Debby brought up that idea, Anne dug in her heels.

She confronted Bill. "Mom keeps getting sicker, and we have no idea what's wrong with her. I think we need to make her go to the doctor, whether she wants to or not."

Bill shrugged. "I understand your concern, Debby, but she's a grownup. We can't make her do anything."

"I'm worried that this ME thing might have something to do with it," she said. "Did you read Ned's letter to Mom while you were here this morning?"

"What letter?" he asked. "I was busy cleaning up Dad and getting Mom to take some aspirin. I didn't see any letter."

Debby got the letter. "I found this on the kitchen table," she said. "I shouldn't have read it, but I did, and it's pretty shocking. Take a look."

Bill looked at Debby's hand holding the papers, but made no move to take them from her. "So Uncle Ned wrote that? When? And how do you have it?"

"He left it for Mom along with the ME. Mom was reading this last night and she left it on the kitchen table. I found it there."

Bill frowned. "Did she say you could read it?"

Debby sighed and shook her head in exasperation. Bill continued to miss the point, focusing on her method when it was the message that mattered. "Okay, no, she didn't give it to me to read. I found it and read it while she was sleeping. When I told her, she said I shouldn't have read it—but given what it says, I think we should all read it."

"I'm going to pass on that, Debby. Whatever the letter says is between Uncle Ned and Mom, and I don't want to read it if she doesn't want me to. And I can't see how the ME is involved in her being sick. None of the rest of us who have used it are sick."

Why did Bill always have to be so unsuspecting and nonchalant? Mr. Smooth. Couldn't he ever be skeptical and jump on anything? "Okay, whatever, Bill," she said. "Anyway, you don't need to stay. I can stay with Mom and Dad tonight. You go ahead home and help Amelia with the kids." Debby was ready to push Bill out the door so she could move on with finding a way to get medical attention for her mom.

"Are you sure?" Bill asked.

"No problem," Debby said. "I'll call you later and let you know how she's doing."

After Bill left, she called Uncle Dan and got him to come over. When he got there, he was at least willing to entertain the possibility that the ME was the cause of Anne's illness. "Although I don't think it's likely," he said. "She's probably right that it's a virus, but she's sick enough that I agree she should see a doctor."

Debby debated whether to show Dan Ned's letter, but decided not to. The information in the letter about the awful family mystery he and her mom were part of should be her mom's to share with him however she chose to.

Dan roused Anne from her sleep and said, "Come on stubborn

little sister. We're taking you to the ER." He ignored her protests. "No ifs, ands, or buts. Debby will stay with Jerry." He half-carried, half-dragged her out to his car and they were gone.

Debby took Jerry to the kitchen and fixed him a green salad and a tuna fish sandwich for supper. He pushed the plate away. "No. Not that," he said. "I want pizza."

"Pizza isn't good for you, Dad." She pushed the plate back toward him. "The salad will make you healthier."

"No," Jerry said loudly as he pushed the plate off the table onto the floor.

Debby looked down at the broken plate and splattered food. Clearly her dad was used to getting his own way. Right now, when he was agitated about Anne being sick, wasn't the time to take a stand about his eating habits. Debby got up, went to the freezer, took out a frozen pizza and turned on the oven to heat it up. "Okay Dad, the pizza will be ready in a few minutes."

As she cleaned up the mess from the floor, she had to admit that the job of taking care of her dad was more of a challenge than she had recognized. Who would do it if her mom was no longer able?

## Clint

Clint had spent the entire day at an Electus planning session, where Commander Zaqar warned the members that the time for Earth to be recycled was approaching. He reminded them that to be chosen to move on they needed to be sure they met the requirements for participation in the new society they would be entering.

Zaqar and his closest assistants reviewed the details of the strict regulations. Members had to give up all their earthly attachments— such as family, friends, money, possessions, and individual identity—so they could start from a clean slate, with their identities and personal histories erased, and with new names for their upcoming transhuman lives. Only those who made the sacrifices would be chosen to move up to the higher evolutionary level.

With the end time approaching, Zaqar updated his rules. To prove their loyalty, all members were to shed their human attachments over the next month and move into a large house Electus had rented in preparation for leaving Earth.

This demand touched off a tiny flame of anger in Clint's mind. He searched for its source.

He had no problem with group living; he had lots of experience with that in the army. In fact he had enjoyed the daily interaction with his buddies who had all given up security and jobs, and left their families and loved ones behind to go to a foreign country and fight for a cause.

What made this different? He would again be leaving his current life and people he cared about to go with a group joined together by a common cause, a cause he believed in. But something stood in the way of his accepting Zaqar's conditions. What?

An image of his best friend, Pete, popped into his head. Pete, the night before he died, sitting on his bed with that big cockeyed grin on his face that meant he was thinking about something serious. Pete was strange that way—his grin was always biggest when he had a profound thought. Almost as if he had to laugh at himself for being thoughtful. "Everything happens for a reason, Clint. We're here to fight for our country, and whatever happens that's a good enough reason for me."

Clint closed his eyes and brought up the scene he had revisited with the ME, the scene where his platoon members died. He remembered the meaning of their deaths. They died for a cause they believed in. They died as a sacrifice to save freedom and liberty. They died for us, so we could live. But Electus members weren't sacrificing themselves for the good of others. They were deserting the others for their own good. They were more selfish than selfless.

Wait! Why couldn't Electus save the planet instead of leaving it and saving only themselves? At the end of the meeting he approached Zaqar. "I'm rethinking our plans and purpose," he said. "Maybe we can do more; maybe we can save others."

Zaqar scowled. "It's too late," he said. "The corrupt society has ignored the signs. They have made their own beds. Now they must lie in them."

Clint shook his head. "They need education. We can do that. We can help them see."

"No," Zaqar said. "They will never listen. Why should we beat our heads against the wall? It's not up to us. There's no discussing anything with them. Why bother?"

"I don't think I could live with abandoning them," Clint said. "I've suffered massive torment remembering army buddies who have died when I survived. It's called survivors' guilt. I think it would hit me the same way if I left my loved ones behind on this planet."

Zaqar scowled. "The army's part of the corrupt system. You should feel guilty and so should your buddies. Now you have to make a choice," he said, turning away.

The harsh rebuke hit Clint like a burst of enemy fire. He instinctively recoiled, then rushed to the door, and grabbed his cell phone from the box where phones had been stowed during the meeting. Outside, he turned his phone on and saw two missed calls from his brother Bill and two from his sister Debby. There was also a text message from Debby several hours ago: *Mom sick. Can you help with Dad?*

Clint knew that if he was going to follow Zaqar's instructions to give up his attachments, he should ignore the messages. But his connection to Electus was crumbling and his connection to his parents was still strong. He wasn't ready to leave his family when he could see they needed him. So he answered Debby's text: *Sorry missed earlier messages. Can stop by now. Would that help?*

Debby: *Never mind. I'm here all night. Can you come in morning?*

Clint: *Morning works. Is mom OK?*

Debby: *Uncle Dan took her to ER. No news yet.*

Clint: *ER?? Sounds bad. I'm coming over to wait for news.*

## Anne

When Dan and I got home from the ER late that evening, Debby and Clint were waiting. I didn't think Clint had been around when I left, but I was kind of out of it when Dan dragged me off, so maybe Clint had been there. Jerry was asleep in our bed, so Dan settled me on the couch. I was feeling much better thanks to the medications the ER doctors had given me.

Clint brought me a glass of water and gave me a sweet hug.

"I thought you'd call with news," Debby said to Dan.

"You can't use cell phones in the ER," Dan said, "and I wanted to stay in there to make sure I heard everything they said."

"So what did they say?"

"Well, it's not the ME that made her sick," Dan said, looking at Debby. "Most likely it was an infected tick. But she is really sick, so it's good we went to the ER."

Clint pulled his chair closer to the couch and put his hand gently on my arm. "So what's wrong with you?" he asked.

"They think it's Rocky Mountain Spotted Fever," I said. "A tick must have bitten me, maybe at the park. I was a little woozy when the doctors were talking, so Dan can tell you about it better than I can."

"They did a bunch of tests," Dan said, "which ruled out a lot of possibilities. They strongly suspect Rocky Mountain Spotted Fever, because they've seen two cases in the past few weeks and she has the beginnings of a rash on her wrists, which is one of the signs. They can't tell for sure if she has it until the rest of the tests come back, but it's very serious and can cause encephalitis, kidney failure or heart failure if it isn't treated with antibiotics right away."

Debby gasped. "Will Mom be okay? How can they treat her if they don't know what she has?"

Dan touched her arm. "She'll be fine," he reassured. "When they suspect Rocky Mountain Spotted Fever, they start the antibiotic treatment before they get the lab results. They started her on doxycycline, which should get rid of her symptoms within twenty-four to seventy-two hours. She'll need to be on it for a week or two to prevent any dangerous complications."

Clint looked at Debby, shaking his head. "Really? You thought it was the ME that made her sick?" He sounded as skeptical as I had been about that theory. "Why would you think that?"

Debby rolled her eyes. "Well it was hooked up to her brain," she said, "and one of her symptoms was a pounding headache, so—duh—we had to consider it."

"You told the doctors about the ME?" Clint asked me. "I thought you wanted to keep it a secret."

"Dan insisted I tell them or he would," I said. "So I told them I'd used transcranial direct current stimulation to apply low dosage electricity to my brain, but I didn't tell them about the ME. I just said I'd read it can improve memory—which is true—so I said I got one of those headsets gamers use and tried it. They knew about tDCS and they said it couldn't cause the symptoms I had."

"She had to give them the information," Debby said to Clint, "so they could diagnose her." She turned to me. "I'm glad it wasn't the ME. I know you want to keep using it. Rocky Mountain Spotted Fever sounds bad, but at least it's acute and curable."

"I agree," I said. I struggled through my exhaustion to thank her for all she had done. "Debby, I do appreciate all your help and your concern. I know I didn't make it easy for you today, and I have you to thank for calling Dan and making me go to the ER. My getting treated right away is crucial for recovering from this illness." I tried to get up to go hug her, but I was too shaky.

She jumped up, came over and hugged me. I could see tears in her eyes. "No worries, Mom," she said. "Just get better."

# Chapter 31

## Anne

I woke up late the next morning. Clint had stayed the night and I had slept so soundly I didn't even hear him get Jerry up and out to the kitchen.

What finally woke me was my phone ringing on my bedside table. Although I could tell I was on my way to recovery, I still had a minor headache and a weak achy feeling. But I was definitely well enough to talk to Joyce, who handles my phone calls at Weller & Associates.

"Hey, hon, how are you feeling this morning? I heard you were pretty sick yesterday."

"Better, thanks. I'm on some antibiotics now."

"Good to hear," she said. "Because it looks like you're gonna need some extra energy today. You got something called a Memory Enhancer over at your house?"

Uh oh. My head began to throb. Had Dan or Debby told Joyce about the ME?

I kept my tone casual. "Why are you asking that, Joyce?"

"Your phone over here where all your landline calls are forwarded has been ringing off the hook. Some really riled-up folks calling you nasty names and talking about a Memory Enhancer."

Where would this be coming from, I wondered. Amelia's group members? Had they gotten tired of waiting for my answer? But even if it were them, there were only seven—hardly enough to ring the phone off the hook.

"Did they say who they are and how they know about the Memory

Enhancer?"

"Yes. They say there's a YouTube video put up by a woman named Laura. I found it and watched it. Kind of hit me in the gut and I guess it did the same for a bunch of other viewers. At the end Laura gives this phone number and tells them to contact you and demand you share your Memory Enhancer. I've just been telling them I don't have any information about it. That's true but some of them don't believe me. Is there something else you want me to say?"

"No, Joyce. Thanks. Is it just this phone number she's giving out? Not my cell number or my address?"

"Yup. Just this. But your address isn't hard to come by. Anyway, you should go on YouTube and watch the video. The title is *Have one more day with your lost child.*"

I hauled myself out of bed and went straight to my office to search YouTube for the video. Laura had put it up twenty-three hours ago and it already had 43,765 views. Good grief. How did people find this stuff so fast?

I steeled myself and pushed the black play arrow.

Laura, the tiny fidgety woman from Amelia's support group sat at her kitchen table holding a framed photograph of a doll-faced little girl with long brown hair and an impish smile who looked to be about six years old. In contrast, Laura's face was pinched and pale, her narrow features taut with grief. Her dark eyes glistened with tears. Looking at her made me want to cry.

"Hi," she said. "I'm Laura from Helena Montana, and this is a picture of my beautiful daughter, Mattie, when she was six. I lost my Mattie to brain cancer five years ago, when she was only eight. It was glioblastoma. We did everything we could—radiation, chemotherapy, clinical trials, but we lost her." Laura choked up, but pulled herself together and continued. "Mattie was wonderful, funny and so smart. She would light up a room. A part of me died with her. It's so hard to move on, and it doesn't get easier with time when you lose someone you love so much. Grief keeps hitting me in the gut. Some days I feel like I can't go on." Tears streamed down Laura's face.

She took a minute, wiped her eyes, and began again. "But all of a sudden, I have some hope for something that could change my life, something amazing I heard about in my grief support group a few days ago. One of our members, Amelia, a mom who lost a baby boy a year ago when he was only two months old, told us about a device invented by her husband's late uncle, a distinguished neuroscientist. It's called the Memory Enhancer and it lets you relive any time from your past through all your senses. The uncle died last month and left the Memory Enhancer to his sister, Amelia's mother-in-law, a retired Montana judge named Anne Weller Barnes. Judge Barnes has been trying out this device and letting her family members try it too.

"Amelia told us she has been able to travel back in time in her sleep through this device to when her baby, Evan, was alive. When she goes back, she's holding Evan, touching his soft baby skin, smelling his sweet baby smell, smiling at him and seeing him smile back. She hears him coo and gurgle. All of this is exactly like it was and she feels it all with its original intensity. Amelia says this has changed her life. Now that she can go back and be with Evan whenever she wants, the deep horrible ache of missing him is gone from her life."

Laura's voice took on a new intensity. "You can imagine how excited all the rest of us in the group were to hear about this Memory Enhancer and how much we want to try it to travel back and be with our children when they were alive. It would change my life to go back and be with Mattie during her good years. By the time she died, her suffering from the cancer and the treatments was so intense that she wasn't herself anymore. Do you know how agonizing it is to watch your child suffer like that? Her last year fills my memory of her so much that it erases the good times. I'd give anything to have those good times back again. If I could hold Mattie, kiss her, hug her, those would be incredible unbelievable moments. I would be happier than I have been in years.

"But here's the problem." Laura's expression flashed from grief to anger. "Judge Barnes refuses to let anyone except her family members try the Memory Enhancer. She says it's too risky, it hasn't been tested enough. We find that hard to believe. If it's that risky, why is she using it? Why is she letting her family members use it? We told her we're willing to be part of a testing program. She, or whoever she wanted, could take whatever measurements they need to on us if she'll just let us try it. But she keeps putting us off. She says she needs time to deliberate so she can look carefully at her choices, weigh the pros and cons, and assess what is the right thing to do.

"We don't want to wait any longer. I want to see Mattie again right now. So I'm asking for your help—all of you who are viewing this video. Maybe you've lost a child. Or maybe you've lost someone else dear to you—maybe a parent, a husband, a wife, a sister or broth-er—who you'd like to see again. We need as many people as possible to reach out to Judge Anne Weller Barnes in Helena Montana and demand she share this amazing invention. Please call her right away."

The video ended with a screen showing my name and phone number in big block letters.

"You sure come off as the villain in that piece, Mom." I jumped and turned around. Clint was standing behind me with that disillusioned look he used to get when he was a kid and I had forgotten to get his favorite cookies at the grocery.

In my mind, Laura's depiction of me was one-sided and unfair, but I had to agree with Clint's assessment. "I know," I said. "If I wasn't the villain Laura described in that video, I would hate myself."

My world was crashing down around me. I struggled to contain my anger, disappointment and hurt as I replied. "I can understand her desperation, but I told them I needed time to consider the situation. That was only two days ago and I've been too sick to think about it."

"But how would she know you were sick?"

"She could have at least checked with me or Amelia to see what was going on before she told her story to the world."

Amelia called me on my cell phone, her voice teary. "Oh, Anne. I saw Laura's video on YouTube. I'm so sorry. After all you've done for me, I feel horrible about creating so much trouble for you."

Her sincere regret came though so clearly that I instantly accepted her apology. Laura was the target of my anger, not Amelia. Anyone can make a mistake the way Amelia did, but Laura's actions were deliberate and hurtful.

"I know you feel awful about all this, Amelia," I said, "but the publicity is Laura's fault, not yours. I can't believe she put up that video."

"I know. And when you're sick, too. Bill said you were in a bad way yesterday. Are you better today?"

I filled her in on my visit to the ER, the Rocky Mountain Spotted Fever and the antibiotic treatment. "So I'm not over it, but I'm much better than yesterday."

"That's good news, but I'm sure Laura's video isn't helping. Are you getting many calls?"

"My landline calls go to the law office, so I'm not getting them personally. But Joyce says it's nonstop and most of the callers are irate. What I can't figure out is how so many people saw the video so quickly."

"Most of them are from Twitter and Facebook, I think. Laura tweeted the link to the video on #bereavedparents and #bereavedmothers, and she posted it on three bereaved parents' Facebook pages. She also put it in some comments on a few blogs and discussion groups. It went viral. Again, I'm so sorry. I can help you with the social media comments if you'd like."

"Thanks, but I don't have a clue what I want to do next," I said. My mind was circling wildly as I tried to get my bearings and think the situation through. But before I could, my doorbell rang. I was still in my bathrobe, but Clint was in the kitchen fixing lunch for Jerry, so I said goodbye to Amelia and went to get it. Hopefully not more grieving parents or, even worse, reporters.

I took a quick peek out the side window and was relieved to see a familiar white-haired man, long-limbed, angular and slightly stoop-shouldered. Max, the husband of my best friend Martha, who had died of cancer last month. I realized I hadn't seen or talked to Max since Martha's funeral. Had that been only four weeks ago? With all that had happened with the ME, it seemed like months.

I opened the door. "Max, come in, come in. I've been meaning to call and check in," I said, reaching out to hug him. "How are you doing? Would you like a cup of tea?"

Max leaned down and hugged me tightly. "No tea, thanks, Anne. Just a short visit," he said. "I hope I haven't come too early. You're not dressed yet and you look tired."

"No, it's not too early. I'm recovering from Rocky Mountain Spotted Fever, so I was sleeping late, but I've been up for a while."

Max pulled back and shook his head. "Rocky Mountain Spotted Fever? That can be dangerous. Are you okay?"

"No worries. I went to the ER last night and I'm on antibiotics now. My energy is low, but I'll be fine. How are you doing?"

"I'm okay, but it's hard. I miss Martha so much." He covered his face with his hands for a moment, struggling to go on. "Oh, Anne. You know. Even though we knew it was coming and everything, I can hardly believe she's gone."

Tears filled my eyes, as I ushered him into the living room and over to the couch. "I do know. I keep picking up my phone to call her and when I remember she's gone, it hits me like a punch in the gut. She told me so many times that she didn't want me to be sad, but I can't help it."

"Me too," he said, his voice a little quavery. He stared down at his empty hands. "When I wake up in the morning, I forget for a few minutes. I feel normal and everything, but then it comes crashing down: I'll never see her, hold her, talk to her, or kiss her again."

I put my arm around his shoulders. "I'm so sorry, Max. How can you and I get through this together? I wish there was something I could do."

He pulled back and looked me straight in the eye. "I know you do, Anne, and that's why I came by—because there is something you can do."

"Sure, Max. Just say the word."

He leaned forward rubbing his hands together. "Well, here's the thing. Gail has a friend who is in some grief support group with your daughter-in-law Amelia and—"

Uh-oh. My stomach did a flip. Max and Martha's daughter Gail must have told him about the ME and now he wants to try it.

"So," Max continued, "Gail's friend told her about the YouTube video, about your device that lets people travel back in time and reunite with people who have died—"

"It's not exactly like that," I broke in. You just revisit—'

"I know what it does," he said with enthusiasm. "I watched the video. I want to try it, Anne. I need to see Martha again before she was sick. A happy time. I need to hold her, feel her in my arms."

"You realize you can't talk to her as the person you are today? You would be just reliving a past time with her as it happened."

"I understand. But even if it is only the past, we had years of marvelous moments. If I could just relive an ordinary day with her and everything, it would be incredible."

I thought about how much joy I had gotten from reliving past days with Jerry when he was still himself. How could I deny that to Max? But there was still the safety issue. Also, I worried that an ME trip wouldn't be the best thing for him so soon while he was deeply grieving.

"Max, the Memory Enhancer hasn't been thoroughly tested or approved as safe. My brother Ned left it to me to try out and decide about. We've only had it a few weeks. Only family members have tried it."

"Anne, Martha was family to you. You two shared everything. Please let me try it. You know she'd do it for you."

He was right, Martha would have done it for me. We were best friends forever until she died. We were always there for each other. I could almost hear her saying, "This matters so much to Max, Anne, please let him have it."

I took Max's hands in mine. "Okay, Max. I'll do it for Martha. But can you wait a day or so? I'm recovering but like I said I don't have much energy and I have a lot to deal with today. And please don't tell anyone, including Gail that I agreed to let you use the ME."

He agreed and I said I'd call him to set a time.

# Chapter 32

## Anne

As I said goodbye to Max at the front door, I noticed several cars driving slowly by, followed by a Channel 12 News van. I closed and locked the door and asked Clint to do whatever he could to keep people away. Jerry was ready for a nap and so was I, so I took him to the bedroom, swallowed my pills, curled up in his comforting arms, and fell into a deeply medicated sleep.

When I woke up, Jerry wasn't next to me. I looked at the clock. It was 4:00 p.m. I'd been asleep for hours. I got up and went to the living room where I found Jerry and Meadow on the couch listening to music. She jumped up, hugged me, and pushed me down next to Jerry on the couch. She pulled up a chair across from us, so close that her knees were almost touching mine. "I'm so sorry I wasn't here to help yesterday, Anne," she said softly. "Clint told me all about it." She stroked my arm. "How are you feeling?"

"I'm much better, thanks. The antibiotics and rest are doing their work."

"I didn't know you were sick until this afternoon. I had a missed call and a voice message from Bill yesterday, but my phone has been messing up, so I didn't see it until about noon today. I called him right away and after he told me everything, I came right over. When I got here Clint showed me Laura's YouTube video. You've had a busy couple of days."

"Did Clint leave?"

"Yes. He left when I came over a few hours ago."

214

"Have people been ringing the doorbell?"

"Oh yes." Meadow sounded exasperated. "Reporters and people demanding to use the ME. I answered a few times, then I put up a sign on the door that says, 'Seriously ill person sleeping. Please do not ring or knock.' But some of them still did. I didn't answer—just looked out the side window and waved them away. Some of them were sitting in the yard until I finally called the police to come make them move. But the police can only force them as far back as the street, which is a public venue, so they're out there on the road."

I got up, went to the window and looked out. Cars and several TV station vans lined both sides of the street. People milled around talking and looking at each other's cell phones. The Twitterverse must be lighting up like crazy with comments about the ME. I'm not on Twitter so I didn't know how to check. "Are you on Twitter?" I asked Meadow.

"No. I mostly use Facebook," she said. "Why?"

"Amelia told me women from her support group tweeted the link to the YouTube video. I want to see what the conversation about it is saying now, what's bringing all these people out. I need to call her."

Amelia answered on the first ring. "Oh, Anne. It keeps getting worse and worse," she said. "People are tweeting stuff like 'spend one more day with your lost loved one' and 'travel back in time through your dreams,' and they give links to Laura's YouTube video. The Memory Enhancer even has its own hashtag now. The whole thing has gotten picked up by more blogs and some of them mention your brother Ned."

"How would they know about him?" I asked.

"I'm thinking from the online news article on the *Helena Independent Record* site."

"Oh, no! Really?" I grabbed my laptop from the table and brought up the *Independent Record* web page. Among the breaking news headlines, I found *Grieving parents beg Helena judge for help.* A short article followed.

*A YouTube video posted yesterday by a grieving Helena Montana mother has galvanized bereaved parents from around the world. In the video, entitled "Have one more day with your lost child," Laura Sutton, whose daughter Mattie died five years ago from brain cancer, describes a device called the Memory Enhancer that lets people return to any time from their past and relive it through all their senses.*

*The article went on to explain how Laura had learned about the ME and why she wanted to use it, and identified me as the owner of the device. The came the surprise ending:*

*Neither Amelia Barnes nor Judge Anne Barnes could be reached for comment today. But Judge Barnes' son, Clint Barnes, who has tried the Memory Enhancer, said it is totally unlike any experience he's ever had. "I went back to 2007 when my platoon was blown up in Iraq," he said. "It's haunted me for years that I couldn't remember the details of what happened and I didn't know whether I had done everything I could for my buddies who died in the explosion. The Memory Enhancer put me right there. I saw, heard and smelled the explosion and was hit by intense pain when I tried to get up from where the blast had thrown me. It was horrible, but I needed to re-member. I am still very sad about my buddies, but now I know I tried to help them even though I couldn't."*

*According to Clint Barnes, the Memory Enhancer was invented by his uncle Ned Weller, who was a prominent neuroscientist at the University of California, San Diego before he died of cancer last month. "Uncle Ned had been estranged from the family for more than forty years. I never even met the guy. So it was strange that he left this invention to Mom, but apparently he thought she was the best person to figure out what to do with it."*

My shoulders and my spirits drooped. Why had Clint talked to the press without checking with me first? I swallowed hard before I spoke to Amelia, who had been silent while I was reading. "I wish Clint hadn't mentioned Ned," I said. "In fact, I wish he hadn't talked to the press at all."

"I know," she sighed. "You for sure didn't need any extra public-ity for the ME. But we can at least deflect some of the social media chatter. I've learned a lot from dealing with the blowback from the Evan's Place website. The more statistics we put out there to combat anti-vaccine disinformation, the more they attack us with their anti-science nonsense. It's essential to keep track of what people are saying and to face accusations head on by stating the facts that make our case. I realize you're not feeling well, but this stuff goes viral in a flash, so it's important to act right away. If you're up to it, I could come over so we can work on it."

Clearly I needed to take some action and I was much better after my long nap—even a little hungry. "Okay," I said. "How would it be if you, Bill and the girls all come? It would be good for Jerry to spend some time with them. He's had a rough couple of days with me being sick and distracted. Would you be willing to pick up some pizza on your way over? We could all eat and then you and I could work on the computer stuff while the rest of them play or watch a movie."

"Sounds good," she said. "We'll keep it short so you can get to bed early."

I warned her about the people outside. "The police are keeping them out of the yard. Park in the driveway and head straight for the door without talking to them. Don't ring the bell, just use your key and come in."

I invited Meadow to stay, but she said she needed to get home. "If you're okay being alone tonight with Jerry. If not, I can come back later and spend the night."

"Thanks, but we'll be fine on our own. Go ahead home, and good luck with the hecklers outside."

She laughed. "Hey. I was a protester in the sixties. Remember? These people don't come close to intimidating me."

I was resting while I waited, snuggling on the couch with Jerry and contemplating the whole mess, when I heard a loud banging on the window overlooking the back garden. I held back my scream so as not to scare Jerry as I sprang up and dashed to the window. A bulky man's face was pressed against the glass—his wide lips and huge eyes giving him a frog-like look. When he saw me, he pulled his head back and started shouting, "Help us! Why won't you help us?" He held up a sign that said, "Give us our dreams."

My heart raced. "Go away," I yelled. "This is private property. You have no right to be here."

He didn't move, so I closed the blinds over the window and went to get my phone to call the police.

Just as I hung up, Bill, Amelia and the girls burst through the front door, slamming and locking it behind them. "We got two huge pizzas," Miranda shouted, "one pepperoni and one cheese. Doesn't it smell yummy, Gramma?"

"Very yummy, Miranda. Thanks for bringing it. I'm starving. If you and your mom will take it to the kitchen and get out some plates and drinks for everyone, we can eat."

I started to follow them to the kitchen, but Bill stopped me. "Mom, I thought you said the police were keeping the gawkers off your property. Three of them ran right up to us in the driveway and started yelling. I managed to get them to go back to the street, but I think this might be more than the police have time to deal with. We should consider hiring some private guards."

"You're right," I said. "There was just a man yelling at the back window. I had to call the police to get rid of him. I'm ready and willing to pay for private guards if you can find some to hire."

Bill said he would get right on it after we ate. Meanwhile Vicky had been unsuccessfully trying to pull Jerry up from the couch. "Come on Granddad. We have pizza." Bill went over to help, and together they guided Jerry to a chair at the kitchen table. Vicky sat next to him, and the rest of us joined them.

"Why are all those people outside your house, Gramma?" Miranda asked.

How to explain without explaining? "It's about a computer program I got from my brother after he died. They want it, but I can't give it to them right now."

"Why not? What is it? Is it a game?"

"No, it's not a game. It helps people remember things that happened in the past. But I don't think it's ready for a lot of people to try it yet."

"Will it be ready soon? There's a lot of people out there."

"Okay, enough questions, Miranda," Bill said. "Gramma's still trying to figure all this out. She doesn't have all the answers right now. Let's eat our pizza and then you can watch a movie with Granddad."

Once Jerry and the girls were settled with their movie, Bill went down to my office to make calls to find some guards to hire, and Amelia and I sat at the kitchen table with our laptops. "I did a little work today creating a website for the Memory Enhancer," Amelia said. "It's a way to tell your story, the story of how the ME came to be and why you want to be careful about how it's used." She brought up a gray screen filled by an abstract picture of a curved tunnel with a light at the end. Overlaying it on the left side in simple white lettering was the headline, *University of California Neuroscientist's Invention Revives Memories.* On the right side were three dark red tabs labeled *About Ned Weller, About the Memory Enhancer,* and *FAQ.*

"This is a rough draft. I haven't added any real information yet. I wanted to have it in the works just in case. We'd have to work on it together and we wouldn't publish it unless and until you're ready."

I had to admire her ability to take prompt preemptive action using her experience as a web designer, but I couldn't focus enough to make thoughtful comments. "It looks interesting, but I don't think the ME is ready to have its own website," I said.

"Sure. It would just be a way for us to get positive information out there to counteract negative stuff. Meanwhile we can respond to what is out there. I set up a Google alert so we get notified whenever the ME is mentioned on the web. That way we can read what bloggers are saying and respond. It's really important to be sincere and honest and keep telling your story the way you want it to be heard."

She showed me how the Google alert worked and then showed me a program called IceRocket that she used to search blogs, Twitter and Facebook for mentions of the ME. Another program, Social Mention, gave her results based on the sentiment of social media buzz around the ME—how many were positive, neutral, or negative, how strong the comments were, what the top hashtags were, who the top users were, how recent the last mention was and so on.

It was fascinating, but it reminded me of my early days in law school when the terminology was unfamiliar and the amount of information was crushing. I mastered it all soon enough, but initially I struggled to keep from sinking in the quicksand. "I can see that it will take considerable time and energy to get on top of this," I said. "It's not going to be something I can do in the next few days."

Amelia gasped, put her arm around my shoulders, and hugged me. "Oh no, Anne. I'm not expecting you to do all this. It's my fault that the ME became public and I'll do whatever you want done to deal with it. I just wanted to show you what is possible. If it's okay with you, I'll respond to blogposts and tweets with whatever message you want out there.

"Thanks, Amelia. That sounds like a good start," I said, grateful to have the burden off my shoulders.

"Great. Then, if you want, later we can put up the website and also start our own blog where we have longer conversations with people than we can have on Twitter. That way we'll find out more about what they want and what they think."

"The movie's over, Mom," Miranda shouted from the living room. "Can we watch something else?"

"No, we have to get home," Amelia said, gathering up her stuff. She turned to me with a smile. "I think we made some good progress, Anne. We can talk on the phone tomorrow about what you want me to say in tweets and blog comments."

Bill came up behind us. "I've got two highly-recommended guards who can start tomorrow," he said, "but I don't want you and Dad here alone tonight. Amelia can take the girls home and I'll stay here overnight."

I protested, insisting Jerry and I would be fine, but Bill had his mind made up and that was that.

# Chapter 33

## Anne

After Amelia and the girls left and I got Jerry to bed, Bill fixed some herbal tea for the two of us and brought it into the living room. "This should help you relax so you can get some sleep," he said. "It must have been pretty creepy having a guy peering in your back window."

"It was. Thanks for the tea and thanks for finding the guards—and for staying tonight." Despite my earlier protests, I would surely sleep more soundly not worrying about someone breaking in.

"No problem." Bill took a drink of his tea, put down his cup, and looked over at me. "Do you mind if I do some muscle stretches while we talk?" he asked.

"Sure. Go ahead," I said.

Bill sat up straight in his chair, bent forward and clasped his hands on his right knee—an evening stretching routine that took me back to his teen years. He held the stretch for a few moments, then straightened up and repeated it on the left side.

He straightened again. "Now that the word is out, Mom, unless you're planning to destroy the ME, I think you're going to have to make a plan to manage it," he said bending toward his right knee again.

A plan? I had no plan, not even a good idea for a plan. He continued his stretches, up and down, back and forth. The rhythm calmed me, but confusion and exhaustion had frozen my brain. "You're way ahead of me, Bill," I groaned. "I'm nowhere near ready to make the ME public yet."

Bill stopped, got up, then lay on the floor on his back and pulled his knees to his chest—another stretch. "The ME already is public. Mom. If you ever want to be able to leave your house again, you're going to have to tell people what you plan to do with it." He held the stretch for a few seconds, stretched his legs out, then pulled them in again.

I left him stretching while I went to the kitchen and got another cup of tea. I knew he was right, but it wasn't just my decision anymore. The ME was the beginning of a new family story.

I returned with my tea and my answer. "I'm not going to decide on my own, Bill. I think of this as a family project now. We have to meet and decide as a family how to handle it."

He finished his stretches and sat up. "Fine, Mom, if that's what you want. The sooner the better, the way this thing is escalating. But we'll have to wait a few days to be able to get everyone together. Can you put up with the aggravation until then?"

I sipped my tea and considered. "With guards we'll be fine. Plus it will give me a little more time to recover from being sick and think about issues we all need to discuss."

"Okay. How about we all go out to the ranch on Saturday? I always think of it as our family place. It would be the ideal spot to come together for a complicated conversation. And it would get us away from the distractions around here."

Instantly I knew Bill was right. Like he said, the 2500-acre Weller Ranch, about an hour outside Helena in the foothills of the Anaconda Mountain Range, is our family place. On the surface it's a working cattle ranch with creeks, high meadows, irrigated hay fields, forest land, two houses—both of which have been remodeled and upgraded over the years—and assorted barns, sheds and outbuildings. But for us, the ranch is much more. It's part of us and we are part of it. It's a place of strong feelings, happy memories, miserable memories. It's been in our family since the turn of the century when my immigrant great-grandfather struck gold in the Montana mountains and used his fortune to buy the ranch and develop a cattle empire. Generations of Wellers have lived and died there.

After the tragedy of Mama's death on the ranch, none of us wanted to go there again. Daddy wanted to sell it, but Grandma Clara was the sole owner and she refused to sell. She hired tenant ranchers to manage the property while she lived with us in Helena. By the time she died seven years later, Daddy had decided he wanted to keep the ranch, which was bringing in a good income. Gradually we began going back there to hike, ride, and enjoy the beauty of the Deerlodge National Forest, which it borders. Our children and grandchildren have enjoyed it over the years. Dan, Meadow and I inherited the ranch when Daddy died—Sandra was a nun who could not own property, and Ned had left the family—so the three of us are the owners today.

One of the houses, originally built as a place for the cowboys to live, is occupied by our tenants, Norm and Freda, who manage the ranch. The other house has always been the family home and we continue to keep it for family use, although we don't use it much.

"Great idea," I said. "The ranch would be perfect. Do you think it will be a hassle for Norm and Freda to open up the house for us on such short notice?"

"No, they'll be thrilled to have us come out. They're always after me to bring Vicky and Miranda out to go riding. The girls will be excited too."

"Okay. You work it out with Norm and Freda and I'll call the family and get them on board. Shall we plan on getting out there around 11:00 a.m. on Saturday?"

"Sounds good. I'll pick up some brisket, slaw and beans from Bad Betty's Barbecue so no one has to cook."

"Yum. Don't forget the jalapeño cornbread. It's Dan's favorite."

We all slept well that night, with—surprisingly— no interruptions. The first of the guards Bill had hired showed up bright and early at 7:00 a.m. prepared for a twelve-hour shift. He was tall, thickset and heavily tattooed. His craggy face exuded a "don't mess with me" air.

Since I had no plans to go out where I might be confronted, I let Bill take my car to get home and then to work.

Right after he left, I got a call from Joyce at Weller & Associates.

"Hon, you're not gonna believe some of these phone messages. I'm not kidding—you can't make this stuff up. One woman said she'd get the church to censure you for keeping her away from her daughter's spirit. A guy said if you don't let him use the ME, he's gonna curse you and bring harsh retribution on your soul. They're calling you names like un-American, abomination to the human race, and a sick twisted piece of shit. No death threats though. I guess they figure if they kill you or blow up your house, they'd never get to try this Memory Enhancer thing."

I shuddered. "Have you talked to any of these people, Joyce?"

"Nah. I'm letting all the calls go directly to voicemail. I listen to the messages, and I've kept them all in case you have a lot of time to waste and want to listen to them yourself. Do you think you might need any of them for legal proof if any of them follow though on their threats?"

My gut heaved. "I don't know, Joyce. How about you keep the messages you think are important and delete the others? Do you think there are any I should hear now?"

"Well, there's one guy who's left several messages saying he wants to buy the Memory Enhancer and is prepared to offer you an excellent price. So if you're interested in selling it…"

"I don't have any plans like that now for sure," I said, "but keep that one in case we might want to consider it. Thanks for all this, Joyce. Sorry it's such a pain."

"No worries, hon. The messages liven up my day for sure."

Next I called Martha's husband Max to set up the ME session I had promised him. We agreed on Thursday morning. "The ME is very specific about time," I said. ""You need to know exactly what date and time of day you want to go back to, so be sure to check it out with your old photos or other mementos and an online calendar."

"I can do that," he said. "Would the time of day be the time in the place I'm going back to?"

"Yes. And online resources can help with that. I was able to pinpoint the time for a celebration Jerry and I had in Hawaii by doing a Google search for the sunset time on that day ."

Max was prepared and raring to go when he arrived on Thursday morning. He beamed. "I'm going back to the trip to Italy Martha and I took five years ago. It was a glorious trip—before her cancer diagnosis when we were both healthy and happy and everything."

I set Max up with the ME and went to hang out with Jerry, who had been spending a lot of time at the front windows staring out at the people.

He was bouncing from one foot to the other and flapping his hands as he stared out at them. "Who are they?" he asked.

I put my arm around his shoulders. "No one," I said, gently pulling him away from the window.

But he resisted, frowning and leaning away from me back toward the window. "Are they lost? Why are they here?" he asked in a wavery voice.

I kissed his cheek. "Don't worry. They'll be fine," I said. "Lets go get some juice and a snack." As I led him toward the kitchen, I worried that whatever was going through his mind about the crowd outside and their continued presence might agitate him more. Bill was right. We needed to get this under control. Unfortunately, despite Amelia's attempts to quash the publicity, social media users continued to hype the ME. It had taken over our lives in a way I could never have anticipated when I brought it home from San Diego.

My timer went off telling me it was time to go unhook Max. His blissful smile told me all I needed to know. "Oh Anne, how can I ever thank you? It was incredible. Martha and I hiking between the Cinque Terre towns in Italy, seeing one breathtaking ocean view after another and everything, eating seafood so fresh it was swimming in the ocean a few hours before. Having that time with my Martha again—I never thought I'd have that." He hugged me and as I hugged him back, I could almost feel Martha with us making it a group hug.

Max pulled back, put his hands on my shoulders and gazed solemnly into my eyes. "This ME your brother invented is a true treasure. I wish I could have one for myself that I could use whenever I wanted to."

I stepped back a bit to move away from his intense desire. "Those people outside are on the same page as you," I said. "And they haven't even tried it. But what if it turns out to have some horrible side effects we haven't seen yet? If I make it available to anyone who wants it, I could be responsible for a calamity worse than Ebola or Bubonic Plague."

His face fell. "So you have to decide between a long testing period or simply letting users take their chances, I guess. Not an easy choice with all the demand that's out there and everything."

Or I could destroy it and put an end to the whole thing. But I couldn't say that to Max after the fabulous memory trip he'd just had. And, given some of my own experiences, I honestly didn't want to consider that option.

After lunch I took a nap with Jerry and woke up with renewed stamina to scrutinize my situation. I would have liked to have taken Jerry outside for some fresh air and exercise, but the crowd was still there, so I settled him on the couch, put on some old Frank Sinatra music he liked, cuddled close, and let my mind drift.

So many recent events—Ned's letter with its shocking discovery, Laura's heartbreaking YouTube video, the hordes of bereaved people demanding to use the ME, Max's joy at going back to be with Martha—raced through my head. I hadn't told anyone about Ned's recovered memory of the shooting. Debby knew because she had read the letter, but I still needed to tell the others. Why hadn't I?

Being so sick had briefly knocked it out of my consciousness, and then had sucked up any strength I had. But beyond that I was worried about how they would react. My heart ached for Ned, but Debby's negative take on the letter had shocked me. How would the others see it? Would they look at Ned as an angry man seeking revenge on the family rather than a victim who had lost his family because of his father's deceit? Would they believe his ME memory was real or would they think he had made up the story to vindicate himself?

I owed it to Ned to share his story with them, and I wanted to do it as fairly as possible without prefacing it with my own beliefs. I decided to read his letter aloud to them as a group, let them respond, and see where it went. I would do it Saturday at the ranch—perhaps a strange location in that it was the "scene of the crime," so to speak. But we rarely think of the ranch that way after all these years, and perhaps, at least for Dan and me, old memories there would intensify the story.

And then there was the ME. The original idea for the meeting was to make a plan for it—but how would we do that? Any way I looked at it, I had gotten myself into a deep hole that I had no idea how to get out of.

Meadow, Amelia, Bill, Clint and I all believed in the ME's value. I couldn't imagine any of us choosing to hold it back from other people it might benefit. At the same time, I couldn't disregard Debby and Dan's concerns about the risks of putting the ME out there for the general public to use. We three are the attorneys in the family, far more knowledgeable than the others about possible liability.

As I frantically racked my brains for possibilities we all might agree to embrace, I tuned in to Frank Sinatra singing, "That's Life." As he crooned the words, "I've been up and down and over and out, and I know one thing. Each time I find myself flat on my face, I just pick myself up and get back in the race."

If only it were that easy, I thought.

# Chapter 34

## Anne

Saturday morning was a perfect example of why they call Montana Big Sky country. A bright and breezy summer day with a blue cloudless sky that stretched on forever above the distant mountain tops. Dan picked up Jerry and me at 9:45 for the drive to the ranch. Jerry fell asleep instantly, but I was fidgety with a fluttery feeling in my stomach like before a big exam. Knowing I would soon be telling them all about Ned's uncovered memory of Mama's shooting was unnerving. I had only just absorbed his revelation myself and I had no idea how they would react.

Once we were out of town, passing through familiar forest and meadows, Dan said, "I need to let you know something before this meeting, Anne." I clenched my fists tightly. Uh, oh. Now what? Did Debby tell him about what she read in Ned's letter to me? I didn't think she would have, but it was possible. Now he could be going to tell me he doesn't want to participate in anything involving Ned. How could I change his mind? Before I could begin strategizing, he went on.

"I got a call yesterday from the university attorney at the University of California, San Diego," Dan said. "She tried to reach you, but the call went to that voicemail that Joyce has set up. So the attorney looked up the firm and called me directly."

Whew. He was on another track entirely. I relaxed a little and replied. "What did she want?"

"The university administration found out about the ME from the *Independent Record* article where Clint said the ME was invented by Ned and identified him as a neuroscientist at U Cal, San Diego. The attorney watched the YouTube video, which was also mentioned in the article."

"So—let me guess—she wants us to know the university may have a claim on the ME because he worked there while he invented it?"

"Exactly. She said Ned had a signed agreement stating he would fully disclose any potentially patentable inventions to the Office of Technology Commercialization. He was supposed to complete an Invention Disclosure Form for any work that could have potential commercial value and potentially be licensed, but he never did it for the ME."

"But he didn't apply for a patent. His only invention is the software, and he copyrighted the code. He didn't create the tDCS headsets. He just ordered them from a site that sells them to gamers. Plus, the ME wasn't developed under a sponsored research agreement at the university, and Ned said he was very careful not to do any work on the ME at the university. It was all done on his own time and in his own lab. He specifically didn't want the ME to be a project of the university."

"They maintain he should have disclosed the ME to the university and then, if he thought he had a valid claim that he was the owner, he should have provided explicit evidence that he didn't use significant university resources and/or facilities in creating it."

"I'm not surprised they're making a claim," I said. "I knew this was a possibility. But knowing Ned's concerns about letting the university control the ME, I can't justify handing it over to them. I'll resist as much as I can."

"Well," Dan said, "I figure the university has rights even if Ned did all development on his own time and at his own lab. It's hard to avoid using any university resources. For example, if he used his university email account or connected to the web on their server for anything related to the ME, they could claim he was using university resources."

"You give up a lot easier than I do," I said. "I'm not ready to admit they have rights."

"No, no, I'm not giving up," he said. "Bottom line, I think there's a good chance the university won't want to pursue the rights because commercialization of the ME could be controversial. I did some research on the process. As a non-profit institution, they'd have to license the rights to a company and eventually the university would get some of the profits—assuming there are any. But a university's main goal with inventions is to make money to fund more research, and they'd rather make it sooner than later. Most university inventions are years away from practical application and are never licensed. There are so many pitfalls that they end up being a drain on university resources because of legal fees and maintenance."

"So what do you think they want from us?" I asked.

"I'm guessing a settlement," he said. "If the research hasn't been taxpayer funded, the university can sell the rights, which can be in their best interests. If we agree to pay them to waive all rights without any admission on our part of wrongdoing by Ned, we can probably get a full and final settlement."

Hmmm…One more debatable question to toss into the family brainstorming session.

When we got to the ranch, Bill and Amelia were already there. Amelia had taken the girls down to the stable where Norm and Freda were waiting to take them riding and fishing. Amelia had packed them lunches so they could make a day of it.

Bill was drinking coffee in a porch swing on the wide deck that wrapped around the front and side of the ranch house. Coffee, juice and muffins were on a rustic wooden table in front of a wicker couch. Jerry and I sat down on the couch, and Dan took the rocking chair next to us just as Meadow, Debby and Clint drove up. A few minutes later, Amelia joined Bill on the swing. I poured Jerry a glass of juice and he helped himself to several muffins, which he began munching noisily.

I had no appetite. All I could think about was Ned's letter. My heart was pounding so loudly I could barely hear their conversation. I just wanted to get through it, so as soon as they were all settled, I took a deep breath and began with Ned's news. "Before we start talking about what to do with the ME, I want to share part of Ned's last letter to me. I only read it Sunday night just before I got sick and Debby read it the next day when she came over to help."

My hands shook as I picked up the handwritten pages and read them Ned's report of his ME trips where he discovered what happened on the tragic hunting trip, ending with his desire for the rest of the family to know the truth.

Everyone was silent except for Meadow who sobbed deeply. I put down the pages and looked around. Tears streamed down Meadow's splotchy face. Amelia was sniffling and wiping her eyes with a tissue. Bill had his arm around her shoulders, his face cloudy. Clint was slumped over, his head in his hands. Debby stared off into the distance with a quizzical look. Dan's deadpan expression revealed nothing. Jerry was so engrossed in his muffins that everything else went over his head.

"Horrible! Simply horrible that Daddy would blame Ned for Mama's death when any of the three of them could have been responsible." Meadow struggled to get the words out as she continued to weep. "I can hardly believe it."

"That's the thing, though," Dan said. "Should we believe it? I can accept that Dad would have lied, but I can't accept Ned's account as proof of that. Don't get me wrong, Dad was quite capable of putting all the blame on Ned. But you have to believe in the accuracy of the ME to be convinced of Ned's story. It could be a fantasy he dreamed, a memory he constructed that told the story in a way he hoped it had gone."

Meadow jumped up and stood in front of Dan, her elbows wide from her body and her chest thrust out. "Good grief, Dan," she screamed, "after all he's been through, can't you give Ned any credit at all?"

Jerry was watching her, but didn't look anxious so I got up, leaving him on the couch, and walked over and put my arms around Meadow. I rubbed her back as she cried into my shoulder. "I believe Ned," I said, "even though it's hard for me to live with the idea that Daddy could do that. I don't know why he did it. Maybe he didn't remember that they all shot, maybe he truly believed Ned was the only one who shot, maybe he was trying to protect Sandra, or maybe he just couldn't face the thought that he might have shot Mama, so he convinced himself it was Ned. We'll never know. And we'll never be able to make it right for Ned." I led her back to her chair and went back to my seat on the couch next to Jerry.

"It's a tragedy," Amelia said, looking around at us all. Her voice broke. "I'm so sorry for you all that this false account split up your family the way it did."

Clint raised his head from his hands, looking dazed. He gave me a pained look. "That poor guy lived almost his whole life haunted by a lie. It was cruel and unusual punishment for something there's only a one in three chance he even did. Why was everyone so quick to believe what your father said had happened?"

"We didn't want to believe it," I said. "But neither Ned nor Sandra remembered anything about the shooting. Daddy was the only one who remembered—or at least he said he did—and he said Ned was the only one who fired his gun, so it had to be him. Ned never defended himself. He just shut himself in his room and refused to talk to anyone. Then he went back to college and never came home. I think we didn't know what else to do but to believe Daddy's story."

"A perfect example of how authority has all the power and no respect for honesty," Clint said in disgust. "And people are too spineless to stand up for the little guy when the man socks it to him."

Silence. Were we afraid to stand up for Ned? I didn't remember feeling that way, but maybe I did. Daddy was a forceful man, who I did find intimidating at times. I don't think I ever won an argument with him over the years. Did I sacrifice Ned out of fear? Honestly I don't think it even occurred to me that Daddy's story wasn't true.

Meadow stopped crying, put her hand over her mouth and looked at Clint, her eyes wide. "You're right," she said, "we didn't stand up for Ned. We believed Daddy. I was only sixteen, but I was old enough to speak up. Why didn't I?"

"Stop, Meadow," Dan said gently. "None of this is your fault and it was all a long time ago. There's no way we'll ever know the truth, and even if we did, there's nothing we can do about it. Let it go."

Then Debby spoke up. "Does everyone except Uncle Dan believe Uncle Ned's memory—or whatever it was—is true?" She stopped and looked around at us all nodding our heads. "So all of you who have tried the ME are one hundred percent sure it shows the truth and what Uncle Ned wrote down is what he saw?" Again, she stared at us. Again, we all nodded, except Dan.

"Wow," she said. "I don't know what to believe. Like Mom said, I read the letter on Monday, so I've had time to think about it. I'm skeptical, but you've all tried the ME and I haven't, and you all believe in it, so I can't simply dismiss it out of hand. Now my question is, are you sure enough that you're going to tell your sister Sandra—the nun—about this? Do you want her to go back and see that all three of them fired their guns?"

Meadow gasped in horror. "No! No we can't do that. Sandra has found peace as Sister Mary Margaret. We need to let her be."

"I agree," I said. "I visited Sandra a week ago and told her about the ME and invited her to come home for a visit and try it. I thought she'd want to see Mama and Daddy again the way they were when she was little. But she had no interest. When I told her about the ME, she didn't bring up the possibility of going back to the accident, so I didn't either. I hadn't read Ned's letter then, but even if I had I wouldn't have told her what he said. Meadow's right. Sandra's found a way to put the past behind her and we should respect that."

# Chapter 35

## Anne

We sat in silence for a couple of minutes until Bill stood up and said, "Hey, we've got Bad Betty's Barbecue and all the fixings waiting in the kitchen. How about a lunch break?" Judging from their enthusiastic responses, everyone was either really hungry or looking for a way to move on from the sad family past.

We ate more quietly than usual, with subdued chit-chat about nothing consequential. Jerry was ready for a nap after lunch, so I got him settled in one of the bedrooms while the others cleaned up the kitchen. Then we gathered in the large living room. Over the years as we remodeled, we've taken down the wall between the dining room and living room, and added vaulted ceilings and sliding glass doors that fill the room with light and open it to the outdoors. The old stone fireplace is still there, the furniture is still overstuffed and comfy, and one of Gramma Clara's quilts hangs on a far wall. It's a composite of the old living room I remember from childhood and an upscale modern ranch house great room.

I opened the sliding glass doors onto the deck and took a minute to enjoy the long view before I faced the group. "Now we have to decide what to do with the ME," I said. "As Bill so aptly pointed out to me the other night, we need to have a plan we can make public in response to the requests and demands I'm getting from people who want to use it. Right now Jerry and I are stuck in the house even though I have police and private guards working to keep the public away. Joyce at Weller & Associates is deluged with phone calls from hecklers, and Amelia is spending hours responding to negative social media comments. That has to change."

They sat silently, faces turned toward me as I continued. "I only read you part of Ned's last letter to me. In the rest of it he talked about his final request, which was to decide whether, and possibly how, to make the ME available to others. If it's alright with you, I'd like to start with the 'whether' part of the question. Do we want to make the ME available? If we don't want to share it, if we think it would be better to destroy it or hide it away, then we won't need to talk about how to make it available."

Meadow spoke up first. "Don't get me wrong, I want to help you as much as I can, but I don't understand why whether or not to make the ME available is a 'we' question, Anne," she said. "Didn't Ned leave this to you to decide?"

"True. He did. But I've chosen to involve you all and now that you are involved, I want us all to decide."

"Okay," she said, "but I think you should start. You've used it more than any of us and you've been in the next room when we used it. So what do you think? Should we share it?"

"For me personally the ME trips have filled a deep hole in my life," I said. "Going back and being with Jerry when he was healthy has been like having him back again. Admittedly, I have also seen some ME downside, but the positives are very strong. Martha's husband Max begged me to let him try it, and I did because as he said Martha was like family to me. Initially he was overcome with grief, but after his ME trip back to a joyful vacation day with a healthy Martha, he was a changed man. He told me how much he wished he had his own ME that he could use whenever he wanted to. I would like to let other people have that experience."

Bill gave Amelia a quick hug. "Yes, I've seen what the ME has done for Amelia and it's amazing," he said. "She doesn't even need to use it every day. Just knowing it's there and she can see Evan when she wants to, has taken away the profound loss that consumed her before. If we can do this for other people, we should."

Amelia nodded enthusiastically. "That's true. It's hard to put into words how much the ME has changed my life. Now that I can go back and be with Evan, my grief has eased off so much that I am a different person." Her smile lit up the room like a sunbeam.

I sensed a strong negative vibe from Debby who was smirking like she saw some truth invisible to the rest of us. "Stop for a minute," she said, tapping her finger on the table. "Wouldn't some people want to use it all the time? It can take over your life in a way that you neglect responsibilities like when Mom was using it so much that she let Dad wander off. Would some of these grieving parents spend so much time revisiting their dead children that they neglect their living children? Mom, you say you let Max use it to go back to be with Martha, and it was amazing for him. Could he decide it's so enjoyable that he begins to spend most of his time sleeping on ME trips, essentially dropping out of current life? He would simply be a passive observer rather than a participant in life."

Amelia tightened. Her smile clouded up. "No, Debby, Bill just said I don't have to use it every day. Just knowing it's possible to see Evan makes a huge difference. And it doesn't take away from my time with the girls. It frees me up to show them more love."

I could see from Debby's narrowed eyes that she wasn't ready to let go. "Well what about someone who gets dumped from a relationship and can't face it and move on," she said. "Could this person decide to basically live in the past when the relationship was still going on? What if you're married to a widow or widower and your spouse gets the ME and decides he or she enjoys going back and being with their former spouse more than being with you?"

Meadow grinned and spoke up so faintly I had to strain to hear her. "Going back to past relationships can also have the opposite effect. People like me, who have an unrealistically rosy view of their pasts, can be stuck trying to recreate something that never was the way they remember it. My memories of the days of flowers and free love were so joyful that nothing since measured up. Going back with the ME helped me realize that my relationships back then were kind of a game where we were all stoned and did whatever gave us pleasure. Recognizing that has helped me revise my ideas of what I'm looking for. And, in fact, I've met a guy I'm interested in getting to know better. Before that ME trip, I would have blown him off."

Dan was laughing so hard, he almost fell off his chair. "What's that Meadow?" he said. "Now you finally see that all that lovey, flowery stuff was drug-induced delusions? And it took the ME to do that? I could have told you that a long time ago, if you'd been willing to listen."

"Oh stuff it, Dan," Meadow said, laughing back at him. "No one here is surprised that profound insights aren't your thing, but I do learn from experience, and I love the ME and it has been great for me."

She turned to Debby. "On the other hand, I do accept Debby's point about the ME's potential for becoming addictive. I've done my share of drugs and spent plenty of time following my bliss, whatever that was supposed to be. I can see where someone who is dissatisfied or miserable in the present could find spending time in their past a lot more enjoyable. Maybe she's right about Max. If he had a ME, maybe he would spend most of his time reliving his past with Martha. Maybe that would even be okay for him. He's retired and no one depends on him. But, like Debby said, what about someone who neglects obligations in the present to hang out in the past? If it happened to you, Anne, it could happen to anyone."

"That's true," I said. "But you can say that about a lot of things. People get addicted to playing computer games, watching soap operas, and using social media. But we don't put an end to those activities in order to forestall possible negative outcomes. Even gambling and alcohol, which are more destructively addictive are still legal and available."

Debby had been looking pensive, her head tilted to one side as Meadow spoke. "Interesting, Meadow. You've showed me a different side to this. I'm still not interested in reliving my past. Most of it wasn't that terrific the first time. But hearing what you've said about how the ME helped you see the past as it really was and how that helped you move on, is helping me see it with fresh eyes. One of the things I've been trying to do with Josh is just that—to get him to see the past as it really was. His therapist hasn't even been able to get him to see that he has a problem. Maybe this would do it. Maybe if he was hooked up to the ME and went back and saw his behavior when he was high, when he was lying, stealing, cheating, maybe he would get it. I'm thinking I might like to see how trying that would work."

"It's good to hear you being more open, Debby," Clint said wrinkling his nose and squinting at her. "But remember that you can't make Josh use the ME. You're going to have to convince him. And he may not want to go back and see himself high and doing bad stuff."

Debby leaned toward Clint. "Of course you're right," she said, "but there are things he wants to do that he can't do right now, so I think we'll be able to make a deal." She sat back, looking satisfied.

Wow. This discussion was jumping—no, leaping—all over the place, in directions I hadn't expected. Everyone was silent for a minute, perhaps re-examining their own positions. Then Bill spoke up, lightening the mood as he so often does.

"This may sound a little frivolous compared to what the rest of you have been saying," Bill said, "but there's also the pure entertainment value of the ME. I went back to some great skiing days when I was at the top of my game, winning medals in slalom races. It was exhilarating to be inside my younger body doing that again. When I woke up I realized what an important part of my life skiing was, and how much I'm missing by not making time for skiing today. I also realized I haven't taken Vicky and Miranda skiing nearly enough. So even the recreational aspect of it can change your life. And what about athletes who have been injured and can't do their sport anymore? Wouldn't they love to go back and experience themselves whole and fit the way they were at their peak?"

Dan straightened in his chair and looked at Bill. "That's sweet, Bill," he said, "but it actually might be a little frivolous considering the possible risk you may be taking just to re-experience yourself as an agile young skier."

Dan slowly looked around at each of us in turn. "I hear what you're all saying about how the ME has helped you, but what you don't know is how it may have harmed you or may harm you in the future. Just for example, what if it interferes with REM sleep in some way? Because of my sleep apnea, I've spent some time being diagnosed at a sleep center. The kind of vivid dreams you report where you imagine you're active sounds like REM behavior disorder, which can be associated with Parkinson's Disease. What if frequent use of the ME increases your odds of getting Parkinson's? Or what if it alters brain function in some other horrific way?"

"Come on, Dan," I said "We can't….."

"No, wait Anne." He held up his hands in his favorite stop gesture. "There's more. Let me finish. What if users start getting confused as to where they are in time? What if their brains start clicking over to the past while they're awake? Would they even realize that was happening? How would they know what is reality as opposed to what is long over and done with?"

Good grief. The stuff he could come up with. I had to speak up to counter that. "Yet it had the opposite effect on Jerry," I said. "He was less confused, at least briefly, after his ME trips. What if Alzheimer's lost memories are actually recoverable and the ME's stimulation of the brain can restore long-term memory? That would surely be worth the risk."

Clint stared at Dan, steely-eyed. "I hope you're not saying we shouldn't let people try the ME because it's too risky. I hope you realize everyone has the right to decide for themselves what is too risky."

Clint's face reddened, his nostrils flared, and his voice shook as he confronted Dan. "My ME trip back to the day my platoon was blown up hasn't interfered with my sleep, it has actually helped me sleep better. Going back, seeing what happened, knowing I did as much as I could for my buddies, has been a huge relief. My mind clicks back to the past less now, not more. There are lots of people out there like me who have traumatic events in their pasts that they can't remember, but they need to remember to stop the hidden memories from haunting them. In fact that's the reason Uncle Ned invented the ME. He had to remember that hunting accident, and I'm sure he got major relief when he finally saw that he wasn't the only one responsible for his mother's death."

# Chapter 36

## Anne

We took a break for coffee, tea, fruit and cookies, and I got Jerry up, brought him into to the living room, and settled him in with a banana and two cookies. As the family regrouped, I considered how best to proceed. In my mind, the discussion was going gradually downhill, like a ball I couldn't quite catch up with. Everyone had weighed in, but agreement eluded us. Typical. Why had I thought we could reach consensus on this, when we rarely agree?

We didn't have a lot of time left, and I needed to come out of this day with a decision about the future of the ME. I decided to move on to talking about how we might go about making the ME available if we could somehow agree that we wanted to do that.

"So we have some strong favorable reactions and some concerns," I said. "Let's look at our possibilities if we do decide to share the ME with the world."

I wanted to lay out the choices impartially. In fact, at that point I wasn't sure which route I favored. "As I see it, we have several alternatives and a few potential obstacles," I said. "The university where Ned worked when he developed the ME has some interest in lying claim to it. Their attorney contacted Dan, saying Ned violated his obligation to disclose any inventions to them, and if he used any university resources to create it, they have rights. But Ned said in the letters he left for me with the ME that he was very careful not to use any university resources, including time they were paying him for, because he specifically didn't want the ME to be a project of a university or

240

scientific institute where it would be embroiled for years if not decades in regulations and red tape. So I will definitely contest their claims."

I could see Clint scowling, his body tense. "So the establishment is trying to screw him even after he's dead. That sucks. Why would we give the ME over to them? We'd never see it again."

Dan smiled and leaned back in his chair, his hands behind his head. "Whoa, Clint. This is just part of the legal game. They want something and we want something so we compromise. I'm fairly confident I could convince the university that it would be in their best interests to accept a settlement to waive their rights. That way they'd profit, but they wouldn't have to deal with the controversy surrounding the ME and the public relations that would require."

"Why should we have to pay some bureaucrats when Uncle Ned was so careful not to involve the university? We'd just be giving in to the corrupt system."

"We wouldn't have to pay them," Dan said, "but it would be a lot less trouble that way, and it would leave us free to go on with other plans without the threat of legal action standing in the way."

Clint sighed and threw up his hands. "Whatever," he said. "What are the other choices and obstacles you were going to talk about, Mom?"

"Okay," I said. "Some of you are concerned about liability from possible side-effects of the ME. Here are the choices I see. If we want more testing of the ME, we could locate or create a scientific institute that would do testing, and delay making it available to the public until we know more about its safety. Or, if we want to respond to the people who want to use the ME right now, we could set up a business to sell it. Or, if we are truly worried that the ME is dangerous, we could destroy it now and let that be the end of it."

"No. Oh, no. You can't destroy it." Amelia said, her body quivering and eyes darting around the room, like a trapped animal. "I know the publicity is all my fault and I am so, so sorry for that. But now that we have to move on, I think it's essential to make the ME available to grieving people like the women in my support group. What it can give them is immeasurable and not available anywhere else. How can we refuse to give it to them?" Tears ran down her face.

"How about this?" Bill said. "How about those of us who want to share the ME with the public start a business to do that. Those who would rather not be involved, don't have to."

Debby leaped on that. "Do you really think it would be that simple, Bill? To sell it, you're going to have to advertise it, and make promises about what it can do for people. But what if it doesn't do what they expect? Or even worse, what if it causes them harm? If some of you start selling the ME and it turns out to have serious side-effects that you are liable for, how would the rest of the family not be affected?"

"We can get errors and omissions insurance to protect us from liability," Bill said. "And don't worry, Debby, we'll leave you completely out of the business if that's what you want. But didn't you just say you wanted Josh to use the ME?"

"I did, but I meant at home like you've used it. Starting a family business is a whole different ballgame. Anyway, who's going to run this business? Do you have time?"

Bill took no time to consider his reply. "No," he said. "I can't run it. Amelia and I have all we can do to keep up with our own businesses while we're raising two kids. Maybe Mom?" Bill said, looking at me.

"No," I said. "I retired to be with Jerry and take care of him. I don't want to run a business."

Bill looked at Meadow. "How about you, Meadow?"

She laughed. "Me? Run a business? With my financial skills, we'd be broke in no time."

"I guess you're right, Debby. Running a new business isn't practical for any of us right now," Bill said. "Maybe we could hire someone to run it."

"You'd still have to supervise, which takes time. I'd say turning the ME over to the university or some scientific institute looks like a better option," Debby said. "We could still have it for our own use in the family, but we could let scientists do the testing and take responsibility for the safety for other people."

Clint jumped up. "Stop," he said, holding his hands out like a traffic cop. "I notice none of you suggested I might run this business. But that's okay. I figured it would go like that. We have something most of us agree can add value to people's lives, but we're keeping it away from them because we're afraid or it's too much trouble."

He stopped and took a deep breath. "So since you're all too scared to take a risk, I took one. I copied the ME software onto my computer and ordered one of those tDCS headsets. And it works—just like yours, Mom. So I'm going to put the software up on the web for anyone to download, and give them the instructions so they can use it. They can order headsets over the web and they'll be good to go."

Waves of shock rendered me momentarily speechless. How could Clint have violated my trust? I spluttered briefly, then recovered my voice. "Clint, how could you do this? What makes you believe you have the right to take my property and decide on your own what to do with it?"

"Come on, Mom," he said, "It's not like I stole your car. This is something that can help people in a major way. I can't sit here and let you throw it down a rathole in the system. In the army I risked my life to fight for freedom—freedom for everyone in this country to live a good life, to enjoy life, to make choices for themselves. This is a much smaller risk and it's one we need to take. When you were a judge, you made controversial rulings, but you were fair. You did what you thought was right, even though it sometimes brought you grief. Now I'm doing what I think is right."

Bill lit up like he'd had a major aha moment. He clapped his hands together and grinned. "I don't know why I didn't think of that. It doesn't have to be a business. This family doesn't need to make money from the ME. Clint's right. We can put the software on the web and let people download it for free. What they do with it is up to them."

"You might have the university suing you if you do that," Dan said. He paused, gazed out the window and continued. "But then again they might not bother. Once it's out there for free download, they'll never get it back in the jar."

"There's still the liability issue," Debby said.

"I don't think we would be liable," Clint said. "I know I'm not a lawyer, but I've done some research on software liability, especially free software. What we would be giving users is a freeware license. When they click "agree" on that end-user license agreement that no one ever reads, they're saying they've read our warnings and they're accepting our terms that we make no warranties—other than that the software doesn't contain malware—and we aren't liable for any damages. Plus this software is free so there is no contract between a seller and a buyer."

"Those agreements may or may not hold up in court," Debby said. "No disclaimer can guarantee liability will not arise. And there can be liability without a contract or monetary payment."

"There's a lot of free and open source software out there, and from what I've read, if providers of free software were subject to contract liability, free software would disappear," Clint said.

So Clint hadn't naively plunged into water over his head. He had put forth the time and energy to explore the possible consequences of letting people download the ME software. I wasn't surprised, since he's always been intense and meticulous about his interests.

Dan was shaking his head. "The more I think about it Clint, the more I think you'd be better off if we settled with the university first so they don't have any claim on the intellectual property rights."

"Uncle Dan, you were an Air Force pilot," Clint replied. "You took plenty of risks doing that. And you were a state legislator who did what you believed in even when it might have led to you losing the next election. But now you're all about playing it safe. We aren't free when we live in fear, we're free when we're bold, when we're willing to take chances to make life better. "

"He has a point, Dan," Meadow said. "Sometimes you just have to close your eyes and jump. I say, let's go for it. Let's give the ME to all those people who are begging for it. It's not like we're breaking any rules. Ned was careful to create the ME on his own and he left it to Anne. Her decision. So what do you say, Anne?"

Sometimes the best ideas come from the most unexpected places. Inside my head I heard the click of pieces moving into place. This wasn't a typical family argument. They weren't baiting each other, they were all coming from principle. Now we had to decide.

In my opinion, the non-lawyers had it right. The cost-benefit ratio was in their favor. Our risk was small in comparison to the value we'd be giving. We should go forward. We owed it to all the people out there who wanted the ME, and we owed it to Ned.

"I've been moved by Amelia's support group participants and by Max," I said, "and I'd like them and other grieving people to be able to use the ME. I like Clint's free software idea, and I'm willing to take the risk of liability as well as the risk of the university suing us for copyright. Dan, I appreciate your offer to approach the university about the rights, but I'm not in favor of offering them a settlement because we don't want to be in the position of conceding they have rights."

Amelia looked like she had won the lottery. "Thank you SO much, Anne," she said. "The ME can help so many people. And Clint, I love your idea of putting it up for free download. I'd like to help you with it if that's okay. I have the beginnings of a website for the ME. You and I could finish it with input from Anne and then put the software up without advertising or promising users it will do anything specific. Word will get around in a hurry."

"That sounds great, Amelia. Thanks," Clint said.

"I love it," Meadow said. "I think it would be cool to start a blog about how the ME can change your relationships."

I put my arm around Jerry. "But beyond that," I said, "my main interest right now is research on the possible effects the ME can have on improving memory in Alzheimer's patients. I'm thinking I could set up an institute where neuroscientists could work on that."

Debby nodded. "I like that idea, Mom, and I'd love to help."

"Me too," Dan said. "I may not share your enthusiasm for Ned's invention, but I do understand why it's important to you. I'll hand the university claims issue over to you, and I'll support you any way you need with legal issues that come up. It would be surprising, but fabulous if the ME could help people like Jerry."

Jerry smiled and said, "I will help you too, Dan."

"Thanks, Jerry," Dan said.

# Chapter 37

## Anne

Back home that evening with Jerry in bed for the night, I got myself a glass of wine, put on my favorite piano concertos, and sat in my comfy wing chair. I let my mind drift and flow with the music as I contemplated the events of the past week, and especially today.

For almost as long as I could remember, I'd had a hole in my heart that I believed could only be filled by family closeness—the kind of connections I thought I remembered from when I was a young child, the kind of connections I thought I saw in other families. But the ME had showed me that the warm affection I remembered from childhood was only there some of the time. The old movies were an artificial rendering where we played our parts for the camera. After the camera was off, we teased, argued, and fought. Life wasn't always the perfect picture I saw on film or visualized in my head.

After ME visits had contradicted my memories and raised red flags about my ability to remember, I had done my own research, reading scientific literature about memory, which confirmed what Ned had written to me about its accuracy.

When we retrieve a memory, we also rewrite it. The next time we go to remember it, we don't retrieve the original memory but the last one we recollected. Each time we remember an event, we embellish it to suit our desires, while remaining genuinely convinced of its truth. Clearly that's what I had been doing with my old family memories—embellishing them. If you think of a typical family interaction as a simple slice of cake, I had added whipped cream, chocolate sprinkles and cherries to mine.

That's why my memories didn't always match those of other family members. Not everyone saw the past in the same way, and we all embellished. Even if several of us saw the exact same events unfold, we each interpreted the events in our own unique way. As we looked back, we saw through our own filters.

I no longer believed I could bring family members together in a way that would create the closeness I remembered—the closeness of the old movies. Not only did they all have their own views of the past, they had their own wants in the present, which didn't always match what I wanted them to want.

I saw that my roadmap for family closeness was a fictional yellow brick road to a fantasy family. I had come to a fork in the road where I needed to choose between accepting the family I had or continuing to try for the family I wanted.

The family I had was there for me when it mattered. I may not have always liked the way they did it, but they cared and they helped when they saw a need. Before they knew about the ME, when I was neglecting Jerry because I was using it so much, they were worried about both of us and they came to talk to me to try to help. I didn't like their stepping in, and I didn't like their suggestions, but they meant well. They put a lot of time and energy into trying to help me.

And they pitched in when I needed them. Debby and Clint stayed with Jerry when I went to San Diego, and Meadow stayed with him when I went to see Sandra. Debby picked up Jerry and brought him home after he wandered off when I was sleeping. Bill dropped everything and rushed over when I missed Amelia's meeting and they couldn't reach me by phone, and he did it again when I was sick and Jerry fell. Debby and Clint took turns staying with Jerry and me when I was sick. Dan took me to the ER, ignoring my protests, and got me the medical attention I so urgently needed.

I could see that I hadn't given them enough credit for what they did. Instead I had looked at them in terms of what they could do to re-create my vision of the perfect family. I wanted them to use the ME to go back, re-visit happy family times, and bring those times into the present. I had a picture of how they each fit into the group and the parts they should play. I tried to be the puppet master. When they went their own ways, I was upset and tried harder to get them back in line. Which led to more resistance or, at best, unenthusiastic participation. I hadn't been seeing them as equal family members.

Today at the ranch as we debated the fate of the ME, I had taken a different path. I had done my best to sit back, let them all speak their minds, and consider each of their perspectives without bias. I acted more like a judge, less like a family member. And I saw a different picture.

As I heard them each speak out passionately about a family concern whose future they believed they had a stake in, I saw a new kind of closeness that came from shared values. They listened to each other, and sometimes were persuaded by each other.

It was like a curtain lifted to let the daylight in. I could see that I no longer needed to have the family change to be the way I wanted it to be. I could accept them as they are and be happy with them.

I knew this didn't mean it would all be smooth sailing or that there wouldn't be conflict. But I hoped we would deal with each other more tolerantly. Strangely, Ned—a family outsider—had left us something that brought us together. Our decisions about how to go forward with the ME had transcended old family conflicts and started us on a path to heal the cracks we had lived with for so long.

## Sandra

As the nuns at the Abbey gathered for Lauds—the morning prayer that hails the rising sun and consecrates the day to God—the new day painted the gray sky with brilliant pinks and purples. Sister Mary Margaret sang the canticles with a joyful heart, cherishing her connection to her Benedictine sisters as they lifted their hearts to God through music. Her commitment to the monastic community was absolute, she was content, her soul was at peace.

# Author's Note

In writing this book, I have drawn on my own family experiences and my own longing to revisit my family's past. My parents died when I was young and they were young (although neither of them was shot), and I and my siblings have felt the impact of that in many ways. I created the Memory Enhancer for my fictional family to help them learn from their pasts, and in the process I learned a lot about myself and remembered much that I had forgotten.

If you enjoyed the story, it would be great if you share your reactions in an Amazon review. Do you think the Memory Enhancer would be a good invention? I'm still not sure, but I expect someone will eventually create it and we will find out.

# About the Author

Lynn Osterkamp, Ph.D., MSW, is the author of three mystery novels, *Too Near the Edge, Too Far Under;* and *Too Many Secrets;* as well as two nonfiction books, numerous articles, manuals and national newsletters. Her professional experience includes hospital and hospice social work, university teaching and research, special education, and serving as a long-term-care ombudsman. She lives in Boulder Colorado.

# Acknowledgements

Many thanks to those who read and edited drafts of this book, especially Marian and Janet from my Boulder Media Women's critique group.

As always my husband, Allan, and my daughter, Laurel, were my go-to readers who went through draft after draft, giving me useful notes and unwavering support. I couldn't have done it without them.

For more information about Lynn Osterkamp and her other books, visit her webpage at:

# http://www.lynnosterkamp.com

PMI Books
Boulder, CO
www.pmibooks.com

www.ingramcontent.com/pod-product-compliance
Lightning Source LLC
Chambersburg PA
CBHW031314170626
46807CB00001B/426